I0738259

THE GOLDEN RIGHT

JUSTIN THRONGARD

Copyright © 2018 by Justin Throngard

All rights reserved. No part of this publication may be reproduced, distributed, or transmitted in any form or by any means, including photocopying, recording, or other electronic or mechanical methods, without the prior written permission of the publisher, except in the case of brief quotations embodied in critical reviews and certain other noncommercial uses permitted by copyright law. For permission requests, write to the publisher, addressed "Attention: Permissions Coordinator," at the address below.

Simple CMS Design, LLC
help@simplecmsdesign.com
www.simplecmsdesign.com/publishing
Ordering Information:
Quantity sales. Special discounts are available on quantity purchases by corporations, associations, and others. For details, contact the publisher with the information below.
Orders by U.S. trade bookstores and wholesalers. Please contact Simple CMS Design: Tel: (208) 740-1534; Email: help@simplecmsdesign.com or visit www.simplecmsdesign.com/publishing

Printed in the United States of America

ISBN: 978-0-578-20338-6
Library of Congress Control Number: 2018903709
Story by: Justin Throngard, Jackie Throngard and Sam Heflin
Cover Design: Sam Heflin
Editor: Casey O'Connell

www.justinthrongard.com

*For Dad,
You taught me
storytelling.
And for Jackie,
You taught me
commitment.*

PROLOGUE

Murray Bench was through with Santa Mira Prison. He just didn't know if he would be leaving in one piece.

He sat alone in the locker room of the gymnasium, bruised and bloodied. The bones in his hands ached from repeated impacts. His ribs throbbed and he was sure that one or two of them were cracked. A cut above his eye caused blood to run down his face and drip off his jaw. In whatever way he left this prison, he wasn't going to be winning any beauty contests.

Outside the locker room, Murray could hear shouts of anger coming from the inmates who'd just watched him take a beating. The guards were attempting to dispel the unruly crowd, sending them out of the gymnasium, but they were resisting. *So this is what it sounds like when you lose*, he thought to himself. The sound was more violent than he expected. Sure, there would be the booing and the hissing that come with any bad performance, but this was something else. There was a hatred behind their voices. He didn't know what to think. He'd never lost a fight before, if one considered throwing a fight a loss.

No boxer wants to "take a dive", least of all Murray. If it had just been his life at stake, he wouldn't have agreed to the warden's terms of going down early. Yet Warden Corenswet knew exactly how to manipulate him: he just had to threaten his friends with misery. It wasn't much of a choice at all. He needed to have the warden's backing and his friends safe. A war was coming with Irvine Graves that could get everyone he cared about killed. Murray's only path was to take the fight beyond the walls of the prison. Outside, he alone would be the target of Grave's wrath.

A drop of blood fell from his chin to the shabby and well-worn boxing gloves that the prison had on supply. Rips in the gloves showed his battered knuckles and, where his hands weren't exposed, there was very little padding left. Murray laughed, despite the pain of knowing that his were in better condition than the other guy's mitts were. The cut on his forehead was caused by his adversary's bare fist, something even a mediocre boxing glove would have hindered.

How long would it be before Ed "Pain" Rains walked into the locker room to clean himself up as well, Murray wondered. Rains was such an egomaniac that he would be out soaking in the glory of his victory for as long as there was anyone around to cheer or curse. He was probably showing off his hands that were covered in Murray's blood to his cronies and saying things like "This is what you get when you want Pain" or "Pain rained today", the latter being Rains' favorite catch-phrase to try to intimidate the others in the block. Murray had thought if one day they were both free men that he would find where Rains lived and set a bottle of ibuprofen and an umbrella on his doorstep, the literal cures for his banal slogan. The only problems with this plan were that Rains probably wasn't smart enough to get the joke and secondly he would never get out of Santa Mira. He'd be spending the rest of his life here after sharing photos of his victims online with the message, "PAIN RAINED TODAY." It didn't take much convincing for the jury to rule a guilty verdict and the judge to give him a life sentence. The man was a moron, yet a very real threat to society.

Murray would be leaving Santa Mira though, and soon. Letting Rains punch him in the face repeatedly when he could have easily dodged the slow lummox's blows solidified the deal to have himself released into the open arms of the California parole system.

What a deal, he thought. *I'm able to get out of here and the warden gets to collect all the winnings he made by betting on Rains. Now I just need to avoid Graves until I leave and then either run from him for the rest of my live or get cut open by him. Great set of choices you've made in life, Murray.*

He removed the athletic tape from his left hand and took off the worn out glove without much trouble. But when he started to do the same to his other hand he stopped. He stared at it for a moment. His right. The Golden Right. The entire reason he was in this awful hell hole in the first place. Just 3 years ago, he was a free man in LA when his best friend and boxing manager, told him its new nickname. It was the same day that Irvine Graves came into his life, just before he destroyed it.

CHAPTER 1

Whoever first said, "I'll punch your lights out" must not have been hit in the head much.

After Greg Williams finished a three punch combo with a right hook across Murray's jaw, all he could see was white light. It was like someone had turned on a flash bulb in a dark room. His eyes struggled to resend information to his brain until finally the first images came through. He could see the crowd around the boxing ring yelling and chanting.

Then another blow came across his temple.

White light flooded his vision again, and when his sight returned he could see he was heading straight for the mat. When he landed, he smashed his left shoulder hard against the floor and felt the shoulder dislocate from its socket. He was blinded again, not from white light but from excruciating pain from his now-dead arm.

His eyes cleared. He could see he was on the mat. The crowd around the ring was yelling at him to get up. He lifted his head gradually to see his manager and best friend, Anatoly Brose, screaming at him from the other side of the ropes. Next to him was his trainer, Sam Davis, who was waving him to come over to the corner. Then the bell rang to end the round. The count by the referee continued. The bell couldn't save him. He needed to stand up.

He found a knee underneath him and then the other. A foot found its hold and by count seven, Murray Bench had got off the mat. The white light and buzzing in his ears had cleared away but the pain in his limp arm was intense. The referee came to him and sent him to his corner. There was no pause on the command from Murray. He reached the stool Anatoly had set out for him and pulled his mouthpiece away.

"Shoulder is gone," he uttered to Sam.

"I saw it," Davis replied while examining the socket the bone had popped out of in the fall. He rubbed around the edge of the arm, making Murray wince briefly.

"Tell me you can fix it," Anatoly added. "Come on, Sam. Fix it!"

"Would you get off me?" Sam barked back. "I'm getting there. Ready, Murray?"

Murray nodded.

"On three. One…," Sam counted and then pulled hard before he continued and before Murray could brace for the shock. The bone snapped back into the socket and Murray grimaced out a quiet stream of profanities that would have made a mother disappointed.

"You son of a bitch," he finished, swinging the arm around to test the fix. "Thank you."

"Watch that hook out there," Sam coached. "The bastard is coming at your head hard, but he's opening up a hole up on his right. Go at his side. Wham! Wham! Wham! I want to see you turn his side into hamburger. Keep your right up and your left low. You can hit him without breaking your arm off."

"Got it," Murray answered between the shots of water Anatoly hit him with in the mouth. "Go low on the right side. Watch the hook."

The bell rang and it was time to start the fight again.

Murray came out of the corner and spent the next round executing Sam's strategy with efficiency. When Williams threw his hooks, Murray either ducked or deflected them and then would strike with his left in the side of Williams's body. Each time, the impact on his left shoulder was painful. His body was telling him to stop. He wasn't listening. The strategy was working. Williams was attempting to lock up with Murray more and more frequently, a sure sign that he was wearing down. The round ended with Murray having done more damage than all the previous rounds combined.

"Nice work out there, buddy," Anatoly congratulated.

Sam rubbed the arm more and kept Murray hydrated. "You feeling all right?" he asked.

Murray nodded his reply and kept his gaze focused on Williams, who was returning the action. The bell rang and the fighters came at each other again. Murray kept the same strategy going and continued to hit Williams in the side with his left. The blows were starting to take their toll on both fighters, yet Murray was suffering more. With each strike, his left was losing force. His arm was going dead. When Williams doubled over slightly from his volleys, Murray went in for the kill. He reared his left arm back and swung it at his opponent's face and missed. The momentum of the punch tore his arm out of its socket again.

The round was only halfway over.

Now he had completely destroyed his left arm. It was useless and hung limp at his side. The pain was incredible, a stabbing that deepened with each movement. Williams took advantage and sent the right hook again and again with nothing to block it. Murray dodged and backed off as much as he could, reeling away from Williams's devastating strikes. Murray was pinned against the ropes and Williams was starting to land uppercuts through his defenses. Murray pushed him off, opening up space. He came out of the corner and attacked with his right. He miscalculated and the blow glanced off Williams's shoulder. The mistake was costly. His failed strike was returned with another uppercut to his jaw.

The white light returned, accompanied by a ringing in his ears. He dropped to a knee and tried to shake it off. When his vision returned, the ref had pushed Williams away from him. The crowd was going nuts. Victory for Williams was eminent.

Left arm still inoperative, Murray stood once again. He wasn't going to quit now. He could do this. His mind flashed back to a painful memory and the face of the man who had caused it. The rage he felt erupted through his body, building into a tense crescendo. He guided his fury into his powerful right, cocking it back like a loaded shotgun. The ref let go of Williams and Murray lunged forward. His right arm launched around and struck against the side of Williams's chin. The boxer teetered sideways and then fell on his back. The crowd exploded in surprise, with Anatoly and Sam screaming the loudest. Three seconds before, Murray looked like he was done and now his opponent had gone to the ground.

The ref came over and began the count, but it wasn't long before Williams shook himself back up to his feet. The referee gave him a quick check and the fight went on. The opponents locked up and Williams tried to put some blows into the body of Murray Bench. Too few, too late. Murray arced his right back and struck Williams in the head. The burly man dropped to a knee, blood running out of his nose. He sprang forward before the ref could get to him, and swung wildly at Murray. The shot he took misfired and Murray replied with his own. With all the power he had welled up in his right, he shot forth in a heavy uppercut that lifted Williams off his feet. Screams of victory for Murray erupted from the stadium before Williams hit the ground.

Three knockdowns in one round, the fight was over. Murray Bench had completed one of the greatest comebacks in boxing history, with only one arm.

CHAPTER 2

"The Kid with the Golden Right -- that's what they're calling you," Anatoly Brose said while showing his Twitter feed to Murray the morning after the fight with Williams.

"Kid? I'm 26. That's a terrible nickname," Murray replied from across the desk. The two of them sat in Anatoly's bedroom office inside of his small apartment in West Hollywood. "Gold is soft. If I have a 'Golden Right' then I have a soft punch."

"Or it could mean your fist is worth a lot of money. Or just that's it made of metal and all metal is harder than skin and knuckles. Whatever." Anatoly often became riled up whenever Murray got too technical. "Stop overthinking things. People are talking about you. It ain't a lot of people talking about you but it's some, and that's where things start."

"Okay. I gotta ask and don't take this the wrong way, but does that really matter? A nickname and some people talking on computers doesn't make me a better fighter, you know," Murray replied.

"Murray, I know this is hard for you to understand, what with you getting hit in the head all the time, but try to keep up." Anatoly could be a bit of an ass sometimes. He had a sarcastic viewpoint on life in general that often made him sound like he felt superior to others. Nothing could be farther from the truth; Anatoly Brose was the most caring man that Murray had ever met in his adult life. Most managers only wanted one thing: money. They would use their clients up for as much profit as they could, as fast as they could, whether it was good for the boxer or not. Most times it wasn't.

Murray had known him for only a couple of years but the two of them became fast friends. When he was just starting out, Anatoly had let him be his roommate until he could get on his feet, all rent free. The two of them would spend a lot of time in those days enjoying the view and drinking beers on the back porch. They talked about what the future was going to be like once Murray could start winning fights against guys in real boxing events, not the little local matches that didn't really mean anything.

Anatoly went on, "See, you want to win boxing matches, which isn't a problem because you're good. Your problem is that no one knows who the hell Murray Bench is. You can't get into good fights because no one cares about you. We need people talking so that fans will want to see you, so that other managers will want to book fights, and venues will want to show the fights."

"All right, I get it. I shouldn't have asked." Murray would often tire of hearing about the business side of boxing.

"So here's the deal. I'm gonna try to capitalize on some of this buzz", Anatoly said while fanatically clicking the "Retweet" button on anything about Murray. "I've got an idea on what we are going to do next, so I want you to go clear your head for a while."

"Wait, are you saying you don't have a fight lined up for this weekend?" Murray asked, confused. "That's the whole reason I thought you made me come over here."

"Kid, you're not getting this," Anatoly balked. "We aren't going to have to set up these matches with random no-names each weekend anymore. I'm going to take things to the next level. Which means bigger fights, more money, and more time between matches so that you're not a walking mass of bruises after each weekend. Now quit worrying about these things. I'm your manager, so let me manage."

Murray stood up to leave. "Fine, you call me when I have a fight to prepare for. Thanks, 'Toly."

"Get out of here, for Christ's sake," Anatoly said with a laugh and went back to his computer screen.

Murray left the office and went on his way back to his own apartment. He had been able to rely on having a paying match each weekend; enough so that he didn't need to live with Anatoly anymore. His winnings were enough to cover the rent in a studio apartment, barely. He still found himself over at Anatoly's often and hadn't even noticed he'd been relying on Anatoly's refrigerator for his primary source of meals. It wasn't until he saw Anatoly eating leftovers from the night before while Murray was eating fresh hot chicken that he realized that he was free-loading. When he confronted Anatoly about it, he was simply told, "You're the one in the ring. You're the one that needs the protein. Without you eating properly, I don't make any money to feed myself dog scraps. Eat the damn chicken, you needy bastard!" From then on, Murray didn't argue but made sure to slip all his extra money into Anatoly's wallet when he used the bathroom or went out for a cigarette on the balcony.

The twenty block trek from Anatoly's small, yet comfortable, second-story two bedroom apartment to Murray's dingy fourth floor studio (with customary window that opened to a brick wall) took five minutes by Uber or twenty minutes on foot. He preferred to walk even if it barely registered as exercise for him. Less money spent on cabs meant more for Anatoly's wallet. The journey, unfortunately, took him through some parts of town that tourists, as well as most of LA's residents, would like avoid. The stretch had its share of crime, corrupt landlords, and even a smattering of cartel importance. It was a breeding ground for drug dealers and mob enforcers. Murray had befriended many of the citizens of this area who were just trying to get by. They knew and loved him. Although he knew that in any group of people, no matter rich or poor, no matter race, color or creed, there were always bad eggs to watch out for.

Murray had never lacked courage when growing up but he'd been taught to avoid trouble, even if that meant looking like a coward. He had always been lanky at best, which was ideal for his fighting style now, but had done him no favors when he was young. Bullies liked to tease him for having such an awkward body, and the taunts only got worse when he refused to stand up for himself. He knew that if he did fight he would have little difficulty defending himself from them. Most were too fat to be a problem if they ever got into a fight, but he never got the chance to flex his superior reach and reflexes.

Violence was never the answer, or at least that was the lesson his father had drilled into his head. Murray had no intention of ever disappointing him, even though the primal part of his brain yearned to teach them a lesson they wouldn't forget.

Murray had loved his father more than anything else in the world. Long before he died when Murray was 20, they lived in a quiet town north of Sacramento. Murray's father, George, was a police officer with the Sacramento Police Department. He'd felt that violence could always be avoided by treating everyone fairly and to make sure that the gun was the last resort, if used at all. He was such a respected officer on the force and in the community that his superiors let him design his own training course around his nonviolence philosophy. George had wanted to make the course mandatory for all new cadets but some on the force still felt that the gun was a tool to earn respect and fear, two emotions needed to keep the peace.

In his tenure with the SPD, he'd only pulled his gun twice, once to stop a mentally disturbed father from shooting his own child, and once on the day he was murdered.

After the funeral, finding no means to avenge his father, impetuous Murray packed and left for Los Angeles. The only thing that he wanted to do was punch someone. He'd spent his whole life following his father's nonviolence philosophy, and that philosophy had ended up getting his father killed. He wanted to be someone who could not only be violent legally, but who would even be paid to be so. A career as a boxer was the first thing that came into his mind. He met Anatoly within a week and the two had begun working together. It was no wonder they became such close friends; both had lost their parents, both had left behind the only life they knew and moved to LA. It made it easy for them to relate to each other. They were all each other had left.

He was passing a corner strip mall that had been built in the 60's and had seen better days. It was occupied by a pawn shop, a pharmacy for pets and a business with a sign that read "EYEBROW THREADING: 100% PURE INDIAN VIRGIN HAIR". He could only assume that it meant people would go in there and get someone else's eyebrows sewn onto their face. The thought made him chuckle a little each time he walked by the shop. LA was such a weird place. He loved it.

He was just outside the pawn shop when he saw a familiar neighborhood face. The homeless man nicknamed TuTone was casually leaning against the wall of the store. TuTone had, at some point in his years, suffered a chemical burn to the left side of his face from his cheekbone to his jaw that bleached his skin white, causing him to have two very distinct skin pigments. It wasn't known how long he'd been homeless or even how old he was but no one could doubt that TuTone was a celebrity around those parts. He appeared to be quite content living on the streets and, despite his poor health and hygiene, was always in the best of spirits. He kept up with the goings on of the people in his community and knew and cared for many of them. He especially liked Murray and the feeling was mutual.

"Murray Bench, the Golden Right! My man!" TuTone called out.

Murray shook his head in disbelief. How did he already know Murray's new nickname? He didn't think that TuTone was big into

Twitter. Yet TuTone was a vacuum for information, so one could never know what news and rumors he had come across at any given point in time.

"TuTone," Murray answered back as the two high-fived each other. "I see you've already heard Anatoly's moniker for me. What do you think?"

"It's got a nice ring to it, but isn't gold soft?" TuTone smiled, exposing several gaps where teeth had once been.

"That's what I said but Anatoly says the ring part is more important than the meaning. Speaking of names, when are you going to tell me your real one? I feel like an asshole calling you TuTone. It seems racist in some way."

"That's a secret I'm never giving up, man. I like TuTone. It makes me feel famous."

"You are famous. Everyone knows you."

"As long as everyone likes me too. Hitler was famous, you know."

"I hope you're not keeping another secret from me," Murray replied sarcastically. "I'll catch up with you next time."

TuTone gave him another high-five and shouted as Murray walked away, "I wanna see you at Sam's gym soon. I want to see you punch through a wall or something, man!"

Murray shook his head and laughed. He was still thinking about TuTone when he turned the street corner and almost walked straight into three men. He could sense trouble with them immediately.

"Hey watch where you're going, man!" barked the first one, a tall slender snake. He writhed as he walked and spoke.

"We should make him pay the toll," the next piped in. He was short, but thick and reminded Murray of the bullies of his youth. "You owe us your money, dude."

"I don't have any money. I'm broke," Murray came back, falsely. This wasn't the first time he'd been shaken down. Each time he hoped the muggers would give up after hearing there was nothing in it for them. Each time he was wrong.

"He's lying," the snake said, followed by agreement from his mouthy comrade.

He looked at the third man who remained silent. The first two were aggressive and loud like peacocks trying to show superiority. The third one said nothing. He just stared and watched as if he was only interested in seeing what would happen. This man had eyes that said he cared about no one and no thing.

Murray tried to back away from the criminals. "I don't want any trouble," he pleaded.

"Yeah well you're the one making it. You just gotta pay the toll," replied the short one, who followed the remark by coming at Murray from his right. The short man pulled his arm back, with his fist clenched but when the punch was finally thrown, Murray was ready. He caught the blow against his forearm and then brought his elbow down onto the neck of the attacker. The short man dropped to the ground, face first. The tall one used his great reach to try and grab at Murray from the left, but Murray lunged away from his grasp and caught him in the stomach with a cross. The wind went out of the man and he went to his knees, gasping for air.

Murray had made a mistake, though. In his movement, he left his back to the center man. The quiet psychopath grabbed him while he faced away. He had pulled a knife out while Murray dealt with the other two, and was now holding it to Murray's neck.

"Don't do anything stupid. A few dollars isn't worth killing someone over, now is it?" Murray cautioned.

"I don't plan to kill you," the wide-eyed lunatic replied. "You think I'd risk a murder rap for your boring ass? You think all of us are just a bunch of uneducated dipshits out here, don't you? Don't you?! But you're not paying attention to where the knife is held. If I just press down, I'll sever your trapezius muscle. Your ligaments will snap back like a broken bungee cord. You'll never be able to use your arm again to lift more than your tiny dick. Now I say to you, don't you do anything stupid and just give us your wallet, fucker."

"Jesus, Johnny. Let him go for fuck's sake," pleaded the short one, who had picked himself back up off the ground. The slender one had caught his breath and was rising back up as well.

"Graves is going to kill us if we're late, man. We don't need cops out looking for us," said the tall one.

"Fine," said Johnny as he let Murray go. "Now, the wallet," he said as he motioned at Murray with the knife still in his hand.

Murray relented to his muggers and pulled his wallet out and handed it forward. The short one grabbed it and began looking at the contents. The tall one pushed Murray to the ground as he went past. Johnny just stood over him and stared, still pointing the blade at Murray. His face was twisted in rage, but it seemed as if his eyes were smiling against the hatred he exuded.

"There's only $20 in here," Murray heard the short man yell. "Steal his watch."

The tall man bent down and pulled up Murray's sleeve. Murray didn't fight.

"Fucker don't got one!"

"What about his phone?"

"It's a stupid flip phone. We can't sell that." The tall man stood back up. He opened Murray's phone and pulled it back until the mount split. He tossed the two pieces on Murray. The short man took this as his cue and followed suit with the wallet. Johnny finally moved and kicked Murray in the ribs.

"See you around, slick," he said and then they ran away around a corner, laughing at Murray until they were out of earshot.

Murray gathered himself and rose to his knees as two people ran to him and helped him up.

"We saw the whole thing," said the woman. "Are you ok?"

"I'm fine," he replied as he brushed the dirt off his pants. "I've faced a lot worse."

"Are you sure? Do you want us to take you to a hospital or the police?" the man asked.

"Thank you for your concern but there's nothing they can do. Goodbye," he said as he departed back on his way home. *Dammit!* he thought to himself. Now he'd lost $20 and his phone. That was just another $20 he was going to have to borrow from Anatoly, plus having to ask him to buy him a new phone. He felt like a kid who'd borrowed the family car, only to have it stolen by leaving the keys in the ignition.

CHAPTER 3

"So was this guy big or something? How'd he get a hold of you?" Anatoly asked.

The pair of them sat on the back porch of Anatoly's apartment. Between them laid an ice chest with Budweiser for Murray and Obolon beers for Anatoly. He had to drive across the city to a small market in Koreatown that specialized in importing Asian, Russian and Eastern European beers. It was the only place he knew that sold a beer brewed in Ukraine.

"No, he wasn't big," Murray replied. "But he was fast and I'm telling you there was something wrong with him. I've never seen someone with eyes like his. It's like he was taking me apart with them, piece by piece to see how I worked." A chill went down his spine as he thought of him again.

"Sounds like some of the Russians that came to Donetsk before my family died," Anatoly said. It was during the war with Russia over the Crimean peninsula when a stray artillery round leveled his family's home, the catalyst for his immigration to America. He'd always dreamed of visiting Hollywood and meeting Stallone and Arnold and acting as their trainers for a new Rocky movie in which Rocky faces off against John Matrix. So with nothing keeping him but painful memories in a nation that was being ravaged by war, Anatoly took what little was left after selling the family gym and everything else he owned and took the flight from Kiev to Paris to Los Angeles.

"I've heard of this name, Graves. Bad things," Anatoly recalled in a deeper accent than usual. He always did that when thinking of his former home. "I heard his name when I wanted to leave Ukraine. A human smuggler, I believe. You want into US? No papers? No problem. There are many men like him. Offer to help someone, then that someone is never seen again. Good thing, I was smart, yeah?"

"If there's worse up the ladder than what I met today," Murray replied, "then I'm really glad you're smart."

"Well don't worry about the money, or the phone for that matter," Anatoly said as he took a drag from his cigarette. Relaxed, his accent had faded away. "Besides, your phone was a piece of shit anyways."

"I thought you were quitting those? How's that working out?"

"Great! I quit all the time. No one quits more than me. If quitting was a sport, I'd be an Olympian."

"Like Zeus or a guy with a medal around his neck?"

"Either."

"What about using one of those vaporizer things?" Murray asked as he finished his beer and grabbed another from the cooler.

"Cigarette juice?" Anatoly answered with his own question. "I tried it. I really liked it actually. I had this flavor picked out that tasted like waffles. Weirdly, people would ask me to blow it in their faces because everyone loves waffles, I guess."

"So what happened?" Murray asked.

"Have you ever been to a vapor shop?"

Murray shook his head, but Anatoly had already started again before he got his answer.

"It's awful. Every single one of them is filled with a bunch of college kids standing around blowing vapor all over the place until no one can see anything. So instead of seeing things they blast dub step as loud as they can to compensate for the loss of their senses."

"What the hell is dubstep?" Murray asked.

"Oh you know. You've heard it. It's that 'wub wub wub dooOOO zoot zoot TINNEEENEE wub wub wub' crap that sounds like a techno music guy got on the bad kind of bath salts and tried to eat his music's face."

Murray had started laughing by this point but Anatoly didn't stop.

"And the dumbest part of these morons standing there not talking to each other with their wub wub music? There's no nicotine in their juice. They just do it because they are trying to make bigger clouds than anyone else. It's completely moronic. It's just a big vaporizer penis size competition."

Now Murray was laughing hysterically. A dog started barking down the street.

"I can't go into places like that. They suck too bad. So here I am, enjoying my death sticks because you know what? The gas station I get them from doesn't try to make buying them like having your brain stuck inside a can of spray paint. Who wants that?"

Murray had fallen out of his chair completely and was slowly trying to recover when the doorbell rang.

The pair looked at each other quizzically. They weren't expecting any guests. Anatoly stood up.

"You order a pizza or something?" he said as he crossed his apartment.

"Yeah, with that $20 I — oh wait, no that was stolen," Murray replied facetiously. Anatoly shot him a look and then turned back to the door.

Murray stared out across the LA nightscape from the back porch while Anatoly attended to the visitor. *City of Stars* hummed in his head as he watched the lights of the hills flicker. Anatoly had a great view.

"It's for you," Anatoly said from behind the sliding glass door of the patio. His face was grim.

"What?" Murray was confused. Why would he be getting any visitors, especially at Anatoly's?

He stood, walked past Anatoly and headed to the door. Beyond the door stood the tall snake and the short bulldog from earlier in the afternoon. Both had black eyes, and the bulldog had a split lip. Behind them was a much larger man in a business suit and sunglasses. He looked like he was Secret Service, but that was clearly not the case. There was no sign of the lunatic with the wide-eyes.

"Mr. Bench, we'd like to apologize," said the bulldog. "What happened this afternoon was unacceptable."

Murray was taken aback a little by this. "Okay," was all he could think to say.

"Our employer, Mr. Graves, sends his warmest condolences," started the snake, "and would like you to know that the one who threatened you will not be bothering you ever again."

"Mr. Graves wants you to know that he has the deepest respect for 'The Kid with the Golden Right' and would like to see you fight soon. He's a big fan. He'd also like you to have this in atonement for today."

The short one put out his hands and showed a $100 bill inside one, a new smartphone in the other. They stood silently, waiting for Murray to take them.

Murray looked at Anatoly who had come to stand beside him.

"Go on," he said. "Take it. Refusing would be disrespectful."

Murray did as was asked.

"Well, thank your boss for me. I accept the apology."

With that, the three left without saying another word. The whole thing seemed oddly rehearsed and was clearly not authentic. When Murray closed the door the pair burst into laughter again.

"Hey whatever works!" Murray said.

"You should have seen your face!" Anatoly gasped out between fits of laughter. "You thought you were gonna get your ass kicked."

"No I didn't, asshole!"

"Bing, bong! Hello, who is it? It's Publisher's Death-house! You're our grand prize winner! Here's some hot lead, sucker! Pew pew!" Anatoly was rolling.

"You, sir, are a dickhead," Murray snarked at him and headed back to the porch, turning on the phone to play with it, the relief of his finances overriding any caution he might have had about taking a gift from Graves. Maybe the Graves Anatoly had heard about was a different guy. Maybe he just didn't care.

Anatoly came outside and sat back down in his chair, lighting another cigarette.

"That's what I love about this town," he said. "You never know what happens next."

The pair were quiet, staring out into the city for a minute before Anatoly spoke.

"See I told you that nickname would work for us. Everyone likes it. It's spreading through this town like wildfire. This is where things start, buddy. Right here and now."

"I hope you're right, 'Toly," Murray replied. "Hey, speaking of boxing, I was thinking the other day."

"Uh oh." Anatoly jested.

"Shut up. All the boxing movies get it wrong. You know what I mean?" he asked. "'Raging Bull' is the only one that ever got it right."

"What about Rocky?"

Murray thought for a minute. The laugh attack and his sixth beer were catching up to him mentally. "The first one and the new one are the only ones that are decent."

"Except for that weird Ruff Riders training montage."

"In the first one? I don't remember that."

"No, in the new one. Where Apollo's kid is getting good and he's running down the street, shadow-boxing as all these ATV guys are doing wheelies and stupid shit around him? It's the stupidest thing."

"Oh yeah. See what I mean? They never get it right."

"I disagree. I really like Rocky IV."

Murray's beer shot out of his mouth. "That's one of the most unrealistic boxing movies ever made! Are you kidding me?"

"I know it is, but I like it anyways," Anatoly confessed.

"But it's such a Cold War propaganda piece about how the Soviets are bad and no matter what they do, good ol' American grit and determination will beat them in the end. Rocky defeats communism! Hooray! I would think that you would have grown up hating that."

"I don't really care about that. I didn't fight the Cold War. I had no love for the USSR. I just cared about good stories. I liked that it was about the old school versus the new. The classic way vs the modern way. That the guy with heart who's trying hard is going to win in the end, not the guy that's just gifted and feels entitled to it. That people who work harder are rewarded more than those that don't. Yes, it's dumb and cheesy but the moral is there and I like it."

Murray really didn't have a response so the pair sat silently for a minute. Anatoly lit another cigarette and leaned against the porch railing, admiring the view.

"Don't worry," Anatoly continued. "Soon, I'm going to get you a fight versus someone like Ivan Drago."

"I will break him," Murray quoted in a horrible Lundgren voice.

Neither of them could predict that when that day came it would be the biggest mistake of their lives.

CHAPTER 4

Three days later, Murray received the phone call that would change his life.

He was just getting out of the shower when his new phone ring. He knew it was Anatoly by the custom ringtone he'd downloaded: Pink Floyd's "Money," Anatoly's favorite song. He picked up the phone and hit Answer.

"Put your pants on and get ready to shit them, buddy," Anatoly said with excitement. "I've got you a fight like you've never had."

"What? What do you mean?"

"Two weeks, StubHub Center in Carson, Murray Bench vs. Tito Pistelli."

"Tito Pistelli?" Now Murray was excited. "I just watched him on HBO last week. He beat Allen Jords last month. You're kidding me, right?"

Anatoly was snickering. "I'm not. It seems like all that buzz we've had lately was enough to get you noticed. An assistant for Pistelli's manager came out to your fight last week and apparently liked what he saw. This is it, buddy. This is where things start for you."

"Anatoly, if I find out you're making this up..." Murray was still in disbelief.

"I wouldn't do that to you, Murray. Not like this," Anatoly replied. "Get your head screwed on. I'm going to come pick you up and then I want to start coming up with a game plan. You need to train, watch a ton of tape on Pistelli and then we need a strategy to beat him."

Fifteen minutes later, Anatoly was outside Murray's apartment honking the horn of his sedan. Murray was already out of the building and at the passenger door before Anatoly could take his hand off the horn.

"You better be ready for this," Anatoly greeted as his friend and client climbed into the passenger seat.

Murray replied, "I've been waiting for this for years, 'Toly. You better believe I'm ready. Let's go."

———

The pair drove to Davis Gym where Anatoly sent all his clients over the years. Davis Gym was rundown and dark with old, outdated equipment. When Murray walked through the doors it seemed like his eyes had a sepia filter placed over them. Everything from the walls to the punching bags to the ring was a mixture of dirty browns and drab yellows, and all of it was faded. He loved the place. It reminded him of characters from a past generation. He felt like the Allies had defeated the Nazis or Carl Lewis won his gold medals right there in that Los Angeles gym.

Sam Davis, the owner and chief trainer, was already waiting for them at the entrance. "Murray, Anatoly told me everything. It's about damn time if you ask me."

Sam was just like his gym. He'd been a heavyweight contender in the late 60's but tore his rotator cuff before he could fight for the belt. He'd been able to make more than enough in his career to pay for his children's educations and to buy the land and the gym that bore his name today. Davis Gym had been the most popular training facility for boxers in California for ten years until the neighborhood started to fall apart. The mafia had turned its gaze on the land around the gym and forced the residents out with violence and corruption. With nobody living in the area, the buildings and streets started to fall into disrepair and people wouldn't travel to Davis Gym anymore. Their local gyms would do just fine for them. Sam had been given the opportunity to sell the gym many times over in the years since but completely refused. This gym was all he had left of the days of his youth and no one was going to take that away from him. Now time had put Sam in the same state as his gym: outdated in mind and faded in form. Nevertheless he could still spot a winner when he saw one, which is why he'd been Murray's trainer from the start. This fight with Pistelli could be just what he needed to bring his gym back to its glory days, with Murray being the draw for new clients.

"Sam," Anatoly said, "I want you to shape Murray into someone who doesn't just stand a chance at beating Pistelli. I want him to have no chance of losing."

"Easy, 'Toly," Murray interrupted. "That sounds a little too much like the Titanic."

Sam put his big arm around Murray's shoulder and walked him towards the ring. "Boy, forget the Titanic. I'm going to turn you into the iceberg."

It was two weeks of hard training with Sam that got Murray prepared for the big fight. Murray and Sam had hardly left the gym during that period. Murray trained until midnight each day and then spent the night on a cot set up in Sam's office. Each morning Sam would open the doors and find Murray in the ring already warmed up and practicing. The pair spent the majority of the time focusing on Murray's agility to avoid Pistelli's heavy blows and building up that golden right of Murray's for the time when a window opened to put Pistelli away.

———

The night of the fight came quicker than expected. Murray was in the locker room getting ready when Anatoly came in. Anatoly had a look on his face that showed his nerves were about to explode. Murray had already been nervous, but seeing his best friend in the same condition put him over the edge.

"What are we doing here?" he asked. "I'm not ready for this. We need more time to train."

Anatoly came over to him and said, "Murray, sit down for a second."

Murray gave Anatoly a gaze of protest.

"Do it," Anatoly commanded.

Murray had never seen him be so forceful before, so he sat down on the bench behind him. Anatoly stood in front of him with his arms crossed, holding Murray's gaze firmly.

"You know what this fight means. Not just to me but to both of us. This is it. This fight is a way into the majors. You know all this," Anatoly said in a stern tone. Then his expression changed and he kneeled down so that he was eye level with Murray.

"What you don't know is that you're the best fighter I've ever seen. There isn't anyone else like you and there never has been. You've got something that can't be replicated or trained for, even if you had an army of Sams. What you can do with your right arm and the power that comes from it is going to change everything. So when you say to me that you're not ready for this and need more training, I have to say to you that you don't. See it's not a matter of whether you're ready or not. You're going to win. It's already done. It's always been done. This is the path that you started walking when we met and it's just another step along it, kid."

The confidence Anatoly had in Murray and the depth of his loyalty left Murray struggling to find the words that could compare to his friend's. The only thing he could muster, "Man...thank you."

Anatoly stood back up and turned to the door. "Well, you're lucky you're a fine boxer, because you are no wordsmith. Come on, Murray. It's time." With that, Murray and Anatoly walked out to ring.

The next time the two of them spoke was time to celebrate. Murray had knocked out Tito Pistelli in the second round with the first full punch he threw, a cross from his "golden right".

Inside the stadium, beyond the ovation erupting for Murray Bench, unfettered by the cheers that exploded around him, a single spectator sat silently. He looked on from his one good eye, the other a ball of white glass. A smile crossed his face. Irvine Graves had found his man.

CHAPTER 5

"Did you see his face? He knew he'd walked right into a trap and was done!" Anatoly said with glee. "He was like, 'I got this', then the next he was like, 'Oh shit', then his face got mashed by your punch. I was rolling!"

Anatoly hadn't stopped talking since Murray, Sam and he walked into the locker room after Murray was announced as the winner by TKO. Murray was all smiles as he sat down and Sam began unlacing his gloves.

"Pistelli was playing it cool," Sam added. "He was trying to wear you down. Locking up with you, then pushing off. It was great strategy when you caught him."

"It was great training, Sam," Murray said gratefully. "This wouldn't have happened without you."

Anatoly was still in a furor. He was pacing back and forth and talking to himself.

"I gotta call the press. I gotta set up some interviews. We need to setup a social media campaign."

"'Toly, please settle," Murray said. "Let's just take tonight to celebrate. We've been at this for weeks without stop. I need the weekend at least, pal."

"The weekend? Ha!" Anatoly said, stopping his pacing. "Not the whole weekend. I'll give you tonight. Let's get you a big steak and then take you to that karaoke bar you like. How's that?"

"Drinks are on me," added Sam.

"Deal," Murray agreed.

Sam had finished unwrapping the gloves and Murray had moved on to removing his shoes when the door of the locker room opened. Three men entered the room. Two were heavies, dressed in suits that barely fit around their broad shoulders. Bodyguards, Murray judged, by the way they carried themselves and walked behind the third man. Their leader was about Murray's height and dressed in a much nicer, all white suit. On his head sat a white Panama hat, covering his salt and peppered hair. He could be considered handsome, had it not been for the white glass-eye that seemed too large a fit. It threw off the symmetry of his face and put his left side in a constant sneer. He smiled in full at Murray as locked his gaze with him.

"No press. This is a private…," Anatoly trailed off as he turned and saw that these men were, without a doubt, not members of the sporting news.

Sam was staring with his mouth open. "Murray, that's-"

"Irvine Graves, at your pleasure," the leader interrupted. "Hello again, Mr. Davis. I hope your gym is doing well these days. Have you had a change of heart?"

"I'm still not selling it," Sam said, standing to face Graves. "I've seen what you do with neighborhoods. I'm not letting you do that to mine."

"Whatever could you mean?" Graves asked.

"You get crime to spread through an area, driving prices down and destroying people's lives. Then you snatch things up on the cheap, force people out of their homes, only to sell them to your rich cronies. I won't let you do that to my block."

"I assure you that is not my intentions Mr. Davis. I am a revivalist," Graves replied, gesturing to his men to stay where they were. "Your gym is just the last piece I require to finish renovating that slum. Don't you want to see it restored to the glory it once had?"

"I'm not selling. Not to a slumlord like you."

"Now that language isn't necessary. You're clearly misinformed about me, Mr. Davis," Graves said, moving further into the room. "Maybe we can get to know each other better soon, but let's leave the real estate discussion for another time. It's not why I'm here."

"Why are you here?" Murray asked.

"Murray—can I call you Murray?" Graves asked. He sat down next to Murray and crossed his legs. "I assume you received my compensation for the earlier troubles with some of the less civil members of the community. Are you enjoying your new phone?"

"Yeah, it's great. Thank you for that," Murray said flatly, put off by Sam's distrust for Graves. "It does make me wonder, what's your business with me?"

"Well, that was one hell of a fight tonight, Murray. I'm sure that Tito Pistelli wasn't the only one that was surprised by the outcome. Myself included, to a degree. You see, boxing is a passion of mine. You might say it's both a hobby and a line of work for me. I like to have people of talent under my employ. Tito Pistelli was just one of the many who I have in my, how should I say, stable of boxers."

"Pistelli is your fighter?" Anatoly questioned.

"Yes exactly, Mr. Brose. It was one of my employees to whom you spoke on the phone about this fight. I wanted to see if this 'Kid with the Golden Right' was as good as people were saying."

"Well then, I should thank you for the opportunity to knock his ass out," Murray quipped. "All flattery aside, what's your point?"

"Straight to it then," Graves said and smiled. "I like that. Murray, I want you to fight for me. I want you to work for my team."

"Not a chance," Sam balked. Graves's guards moved forward, but were waived off by their leader, who stayed focused on Murray.

"I'd like to hear from Murray on his future if you don't mind," he returned.

"The answer is no, then," Murray stated plainly.

"That quick?" Graves asked, visibly surprised. "Give it a little thought, please. I can offer you opportunities you wouldn't have with your current... management." Graves looked at Anatoly. "I can make you famous."

"He'll use you up and spit you out, Murray," Sam objected. "He'll drop you the first chance he gets."

Graves eyed Sam with distaste, a glint of anger in his eye, and then turned his focus back to Murray.

"It doesn't matter," Murray stood and looked down at Graves. "Even if you weren't trying to force my friend out of his livelihood. Even if you were going to bring me fame and fortune. Even if the sun rose and sat in your ass, I wouldn't fight for you, Graves. I work with Anatoly and Sam. End of story."

A warm smile found its way across Anatoly's face.

Graves sat silent for a moment, then stood.

"This is a miscalculation on your part, Mr. Bench," he warned. His change of tone did not go unnoticed by Murray, accentuated by the gnashing of his teeth. "Points in time like this change one's life. I've offered you a future, the future you have sought for your whole career and you turn me down. This is not a rejection I would recommend," he looked at Murray's friends, "if you care about the future of others."

"You piece of shit..." Sam started.

"Graves, I think it's time you leave," Murray interjected, his temper was rising. "I'll make you an offer. I'll be happy to pretend I didn't hear your last sentence, and so not beat the ever living fuck out of all three of you right here and right now. You want to do business with me? Well, you go through Anatoly, professionally. But you ever make a threat again, veiled or not, I'll make you crawl back into whatever shithole birthed you and we'll never hear from you again. Got it?"

Graves' face twisted in anger, the glass eye accentuating his rage. He moved right into Murray's face.

"No one threatens me, Murray Bench," he said through his gritted teeth. "And no one refuses me."

Murray held his ground, staring Graves right back in his living eye. He braced for the incoming attack, ready to strike back.

The attack didn't come. Graves closed his eyes and breathed slowly for a moment. *Did he just count to ten?* Murray asked himself as Graves turned back towards the door.

"But tonight is a night for celebration. I will leave you to that," Graves bowed and then walked out of the locker room with his bodyguards in tow.

"Don't let the door hit you-" Anatoly shouted, but was cut off by the slamming of the door by Graves.

"Well that could have gone better," he finished.

————

Graves and his men walked through the hallways of the stadium. He strode forward in long, rapid steps, his fists clenched at his side, his body shaking with anger. The heavies behind him kept their distance, knowing full well of the repercussions of stepping over a line when things had gone poorly for their boss. One false move could push him over the edge. After finding the exit, they met one of his men outside, waiting by Graves's car.

"Well?" he asked.

"That cocksucker is going to pay, Whiteley," Graves shouted and entered the back seat of the vehicle. He stopped with one leg out and waved Whiteley over.

"If Bench will only fight for that communist, then let's leave him with no choice but to join me. Get Officer Johns on the phone. I want to send a message that Bench will understand."

"You got it," Whiteley replied.

Graves closed the car door, leaving Whiteley to watch the vehicle drive away. He glanced at the other man standing next to him and nodded, confirming Graves' orders.

CHAPTER 6

The next day, Murray awoke inside of a jail cell. His head was pounding, not from the hangover, which was significant, but from the huge, throbbing lump on the back of it. He tried to sit up and was overcome with dizziness and went back down. He blinked his eyes over and over trying to get anything in his brain to make sense. Where was he? He'd remembered the bar and celebrating his victory with the locals. He remembered having drinks bought for him by almost everyone there. What happened? His head was still a fog as he tried to sit up again.

This time he was able to fully sit upright but the throbbing made him put his hands on his head in pain. He felt the lump on his head. It wasn't from the fight. The only blows Pistelli landed were body shots. Had he fallen down?

He looked around at the cell he was in. He was alone in it and there was no sound from anyone else in the jail. Across the hall from his cell lay another cell that was empty. *All right*, he thought to himself, *put it together, Murray.*

Another wave of memories came to him. He kept remembering images of the fight. The body blows, Pistelli pushing off of him and opening himself up, the knockout punch, the crowd erupting, and the first person in the ring to rush him was....Anatoly. And then it all came back.

The first thing he remembered when he thought of Anatoly was the sight of him lying on the concrete with blood running from his nose and mouth; he was unconscious. Another flash came of Murray hitting a police officer in the mouth and putting him to the ground.

The car.

Oh God, Anatoly was driving me home.

Memories were cascading in.

He refused to let me walk.

I don't remember getting in the car at all.

Another wave of pain took the thoughts away. Murray rubbed his temples in an effort to at least ease the pain of his hangover; the pain from his injury was a lost cause. As it subsided, he kept seeing flashes of Anatoly's still body on the concrete. He saw someone kick him in the ribs. Who was it? Another memory showed someone striking Anatoly in the face with a stick or a bat. Another of Anatoly speaking to someone by the parked car and apologizing.

Was he apologizing for something I'd done? Murray asked himself.

At that point Murray pulled himself together well enough that he knew he had to find out about Anatoly. The last thing he could put together was Anatoly laying still, the kick in the ribs and then blackness. He stood up shakily and made it to the cell door. Almost perfectly on time, he heard the sound of a door opening at the end of the hall and footsteps approaching. Just as Murray was about to shout, Sam Davis' face appeared.

"Oh God, Murray. I'm so glad to see you're okay," Sam said with a look of worry. "How are you holding up?"

"I've been better, Sam," he replied. "I feel like crap. What the hell happened? Why am I in here? Where's Anatoly?"

Sam face's changed quickly to a look of surprise. "What do you mean? You don't remember?"

Murray shook his head slightly. "A little, but really only up until leaving the bar."

"Oh no... Murray, I think you better sit down."

"I just got up and it took a lot of effort to do that. Just tell me what's going on."

"Murray, sit down!" Sam barked. The tone of his voice and the volume were enough to send shocks of pain in Murray's hung-over brain. However painful it was to stand up was nowhere near as bad as having to hear that again. Murray sat back down on the bed.

"Murray, I've got to tell you some things and they aren't good. You aren't going to like what I have to say."

"Just get to it, Sam. I can deal with it. I'm sure whatever is going on, we can manage."

"Murray, they've got you on quite a few charges. You're going to see a judge on Monday, which means that you are in here for the full weekend. I've got an attorney lined up. He's the best in the business at police violence cases. He's not cheap, but your winnings should make a pretty solid start. I'm going to help out with the rest."

"Sam, I have no idea what you're saying right now. I did something stupid. Okay, I'll deal with that when I can think. Just tell me where Anatoly is. Is he here too?"

Sam looked down the hall, searching for a way to avoid what he needed to say. The expression on Sam's face was of doubt and fear. He found no help in his search. He was the only person there who could do this. Sam shifted his face back to Murray.

"Murray, Anatoly's gone. They killed him."

The floor dropped out from below Murray. Gravity crushed down on him. The blood left his veins and was replaced with emptiness. He became dizzy, nauseous and then his hands started to shake. He realized he knew everything. His earlier flashes of memory must have been a mental self-defense mechanism. The whole story was there, just waiting to be unlocked.

After the fight and the incident with Graves, the three of them went to the bar to celebrate. People were cheering and patting

Murray on the back. The bartender even made him sign an autograph on a copy of the program from the fight to hang on the wall of the bar. People were buying him drinks. Anatoly and Sam were drinking with him. People were singing karaoke tribute songs like "Eye of the Tiger" and "My Way" to him. A woman kissed him. Sam took a cab home around midnight, while Murray kept drinking and Anatoly switched to water. They stayed and shut the place down. Stumbling on the streets, after the bar closed, Murray said he would walk home, but Anatoly insisted that he was in no condition to make it through the tough neighborhood on foot; he'd drive. Murray hung his head out the window and vomited. Lights flashed behind them. The police were pulling them over. Anatoly spoke to two of them. They administered a sobriety test on him. Another police car arrived. Murray stood with the two new officers and told them he was the best fighter in California and that he could take any of them. He shadowboxed near one of them and barely missed hitting the officer. Losing his balance, Murray hit the ground. Anatoly shouted to stop and moved towards Murray to help. The two officers grabbed him and slammed him into one of the cars. They called him derogatory names like "Communist" and "Ivan". They must have thought he was Russian. Murray stood up and saw Anatoly being hurt by the cops. He rushed over and tried to push them off. An officer swung his nightstick at Murray, who instinctively dodged it. The stick struck Anatoly in the face and he went down. Murray yelled at the cops, but they started kicking Anatoly, who was now bleeding profusely from his nose, ears and mouth. Murray swung at the cop who hit Anatoly with the nightstick and struck him full force in the face. Another came at him and swung his club, which Murray ducked and then used his full momentum to land his fist squarely in the cop's stomach, bending him over and crumpling him to the ground. He turned and saw another reaching for his gun. Murray cleared the distance in one bound and leveled the cop before he could get his gun out of his holster. Then he felt a blow to the back of his head and went down. His last sight was of Anatoly lying bleeding with an empty look on his face, before the blackness surrounded Murray and he passed out.

———

"Oh Jesus, Sam" Murray cried.

"I know, kid. It's awful. There's more that I gotta tell you though." Sam replied. "They're going to charge you with first degree assault on a law enforcement officer, three counts of second degree assault on a law enforcement officer and reckless endangerment. Not to mention resisting arrest."

"Oh Anatoly. What have they done to us?"

Sam went on, "They are saying that because of who you are they consider you a trained expert and a punch from you can be lethal. So when you hit the officer, you committed assault with a deadly weapon. They say it's the same as if you had shot the officer. Murray, are you listening to me?"

"There's gotta be some sort of mistake, Sam," Murray said. "A mix up or something. Why would anyone hurt 'Toly? The hospital must have got it wrong. He's fine."

Sam frowned in discouragement. He had no experience in comforting someone with loss. He didn't know what to do or say.

"There's no mistake, Murray," Sam stated as truthfully as he could. "I was at the hospital. He's gone."

"But how can this happen? Anatoly wouldn't hurt anyone," Murray seethed, clutching the cell bars so hard his knuckles were turning purple. "They killed him and stuck me in here to rot. Why? Why would this happen?"

"Listen, I know," Sam pleaded. He couldn't find the right words to say. "This sucks but we've got to talk about what to do next."

"Do next? I'll tell you what we do next," Murray said, turning directly at Sam. "I'm going to find the bastard whose fault this is and I'm going to choke the life out of him."

"Come on, Murray. We need to come up with a plan to get you out of this."

"You do that and find out who these cops are."

"The attorney and I looked into them. Officers Johns, Rodihan, Greem and Crockett. These guys have a rep for being a little rough, Johns and Rodihan especially."

"A little rough? They killed my best friend, Sam!" Murray shouted pushing back his grief. "What am I supposed to do? Let them get away with it? They killed him for no reason! They have to pay!"

Sam went quiet. What could he say? He couldn't fault Murray for the way he was feeling. Sam was angry too. Yet, he knew that anger and some sort of vengeance wouldn't bring Anatoly back. He had Murray's future to worry about, and that meant focusing on getting him out.

"There's nothing I can say to you that will take away this pain. You have to find a way to deal with it on your own. I'm here for you, though. You want to talk about things? I'll come running. Right now, I'm going to go talk to my attorney and see what our moves are."

"Ok. Tell him I want to sue the LAPD too, or… see if I can, I guess," Murray asked. He had no plan. He didn't know what to do but doing anything was better than doing nothing.

"All right, buddy. I'll call you the first chance I have something. You gonna be ok?"

"Yeah. I'll manage. I just…"

"Hate this? Me too. It isn't right," Sam said giving Murray a half-smile. It was the best he could manage. Then he turned and walked out of the jail.

Murray paced back and forth, his fists clenched, his teeth gnashed.

"What am I going to do, 'Toly?"

CHAPTER 7

10 year-old Murray sat on the bench seat of the red and white single-cab pickup truck that bounced along the washboard dirt road. Through his open window, pine trees passed by and patches of melting snow splashed under the truck's tires. Nothing made him feel like a grown-up more than resting his arm out of a vehicle's open window. Air conditioning was for city people, not rugged tough men.

He looked over at his father, who was busy navigating the truck through the large ruts and trenches in the road that the spring runoff had caused. Some of the ruts were over a foot deep and getting a single tire jammed into one could high-center the truck or, even worse, break an axle. That would put an end to their adventure pretty fast. Still George had been up roads like this his whole life. He knew how to manage the twisting dirt paths that led deep into the California forests and he would get them to where they were going.

"Dad, how much further?" Murray asked. "I gotta pee."

"We're getting there, buddy," George replied. "I warned you about drinking that many root beers before we left the diner. How many of those did you have anyways?"

"Only about four."

George finished his Coors and tossed the can out of the driver's window and landed it perfectly in the back of the truck bed. The can clanked against the tailgate, next to the other three cans that had found the same destination.

"I guess we're about even on the count then. I think I'll be ready to drain the main vein shortly too. We've still got a little ways to go, so I guess now is as good as time as any."

George slowed the truck to a stop and the pair jumped out onto the muddy trail. The truck sat in the middle of the one lane road but George wasn't worried about blocking someone else's travel. This road was a dead end about 20 miles north of them. There would have been tire tracks in the wet dirt if there was anyone ahead of them and they would have run into someone at the diner if they were going to be followed.

Murray walked over to the edge on the right and looked down the hill the road cut into. There was a twenty foot drop off that was covered in rocks and small trees but just beyond those, he could just catch a glimpse of a stream. He loved streams like these. Ever since his dad took him fishing for the first time, he loved to explore the little pools and search for rare stones inside them. He'd created quite the collection of geodes, quartz and pyrite that he'd found during the trips he and his father made into the forests and mountains of Northern California.

"Dad, there's a creek down there. Can I check it out?" he yelled as he made his descent without waiting for the answer.

"Yeah, hold on for a damn second though," George answered. He finished his business, zipped his fly up, and then walked over to where Murray had begun his trek down the embankment.

"Well it looks like you've found one hell of a spot to take a leak at, Murray." George said as he looked out past the stream. On the other side was a clearing in the woods with a grassy knoll and a rocky outcropping. A little brook split the clearing in half where the waters trickled down into the stream. The area looked completely undisturbed by any hunters or campers that would periodically come this way. It was an ideal camping spot but you would never be able to see it from the road. George had been up this road dozens of times and he'd never known of its existence.

Murray ignored the statement and kept moving down the small hill to the stream. George didn't mind the lack of conversation from his son; he wanted to let the boy have his fun. He reached into the bed of the truck and pulled out a backpack and a long case that contained the three rifles and three pistols they'd brought with them. The plan had been to take Murray to the same spot his father had taken him when he was old enough to learn how to use a firearm. The pair had already been there three times this year and Murray was a quick study. On the first trip, he missed his first two shots at the beer cans George had set up at a distance of ten feet. From then on he'd hit each one without mistake. This trip was the first time Murray would be learning how to fire a rifle and George was anxious to see how the slender boy would do with the recoil of the bigger and heavier weapon.

"Murray, I need you to carry the backpack," he called out to his son who had already reached the stream.

"Hold on, Dad. I want to see if I can find some gems." Murray shouted back, his gaze fixed on a small pool on the other side.

"You'll have plenty of time for that. I think we're going to set up here for target practice."

"Really? All right!"

"But I need your help. I can't carry the guns and the pack while climbing down."

Murray hustled back up the side of the hill, took the backpack off his father's arm and without pause ran back down to the creek. The footsteps he made on first trip down made for a nice little staircase that he could use at a much faster pace. George followed behind him and shortly both were standing next to the creek, scanning for a path to reach the other side. The stream was shallow with its greatest depth reaching about six inches, but neither of them were very interested in wading in the cold mountain waters in their fabric hiking boots. It was Murray who saw the fallen tree downstream first.

"Dad, we can walk across that log," the young boy exclaimed.

"It's worth a look," George replied and then walked along the stream.

The pair reached the log and George took the backpack from Murray and began to climb across the eight foot span that bridged the creek banks. Once on the other side, he set the backpack down and went back for the guns. Murray slipped as he crossed but caught himself and soon the two were safely across with their gear. George moved the equipment up to the top of the grassy knoll, while Murray ran straight to the pool he wanted so desperately to look in earlier.

"I thought you had to pee?" George shouted out as he opened up the backpack and pulled out some boxes of rounds and one of the beers he'd stashed inside.

"Oh yeah!" Murray shouted back and ran up to the tree line to find a good spot for privacy. George continued unpacking and then opened the gun case. Inside was the Sig Sauer P226 he carried when on duty, a Beretta 92, a Ruger .38 snub nose, a .22LR lever action with a walnut stock, the same rifle he'd owned since he was Murray's age, a Remington .30-06 bolt action in black he'd bought just last year, and a Colt M4 Carbine. The last rifle wasn't for the boy, not yet. The assault rifle had been issued to George by the SPD as part of their increasing focus on fighting the gang violence that had risen in the Sacramento area in the last few years. It was mandatory that each officer become fully trained in the use of the powerful weapon, and George saw this trip as the perfect time to practice. Spending time with his son was just an added bonus.

Murray had lost his mother to cancer when he was too young to remember her. Since then, Murray had grown up with only his father and the entire SPD to raise him. George's pay was not nearly enough to hire someone to watch Murray on a full time basis while George was on duty. Murray would often have to sit at the station while George finished his shift. It wasn't much fun for the boy, so

George would take any opportunity he could to perform his work duties and keep his son happy at the same time. These trips into the woods were their favorite such opportunities.

"DAD!"

"What is it?" George replied as he continued to unpack the equipment. He loaded a clip into the carbine and looked down the sights. *Spot on. No need to adjust anything,* he thought. *I should have brought something bigger than beer cans for this thing.* He walked down to a good size stump and placed three cans on top.

"DAD! COME QUICK!"

"Give me just a minute. I'll look at the rocks you found when we're done with practice."

That boy is always finding something new that has to be shared immediately. He just can't ever wait. George turned from the stump and stopped. *Smoke!*

The smell reached George before he saw it. Smoke was billowing up from beyond the knoll in the woods. George dropped the gun and ran towards the fire. Cresting the knoll he saw Murray. The boy was kicking at flames that were spreading through the layers of pine needles at his feet. With each kick the boy was only spreading the fire further.

"Murray stop! You're making it worse!"

The boy was panicked. He kept kicking the fire, sending balls of burning pine needles into the air. George reached him and pulled him away.

"Go to the truck and grab the bucket! NOW!" George yelled out. Murray did as he was told. George jumped onto the flaming underbrush, smothering it with his shoes as best he could. It was a losing battle. The fire was growing at a rate faster than he could squelch it.

"I'm coming!" Murray yelled out from the other side of the stream. George stopped and ran to him. He grabbed the bucket and dunked it into the stream, filling it as full as he could get. He ran back to the flames and doused what he could. Then he ran back to the stream and started again.

Three trips later the pair had the fire tamed. George had sent Murray back to grab the shovel and George was piling dirt on top of the few embers that were left. When the final flicker was out, he turned to the boy.

"Is this you? Did you do this?" George asked, infuriated.

"Yeah but it wouldn't have gotten out of control if you'd came when I called," Murray shouted back.

"Why you-" George stopped. Losing his temper now wasn't going to help the boy learn. One deep breath later and he was ready. "You're right. I should have come when you called. I'm partly to blame, son. But let me ask you this. Who started the fire?"

———

Who started the fire?

His father's voice still repeated in his head as Murray woke from his dream. He sprang up in his bed, his eyes blinking at the light hitting him directly. The guard aimed the flashlight away and continued on his patrol of the jail cells. Murray's heavy breathing calmed as he recognized his surroundings as the cell he'd been shuffled into the previous day.

His mind returned to the dream as he laid back down and closed his eyes. *You just don't quit, do you Dad?* he asked himself. *Even now, you're still teaching me lessons.*

That moment in time had stuck with Murray his whole life. He tried to live up to what his father was teaching him. Don't blame someone else for your own mistakes. Stand up and take responsibility for your actions. Be the man you want to be. Fifteen years later, and it was still relevant.

The next morning, Murray called Sam from the jail phone.

"Sam, call that attorney and tell him you've changed your mind. I won't be needing him."

"Now hold on," Sam replied sternly. "You need a good attorney. We need to fight this. They can't do this to you. Especially not after what they did to Anatoly."

"Sam, do it. This is my fault. I'm going to plead guilty."

"Murray, you're not thinking clearly. The whole city is behind you. There's people protesting your arrest as we speak. The news has your face on it every hour. We can win this."

"I said do it, Sam!"

"Murray...."

"Take the money I won and give it all to charity. Something Anatoly would respect. Every cent."

"Murray, they're going to throw the book at you. You'll be sending yourself to prison."

"Sam," Murray's tone had changed to calm as he spoke softly. "My best friend is dead. Whether some cops beat him to death or not, it's my fault. I put him in that car. I put him behind the wheel. I started the fight with them. They took part and will find their own judgment, but I'm the one that started the fire."

Sam was silent in disbelief. He opened his mouth to protest once more but he knew Murray had made up his mind. Murray's convictions were something he'd never been able to dispute. He knew that there was no changing his mind. Sam swallowed the lump in his throat and then just said, "God help you, Murray".

CHAPTER 8

When Murray faced the judge on Monday, he stood next to a public defender. Murray planned to plead guilty on all counts. His attorney, John Sloan, was fresh out of law school and was all too happy to hear that his first case would end without a trial. Murray had barely told him anything and with no witnesses aside from the police officers involved, the young defender knew there was no chance for him to win this one.

The media didn't agree with Sloan's pessimistic outlook of the case. They had been covering Murray's situation to a great degree across the nation. They were calling it a case of police brutality and that the imprisonment of Murray was a tactic to cover up the death of Anatoly. The public was in full support of Murray being freed and wanted him to fight the charges. Sloan was thrilled that he was going to get a lot of publicity but was even happier Murray wasn't going to give him the chance to embarrass himself.

Murray was dressed in a suit and tie that Sam had brought from Anatoly's house. Sam and Sloan had both insisted that Murray wear it. It was the only thing they could convince Murray of doing. It was too small, but he still looked good in it. His head injury was starting to heal and the bruises on his ribs from the fight were subsiding. He looked like he could have been there as a witness to a trial instead of someone facing a long prison term.

"All rise," the bailiff declared as the judge entered the room.

Murray stood with everyone else. He showed no sign of fear or worry in his face, just regret.

"Court is now in session. Judge Simpson presiding. You may be seated," the bailiff finished as the court found their seats.

Judge Simpson was a white man in, what Murray guessed, was his early sixties. Sloan had told Murray about Simpson, what little he knew. He'd been a judge that had presided over cases involving drug and alcohol related incidents for the last 15 years. He'd done it more than any other judge in the state. He knew each and every police officer on the force and not one defendant had ever been found not-guilty after testing positive for drugs or alcohol. Sloan was indeed glad that Murray was pleading guilty.

Judge Simpson spoke without looking up from his notes. "Mr. Bench. You are charged with the following: one count of first degree aggravated battery on a law enforcement officer, three counts of second degree aggravated assault on a law enforcement officer, assault and battery with a deadly weapon, reckless endangerment, and resisting arrest. How do you plead?"

Murray stood looking Judge Simpson in the eyes silently. Just one word would change his life forever. *Just say it, say it!* Behind him, the audience became restless. What was happening?

Judge Simpson tapped his finger until his patience was up.

"I need an answer, son."

The break in the quiet jarred Murray's resolve and he forced out the word.

"Guilty."

Gasps of disbelief filled the room and were quickly followed by warnings of injustice. There was a curse and accusation of corruption from the back, and someone spoke up "Those bastards are going to get away with it!"

"Order!" barked Simpson. He glanced at Murray. "Son, I take this type of case very seriously. While I appreciate you not wasting the court's time by pleading not-guilty to a crime you clearly committed, do not expect that action to give me cause to take it easy on you. Our police officers are the main force in keeping law and order in this city and no one is going to get a slap on the wrist for attacking those brave men and women. You are hereby sentenced to 10 to 15 years in Santa Mira State Prison with the possibility of parole after five years. Next case." Judge Simpson's gavel hit its mark and sent a flood of dismay through the room.

Murray was led by the bailiff out of the room as the crowd of people began shouting louder and booing even more. Judge Simpson was still shouting for order and hammering his gavel as Murray was escorted to the exit. He looked back into the courtroom at the people protesting the decision, standing, yelling and pointing at the judge. All their efforts were directed at Simpson. All except one man who stared at Murray in disgust from behind his glass eye. Irvine Graves held his gaze until Murray was pushed through the door.

———

It was midnight when a pair of guards walked into the jail and up to Murray's cell door.

"Time to go, kid," one said as he started unlocking the door. The other guard had a night stick out and was hitting the bat into his empty hand, all while remaining completely silent.

Murray had been sleeping and awoke in confusion. "Now?" he asked. "It's the middle of the night."

The guard entered the cell and Murray stood up. The armed guard waited outside the cell, still attempting to be intimidating with the nightstick. Murray looked at him in wonder as the first guard handcuffed Murray's wrists and then shackled his feet.

"Not my problem buddy," the vocal guard said, uncaring. "Apparently, you've got some fans outside and we need to move you out tonight before more arrive in the morning. We try to keep pandemonium to a minimum here."

He led Murray through the jail and into a large room with rows of walled cubicles. Murray continued on a path that led toward the front of the office but the guard cut him off, grabbed his arm and took him to the back of the room, where the cubicles blocked the view from the front of the police station. They passed a section of the room that was more open, and Murray could see more of the station. At the end of the rows of desks and filing cabinets was a long desk encased in windows to separate the office from the entrance.

A group in the reception area caught sight of Murray and stood up, rushing the windowed reception desk. They yelled at the police officer at the desk and created a cacophony that Murray couldn't understand. As Murray walked further, he lifted his head as high as he could get to see if he could make sense of the scene at the front. Just as the guard pulled Murray away, he was able to see the face of one person he knew. It was the face of a man who was directly in front of the officer at the reception desk and clearly the one making the most noise. It was Sam Davis. The guard pulled Murray again and led him through the exit doors.

Outside, a white transport bus had been backed up with its double doors open, ready to receive Murray. Eight armed guards formed two rows of four on either side of the bus. The sounds Murray heard from the crowd inside were nothing in comparison to the yells and screams outside. While Murray couldn't see anyone, he could tell that outside the fenced parking lot were considerably more people than inside the small reception area. Their voices were heard much more clearly, as they weren't just yelling, they were chanting, "We want justice! Let Murray go!" Their chants did nothing to relieve the guilt Murray had stored deep inside himself. In his heart, justice was being served for the killing of Anatoly Brose.

Murray was pushed into the bus and then forced into a seat by the guard with the nightstick. Murray was still handcuffed and the impact of landing in the seat shot pain through his wrists. The armed guard then leaned close to Murray and curled his lips in hate as he spoke "Santa Mira's gonna eat you up, boy. It's what you deserve for attacking a cop, you piece of shit." Murray looked back at him again in the same wonder he felt in his cell. At no point had Murray felt any fear of this bitter man, he just wondered what could make him so angry towards Murray. Now he knew.

The doors of the bus slammed closed and Murray felt the bus jolt as the driver shifted into gear. Murray looked around and saw that it was empty except for the driver and a guard sitting backwards behind a fence at the front. He was holding a shotgun and stared back at Murray.

Murray looked out the windows and saw rows of people behind the fence of the station. Inside the courtyard were at least forty police officers in riot gear all facing the fence. There were SWAT trucks on either side of the yard and Murray spotted an officer sitting atop each, armed with a fire hose in case the protesters turned violent. Outside the courtyard, Murray could see signs being waved as large spotlights circulated through the crowd. He was able to read some of the signs clearly.

"LAPD KILLED BROSE"
"JUSTICE FOR BROSE"
"LET MURRAY GO"
"WHEN WILL YOU START KILLING US?"
"JUDGE SIMPSON IS GUILTY"
"TRIAL FOR THE BROSE FOUR"

"Brose Four?" Murray muttered as the bus pulled through the gates and onto the road. "What's that?"

"The four officers who arrested you," a voice from the front of the bus said. Murray looked up and saw the guard with the shotgun was speaking to him. "It seems these people have it in their heads that you didn't try to kill those officers and that we should all just play patty-cake instead of defending our lives from someone attacking us."

The bus driver turned his head and added, "City has gone nuts. I'm all too happy to be getting out of here. Maybe if The Four hadn't killed that Ukrainian guy..."

"Hey, one of those guys is my friend. This asshole broke his eye socket and ruptured his fucking eye. Doctors say he's going to need to have a fake eye and a face made of plastic. His fucking bones shattered into his brain. If this shitwad had hit him a half inch further in he'd be dead. If anything, they should have killed this piece of shit we're caring for."

"None of that is true. Did you read that on Facebook or something? The news says that they are all fine and were released from the hospital," The bus driver said and turned his eyes back to the road.

"The media lied. You can't trust them. They're biased against police."

"Fine, sorry. Whatever." The bus driver retreated from the impossible argument and fell silent.

"You better be. It's my friend lying in a hospital," the guard defended and kept his eyes fixed on Murray.

Murray decided it'd be best to keep his mouth shut for the rest of the trip. The chants and cries of the protesters were starting to fade as the bus pulled away from the police station and began the six hour trip to Santa Mira.

As the bus entered the on-ramp to the I-5 North, Murray watched out the window at the lights of the city he'd called home for the last seven years. Somewhere in those lights was Sam Davis's gym. He wondered if Sam had gone back to take care of things there, now that Murray wasn't at the jail anymore, or if he was still behind the glass yelling at the desk sergeant. He thought of the West Hollywood neighborhood that he walked through every day and whether anyone from it had been outside the jail holding signs and chanting. He thought about them finally having enough of the corruption and the ruin brought by crime-lords like Irvine Graves. What was he even doing at the plea hearing?

As the city lights faded away and the bus passed San Fernando, his final thoughts were of him and Anatoly sitting on the back patio, drinking beer and talking about boxing greats. "Murray, someday two guys are going to be drinking beer and talking about you. You'll be a legend."

Murray's last views of the outside world, the world he knew, were lost in the blackness of night as he drifted away to sleep.

CHAPTER 9

When the bus turned off the I-5 and onto I-580, Murray woke up and saw the morning sun. He watched it rise over the San Francisco Bay as the bus headed north through Oakland and Berkeley. He knew this would be the last moment he would see a sunrise without bars or walls blocking his view for quite a while. By the time the bus reached Richmond, the sun had fully risen and the spectacle was over. It was now that the reality of his future set in.

Murray tensed as the bus drove over the San Rafael Bridge. "The end of this bridge is the end of the road for us," the angry guard spoke, then added in a hateful tone, "And for you." They drove onto the less-than-scenic two story bridge that spanned the bay in the north, the last stretch of the journey ending in a drab view, a dismal omen of what lay ahead.

The fear began to settle into his consciousness. He had no idea what hell he'd be facing inside. Everything Murray knew about prison he'd learned on television and film. He figured he was going to have to defend himself immediately. He was the son of a cop and well known for his boxing. He thought every inmate with something to prove would be challenging him. Each guard would be watching him and wouldn't give him an inch since he was in prison for attacking the police.

Murray shadowboxed in his mind to prepare his defense against the many potential ways his aggressors could strike. He ducked punches aimed at his head, dodged knife attacks to his torso and blocked jabs aimed at his throat. He tried to mentally prepare for every potential situation he might face inside as the bridge ran out of road and the bus made the left turn onto Main St. in the coastal town of Santa Mira, California.

Houses lined the little two-lane road as it ran along the coast. Residents were bringing their trash cans out and leaving them beside the road to await the garbage truck. People walked along the paths running next to the waters of the bay. A woman on the deck of a two story house watered her hanging plants. A man was painting his fence that ran parallel to the road. No one paid him any attention. The citizens of Santa Mira were uninterested in either the prison bus or the cargo it carried. It was quite a change from the near riots at the police station that Murray had experienced the last time he saw any human life that wasn't the silent bus driver or the angry guard whose stare couldn't be broken.

The bus pulled up to at a stop sign next to a little post office and Murray's gaze turned to what lay ahead. In front there was a small metal gate that resembled the type you might see outside someone's house in the neighborhoods of Beverly Hills. Next to the gate was a very unassuming sign that read:

Department of Corrections

California State Prison

Santa Mira

Just off to the left and sitting quietly atop a little hill that itself sat atop a jetty out into the bay, Murray saw the walls of Santa Mira Prison. It looked like it had been built as part warehouse, part dam, part castle, and part mansion. On the outside it was not the gulag that Murray was expecting. It seemed as if the whole thing could have just been some government building inside of a quiet little town, instead of the fortress that the California justice system used to dump their convicts bound for death row.

The bus pulled onto the prison grounds and, after passing through several additional gates and checkpoints, drove into a parking lot where several other buses were parked. The driver pulled up alongside a small building next to a fence and stopped, lurching the bus forward as he braked. "Let's go, tough guy," said the angry guard as he stood and walked toward Murray. He grabbed him up from his seat and Murray felt the pain of blood rushing back into his hands. He'd been cuffed the entire trip and hadn't even noticed his hands were completely asleep. He exited the bus to find two more armed guards standing outside who led him into the small building. "Ten minutes, asshole," he heard the bus guard yell as he walked inside. "You're going to make it ten minutes before you're dead," was the last Murray heard from the guard as the doors closed behind him and Murray became a resident of Santa Mira Prison.

———

Murray's initiation to life beyond the walls of Santa Mira were not what he had expected. The mental training for an attack he had prepped for on the bus was useless. No attacks came. In fact, he spent most of the time alone.

He was first brought into a tiled room, where he was stripped and intrusively examined for any contraband. Finding nothing, the staffers brought him into a shower. Cold water sprayed him at high-pressure. Only shampoo was given to him and he was told to scrub his entire body with it. No towel was provided before they handed him an orange jumpsuit.

He then sat alone in a concrete room for an hour or so. They'd given him a prison conduct manual to read and after doing so multiple times, he was handed a clipboard and a short pencil then was told to fill out a questionnaire.

The test had started with some basic questions that Murray understood the relevance of such as *Do you have any hobbies, Are you interested in sports, Did you go to church often* and *Have you any ambitions in any line of work* and so on. He wrote brief sentences to answer each of these questions, mentioning his interest in boxing, that he wasn't a religious man, he had enjoyed his life and that his upbringing had been what he considered normal until the time his father died.

The second block of questions was much less direct and Murray didn't really know the point of them or how to answer. The first of these questions asked "It's a fine day, isn't it?" Murray stared at this question, not sure how he felt. *Well no, it's not a fine day. My best friend is dead and I'm in prison. I'd say it's a pretty shitty day,* he deduced immediately but then he had a change of thought. *If I write something negative, they'll think I'm a problem. Maybe anger issues or they'll think I'm a risk to myself.* He wrote in the answer: "The weather is quite good today." He moved on. The second question asked "Do you think the country is being run right?" *What the hell does that matter?* He wrote into the answer, "Yes, I feel that the country is on the path to greatness." He couldn't even begin to guess what the correct answer was but he thought positivity was going to work out better for him.

He couldn't get to the third section of questions as the door opened and a young guard came in. This one had a friendly face and said, "Don't worry about the rest of that. I think it might have been written in the 30's but it's the only one we got. The docs only use the first section anymore." Murray handed him the clipboard and pencil and stood up. "Come on," the young guard went on, "We've got to get you documented now."

Documented must have been code for standing in line for hours. When he reached the front of the line, he was fingerprinted (again) and asked if he had any tattoos to document. Answering no, he moved on and into a medical exam room. His blood was taken, then he was pushed into another queue. This line ended with his name being written next to the name Schroeder, a case manager of some sort.

Finally finished with becoming a citizen of Santa Mira, Murray was led into the west cell blocks. The guards found him a cell with three other inmates inside. All had been through the same process and were now waiting a couple of days for their tuberculosis test results to come back before they could enter the general population. Murray was in for a serious wait before his time at Santa Mira really started.

———

It was about noon of Murray's second day at Santa Mira that a guard came to his shared cell door and told him to follow. Murray said farewell to the group inside and went with the guard. The guard led him down to the first floor and outside to the prison yard. It was the first time Murray had smelled fresh air in two days so he sucked in as much as he could. He wished that it wasn't cloudy so he could also feel sun on his skin but he was happy with this nice change.

The yard was fairly quiet at this time and very few inmates were outside; those that were looked like they had jobs to perform rather than just hanging around. Lunch time, Murray thought. Everyone else is inside eating.

From the main prison yard, the guard led Murray through a narrow alley between the building that Murray had registered in and the East Block to a set of buildings that looked like they might be used as offices or for administrative purposes. They entered through two large double doors that led to a hallway and then an elevator. Inside the elevator, the guard hit the button for the 4th floor, followed by a security code that allowed passage to the top floor. Murray and the guard rode the elevator in silence until it reached its destination and opened its doors to a large hallway with stained wood walls and smoked glass windows.

They were greeted here by a new guard with a face Murray would never forget. The guard was a mountain of a man with broad shoulders and thick biceps that stretched his uniform. He was built like a linebacker, strong but athletic. It was his face that put Murray at unease. From his right cheekbone down to the front of his jaw ran a deep scar that had several points that split off into smaller scars. It looked as if he'd gone in for surgery by a doctor that only had power tools to work with. Above the scar were two cold dead eyes that didn't appear to move but stayed locked on to whatever they were looking at, like he was looking at something behind Murray instead of returning his gaze. His mouth was curled in a constant frown as if he had eaten something so distasteful that his mouth was permanently fixed in an expression of disgust. On the front of his uniform was a name tag sewn into his shirt above his right breast with the name "Mitchell".

"Murray Bench," the guard that led Murray to this point introduced him to Mitchell. He promptly returned to the elevator having fulfilled his human courier duties. Mitchell grabbed Murray by the arm with a firm grip and escorted him to the end of the hall with two thick wooden doors and a placard on the right that read:

Offices of the Warden

Brett R. Corenswet

Inside the office was a slender man in his early 50s wearing an expensive yet tasteful blue suit. He stood behind a desk and gazed out of a large window that looked down on the prison yard. He had his right hand up to his mouth as if he was thinking deeply. He reminded Murray of a famous picture he'd seen of John F. Kennedy that always portrayed JFK as having the weight of the world on his shoulders but was always just one emotion away from blowing the whole thing up.

"Mr. Bench is here," Mitchell spoke to the other man as he brought Murray into the office. Mitchell stayed behind Murray by the wooden doors.

"Thank you, Steven," the suited man replied without turning from the window. "Murray, as you may have guessed, my name is Warden Corenswet and you should address me as such. I am going to speak to you now and you must not say anything until I am finished. Is that clear?"

Murray nodded, guessing that it didn't matter that his nod went unseen. Silence was the only answer Corenswet wanted.

Corenswet continued, "I apologize for the amount of time you've had to wait to meet me. I couldn't really treat you differently than any other new inmate just because you're a celebrity and all."

At this point, Corenswet turned and sat in a large leather wingback chair. He motioned for Murray to also sit down in the chair across the desk.

"Murray... may I call you Murray?" he asked. Murray nodded back, not failing to notice that this formality had already been broken.

"Murray, five years ago I became warden of this prison. When I started, Santa Mira was a dirty, overcrowded and violent place. The prisoners were undisciplined. The staff was careless and many worked more for the prisoners than the warden. The infirmary was overloaded with the sick and the injured. The previous warden had been fired for not caring much for the health of the inmates. Yet I was able to turn that all around."

Corenswet brought his hands together and turned away from Murray, looking off in the distance as if he was recounting a fishing tale. He went on, "I oversaw the installment of a new medical complex with a trauma center. I cleaned house of guards I knew were too corrupt and brought the others back in line. I instituted a series of work programs to keep the inmates busy, as well as provide them with useful skills. But pertinent to this discussion, I turned a dilapidated mess hall into a gymnasium outfitted with weights, aerobic equipment, and a boxing ring." He turned back to Murray and raised an eyebrow in delight as he spoke the last words. His eyes had a spark of anticipation that Murray had seen in eyes of other fighters he'd faced throughout his boxing career. It was the look of a predator circling what it thought was going to be easy prey.

"I must say that I am quite thrilled that you've come to stay with us here. On the other hand it is no coincidence that you are at Santa Mira. You see I went out of my way to bring you here. Why send a local celebrity in such a high profile case to the most notorious prison in the state and the only one with a death row? It could be that you were needed to really make an example of. It could be that the other prisons weren't suited to your particular disposition. Or it could be that the man who married the cousin of the California Attorney General is the warden and simply had to make a little phone call asking for a favor that brought an up-and-coming boxer to my neck of the woods."

Murray sat still, not sure how to feel about this revelation, yet knew he must not lose his composure or utter a sound. What was done was done and his best bet was to play his role out in this little drama.

"You might be feeling a little anger about that, but I assure you that I've done you a great deed by bringing you here. I know you thought that your career in boxing was over, but I'm telling you it is just getting started. You remember the boxing ring I mentioned? Well, it's very popular with the inmates now. One of the other contributions I made here was to institute a zero tolerance to violence, with one exception. Inmates and guards may use the boxing ring to release their inner demons upon each other. Now, I'm a bit of a betting man, and if the odds are stacked too much there is no money to be made. I need someone I can count on to win, but who no one else will bet on. Someone that is too lanky and scrawny to be much good here. Someone who never grew up on the streets or was part of a gang. Someone with no respect or street cred. Murray I'd like to have you be my winning bet."

CHAPTER 10

A couple hours later, Murray was standing in the boxing ring facing off against Marcus Cameron. Marcus was about 20 years old, looked like he might weigh 180 pounds and stood about 5'9". His stature was not impressive but he strutted around the ring as it if he was Hercules. Murray could tell that the kid was there because of his own stupidity, probably by selling drugs and getting caught easily. He was heavily tattooed on his torso and arms with guns, skulls and gang slogans written in Old English-style font.

The gymnasium was filled with other inmates exercising and weight training. Some were running laps, using the treadmills or elliptical machines and very few paid any attention to the boxing ring that was in the center. There was a small group around the ring, mostly comprised of friends of Cameron's or perhaps those that had placed bets on him. There was lots of yelling from this group.

"Kick his ass, Marcus."

"That skinny-ass white boy can't beat you."

"You'd better catch a square, punk."

High above the ring, Murray could see a windowed room that looked down on the fight. Inside sat Warden Corenswet with Mitchell standing behind him. Murray couldn't tell if Mitchell was looking at the ring with his dead eyes, but Corenswet looked at Murray and gave him a reaffirming nod. Corenswet had put this little exhibition match together very quickly. He was all too eager to start placing money on Murray to win, betting against other guards and inmates who still had access to outside money.

Murray looked at Cameron, who upon meeting his gaze slid one of his gloved hands over his own throat in an attempt to intimidate Murray. Corenswet told Murray that Marcus Cameron had only been at Santa Mira for less than a month but was already building a reputation for being mouthy. Corenswet had called him a "jitterbug". He said that it was time someone put Cameron in his place, and since the only place where someone could inflict pain on him was the boxing ring, Corenswet might as well make a few dollars in the process.

Murray shrugged off Cameron's taunts and put in his mouthpiece. There were no managers for the fighters. Both opponents' corners were empty. An older inmate came into the ring and waved over both fighters to the middle. There he explained the rules: there were no rounds, the fight went on until one fighter was down for ten seconds or knocked out, there was no hitting below the belt, there was no kicking and lastly, there was no hitting someone while they were down. Cameron stared at Murray the entire time the rules were explained until the makeshift referee left the ring and from the ground yelled, "Fight!"

Cameron came at Murray quickly and instantly threw a right with full force. Murray lowered his head and dodged the blow, but before he could counter, another punch was heading his way from the other side. This punch Murray blocked with his right forearm as another jab hit him in the ribs. It was a fairly light blow compared to the punches that Murray was used to, but the poor condition of the boxer's gloves was enough to make Murray feel the knuckles of his opponent against his body. Another jab came to the same spot and then another, sending jolts of sharp pain through his ribs. The punches weren't going to cause any permanent damage but the bare bone to bone contact was enough for Murray to flinch.

Murray pushed Cameron away to gain some distance. Cameron took this as a sign of weakness and spun and waved his hands in the air to his supporters. They cried out with shouts of encouragement to Cameron. "Gut this fish, dog" Murray heard one shout. "Chin check that bitch," another screamed.

Cameron turned to Murray and lunged forward and instantly pulled back, making a childish expression and laughing. Cameron was trying to play cat and mouse with Murray but he didn't know that Murray was a lion playing with a house cat. He brought his gloves up to his face and waited for Cameron to make his move. When Cameron had finished laughing he turned his head to his fans and smiled once, then came at Murray with the same right hook that started the match. Murray ducked the punch again compressing his body down this time and with all his momentum snapped up like a spring with his golden right leading the way. The blow struck Cameron right in the cheek, causing his head to spin and twisting his body into a pirouette as he dropped to the ground, unconscious. The sound of his body landing on the mat was loud enough to stop the other inmates from exercising, turn their attention towards the sound and to stare at the ring. The spectators were silent as they stared at the pile of Marcus Cameron that had folded up before them. The silence was broken by the muffled sound of Warden Corenswet clapping in knowing triumph from the windowed room above the ring.

Murray turned to his corner and began removing his gloves before anyone else moved. Finally one of the onlookers turned away in disgust and the rest shortly followed suit. The older inmate came back into the ring and lifted Cameron's arm, which fell in a thud when let go. He waved to another inmate who came into the ring and helped lift Cameron up so that they could wake him up with smelling salts.

Murray walked into the locker room as Cameron was placed on a gurney and carried out of the gym on his way to the trauma ward of the prison. As he sat, pulling the rest of the tape off his knuckles, Warden Corenswet and Mitchell came in.

"Well Murray, you've proved me right again," the warden said through his wide grin. "I want you to know that today was just a first step into a successful career here. I plan to make a lot of money off you so I want you to stay healthy."

"I will, sir." Murray replied, speaking to the warden for the first time.

"I'm going to have my guys keep an eye on you, so keep your nose clean. No fighting unless I set up the match. No lipping off to guards. No getting mixed up with any of the gangs. No gambling. No games, Murray. I mean it."

"I understand."

"Good. Now I want you to clean up and then report to the vocational office. I'm going to set you up with a Cadillac job."

Murray looked at him in confusion.

"An easy job. A cush job. Don't worry, you'll learn the lingo soon enough." The warden stood up and left Murray alone in the locker room with Mitchell.

Murray took a quick shower, dressed back in his prison jumpsuit and left the locker room with Mitchell. The gym was still crowded with inmates exercising but this time, as Murray walked by they stopped and stared at him. Some glared in hate as he walked past them and out of the doors.

Mitchell led him through the main prison yard that was full of inmates and guards. Murray now noticed that the guards were giving him the same looks of contempt that he was getting in the gym from the inmates. Some spat at the ground as they saw him while others spoke to each other with disgusted looks on their faces, slinging unheard insults in his direction. Murray looked at Mitchell as they walked past these guards but Mitchell's face was fixed in the same manner as when Murray met him: dead eyes looking at something past his destination, mouth curled downward in distaste.

Murray and Mitchell walked past the main yard that doubled as a baseball field and past the basketball and tennis courts, until they reached a concrete wall which stood about 10 feet high and ran the length of the yard. The pair came to a small door along the eastern end of the wall.

Beyond the wall was a group of large buildings looking like the industrial shops and factories that usually lie at the edges of towns. There were two big square buildings on the ends with three smaller ones in between them. Surrounding the buildings were trucks and freight vehicles. Men were loading and unloading various items in and out of these vehicles. The building in front of Murray had a large sign over it that looked to have been hung in the early 60's. The dilapidated sign read "Furniture Factory and Print Shop" in faded and peeling paint.

Mitchell closed and locked the door behind him and nudged Murray onward with an elbow. He shuffled forward as Mitchell pointed towards the small buildings over Murray's shoulder. The giant remained silent. They walked past another long and narrow building on the right which had another dilapidated sign proclaiming the building was the clothing factory. The path beyond led to a small set of offices that Mitchell guided Murray towards. Murray walked up a ramp and into the offices.

Inside, there was an inmate sitting behind a reception desk. He was an elderly man, clearly in his late 60's. His grey hair was combed in a part on the side and his glasses sat perched on the end of his nose while his eyes gazed at a computer screen from under his bushy eyebrows. As the pair approached the wizened man looked up at the two of them.

"You must be Bench," he said while looking at Murray. He briefly looked at Mitchell but then quickly returned to the computer screen. Mitchell took this as a sign of his escort duty being fulfilled, turned and left. Murray was all too happy to be out of the presence of the foreboding prison guard.

"They call that one 'Dragoon' around here. The warden has been known to use him to pressure his opponents into changing their views, usually by force. Life is better when he is not around." The inmate shuddered and focused on something on his computer.

"Corenswet just emailed me that you would be in shortly. Sounds like we're to set you up with a Cadillac." He then looked back at Murray and waited for a response.

"The warden said he wanted me to report for a job, yes." Murray replied, not totally sure what he was supposed to say.

The little man looked back at his computer and clicked the mouse through various screens. "Well I'm afraid that the job the warden mentioned isn't one that I would consider easy, but I'm sure it will be suitable for a man of your stature and age. You're going to work in the furniture shop, which we call the FF. I'll walk you over there." The little man stood up and walked up to Murray. "My name is John Dormus, but everyone calls me Mouse."

Murray shook Mouse's extended hand. He was the first friendly character he'd met at Santa Mira.

CHAPTER 11

The 'Cadillac' that Murray had been 'volunteered' for was anything but an easy job. He was put to task in the textile department of the FF. Mouse explained that he would start as a mover. He would move the rugs and carpets from station to station and when complete, move the finished products into the warehouse section of the FF. In between moving product, he would train at each station, learning how to build the machine-made rugs and carpets, how to repair the rugs that were brought in from local dealers and eventually how to hand knit wool rugs. He would work in this capacity until he'd become adept at each of the machines, workstations and tasks.

"It'll be quite a while before you're good enough to work on your own," Mouse told him as Murray wondered at the size of some of the rugs. "Couple hundred pounds, some of 'em are. You'll be doing most of the heavy lifting but there's a few guys around that'll give you a hand on the big ones."

Mouse brought Murray to a large table in the middle of the work area. Tools and fabric were neatly organized around the outside of the table in apparent perfect order. Occupying the majority of the table and part of the floor was a tapestry that Murray guessed as 12' x 15' in size. An elaborate pattern ran along the outside with images of castles, knights and lions stitched neatly within the pattern. At the center was the image of a knight in black armor, sword drawn, facing up toward a flying dragon spewing flames to the ground in front of the knight. It was the most elaborate and awesome piece of art that Murray had ever seen.

Mouse looked around and said, "We started repairing tapestries for the state-owned museums a few years ago. A lot of them come out of Hearst Castle up north. Always wanted to go there, but, well…," he paused, a memory drawn then dispersed. "I guess things didn't work out that way. Anywho, we don't do all of 'em but we do the ones that are too large to repair onsite. There's only one person who works on these. He's as much of a boss as one can be here. Now where is he?" Mouse looked around the area. "He's an elusive one."

Murray felt odd momentarily, as if he was being watched but he could see no one aside from Mouse, who was still looking behind boxes and tool racks. He felt something brush his arm and was startled to see a man standing next to him. He fell back on his heels in shock and was just about to fall into a shelf when the man lunged forward, clearing the distance between where he stood and Murray's backward plummet at an incredible speed. Murray felt as if he was falling backwards in slow motion but the man was moving faster than Murray had ever seen; he reached out and caught Murray's prison jumper in one swift motion. He pulled Murray directly up onto his feet and braced him until he found his balance. Murray was now looking directly at him, still in shock.

The man stood at about 5'9 and was clearly of Asian ethnicity. His age was hard to determine. You could have told Murray he was anywhere from his mid-30s to his late 50s and he wouldn't have thought twice about it. He was lean but very strong, as he had supported all of Murray's weight with one arm. His hair was full and dark and a mustache run from his upper lip down to the sides of his chin. His gaze was fierce as he looked at Murray.

"Ah, there you are," Mouse spoke. "Murray, meet Jan Liu."

The man holding Murray's arm now changed his expression to a smile as he let go and gave Murray a bow. Murray didn't know how to react so he did nothing in return. Liu shot a waiting expression with an eyebrow raised over to Mouse.

"Oh, sorry," Mouse came back. "*Master* Jan Liu."

"At your service," Liu bowed again.

"Master? Of what?" Murray asked.

"Oh, a little of this, little of that," Liu answered releasing the bow. "Here I am the master of tapestries."

"Liu runs this department. You'll be working with him. He'll show you how to do things around here," Mouse continued. "Jan, this is Murray Bench. Corenswet sent him over here personally."

"It is a pleasure to meet you, Mr. Bench." Murray expected another bow with this but instead was met with an extended hand. He met the handshake firmly.

"You can just call me Murray, Master Liu." Murray said.

"And you please do the same and call me Jan. Only John here must call me Master," Jan replied with a chuckle.

"I lost a bet," Mouse said.

Liu smiled. "One of many. Come, I have much to show you."

"You're in good hands Murray. I'll leave you to it," Mouse said as he started to leave. He stopped abruptly and turned back to Murray. "Hey, I know that you're new here and I get the feeling like you could use a few friends. Why don't you join me and some of the other boys at chow time?"

Murray smiled and said, "Definitely. I'll find you. Based on the looks I got on the way over here, I'm going to need all the friends I can get."

Mouse exited and Murray was left to begin his work. He spent the rest of the day learning where everything was and where it all belonged. Jan took him throughout the entire department and showed him an overview of the steps each article went through as it was created or repaired and then shipped out. The department made carpeting for all the State's correctional facilities as well as law enforcement and administration offices. Area rugs were made by several machines and then shipped out to different government offices. Hand knotted rugs were sent out to the more publicly visited agencies like the Office of the Governor and city official departments. Lastly, there were the tapestries that only Jan repaired.

At about 6pm, Jan told Murray that it was time to call it a day and head back to the blocks for dinner. Tomorrow would be the real start of Murray's work. Murray invited him to join him with Mouse for chow, but Liu declined. He had to continue to work on the dragon and knight tapestry and would be staying at the FF through chow time.

Murray thought that seemed odd. Weren't there certain rules in place that prevented inmates from not following the same schedule? Maybe this place wasn't as bad as he'd always thought it would be. He'd now made several friends, had a job, and best of all was able to keep boxing. Still, it had only been a few days that he'd been in lockup and it wasn't always going to be good. Eventually something bad would happen, but he could handle it. There was hope. He'd serve his time with his head down and mouth shut and be able to get out of here once his sentence was served. For the first time since he woke up in jail, Murray felt a bit of optimism as he walked across the FF to the door that led to the prison yard.

He was still smiling as he walked through the door, when he heard footsteps behind him and a voice say, "Hey, new boot!" Murray turned in time to see four men coming towards him, three of whom he recognized as part of the crowd from the boxing match and the fourth as Marcus Cameron himself. Marcus rushed at Murray and swung a broken pipe at his head. He ducked the blow and countered his attacker with a right cross to Marcus's ribs. Cameron went down in a pile, gasping for air. The next attacker threw a punch at Murray's face but Murray caught the blow with his forearm and struck back with a left, just before a bat swung at his face. He ducked it and the weapon clanged against the side of the building. Murray took the break in the incoming blows to run.

He was too far outnumbered and his attackers being armed was enough to make him retreat. He sprinted away, hearing his pursuers gather themselves and run after.

He had just enough of a lead that he could try to lose them. If he could find someplace to hide, he might be able to get away. But where? He had no idea where he was or what was ahead. He had no choice, he had to keep going.

Along the side of the FF he continued, daring once to turn back to look at his attackers. His physique was playing in his favor this time; he was gaining ground but he hadn't ditched them yet. Luck was on his side again as his glance allowed him to see that the FF had a second story with windows lining the upstairs. Just a few more steps and he would be turning the corner around to the front of the building. As soon as he rounded the corner, he found his way up. Ahead was a pile of trash. He bounded up a stacked crate, then leaped off a barrel at the top of the stack and finally grabbed onto the roof of the building. He pulled himself up with the last of his strength and then dove in through the open window to the second floor.

He lay flat on the ground, attempting to catch his breath. Outside, he heard Cameron's crew continue pass him. He'd manage to escape. Another deep gasp of breath was needed when he realized he cut his forearm on the roofline. He hadn't even noticed it until now. It wasn't much but he would need to get attended to at the infirmary next.

"I can patch that up for you."

Jesus! Murray jumped up to find Liu staring back at him.

"You scared the shit out of me!"

"Today it looks like lots of things are scaring the shit out of you," Jan said with a laugh. "You will need to watch yourself out there in the future. Otherwise the prison laundry won't be able to keep up!"

CHAPTER 12

"Ready? On three. One, two, threeee-aggghhh!"

Murray strained with the weight of the rug and his coworker wasn't faring much better. A few inches above the ground was all they could manage before having to give up and let it drop. They needed to get three feet higher.

"Lift with your legs!" yelled the helper from across the rug. Murray hardly knew this guy and only knew to address him as "Stiff".

"I am lifting with my legs!" Murray barked back. "You got it just as high as I did."

"That's because you were lifting with your back!"

Murray waved his response off. He was just about to suggest getting one of the four forklifts used in the loading area when the doors of the warehouse opened. Five men entered: four guards and the warden.

"Murray! What are you doing lifting these? I said you were to have a Cadillac," the warden said as he strolled in, his entourage tailing behind.

"This is what was assigned to me."

"We'll have to change your tasks," Corenswet replied, eyeing the large rug beside his boxer. "I don't want you throwing your back out. I need you in excellent condition at all times."

"Then it would be a good thing to keep this up," Murray said. It wasn't in his interest to shirk his duties after just arriving. What better way to be singled out by the other inmates as the warden's pet? It would be like painting a target on his jumpsuit. However, he knew that he couldn't disobey the warden either. "I need to exercise to win. Strength-training, you know?"

"Hmmm," the warden hummed. He thought for a minute after looking at Murray's physique compared to the other inmates who worked in the loading dock. "You need this strength training in your legs?"

"You saw how I beat Cameron. It's all in the legs, sometimes."

"Very well. Continue with your duties, but do not do anything that could put you in the infirmary. Understand?"

"I do."

"Then it's settled." Corenswet smiled and then sat down on the rug. Murray hadn't seen him smile before. It didn't seem a natural occurrence to him. The warden continued speaking after letting the expression fade.

"Speaking of Cameron and the excellent lesson you taught him, I'd like to set up another fight. When do you think you'll be ready?"

Murray had known that this was coming, he just didn't expect it so soon. It was only his second day out of prison quarantine.

"I don't think the lesson took to Cameron. The aftermath of the fight didn't go really that swell."

"I heard about the attack. I've got to give you my apologies for what happened" Corenswet said. "I can assure you that I take full responsibility and I promise you that it will not happen again."

"Warden, I appreciate the sentiment but this was not your fault. Those boys had it out for me." Murray stopped talking when he saw the warden's expression change and Mitchell took a step towards Murray. Apparently, you couldn't disagree with the warden, even if you were defending him.

Corenswet's hand went up to stop Mitchell. "Do not question me, Mr. Bench. What happens within these walls is for me to decide. Those men attacking you is no different than if I'd been the one holding the bat. But as I've said, they won't be bothering you anymore. In fact, no one here will ever be hearing from them again."

Murray's face went white. Who was he dealing with here, really?

Corenswet saw the expression in Murray's face. "Oh no, dear boy. You don't think I had those men killed, do you?" Corenswet laughed as he continued. "What kind of a monster do you think I am? This isn't one of those prisons where the warden sticks rule breakers in some hole in the ground to rot or has a private sniper that shoots inmates from a tower and then calls it a failed escape attempt. No, no. I had them all transferred to one of the other state prisons."

Corenswet rose and began examining the loading area as he spoke. "Their kind are not wanted and that type of behavior is a one way ticket out of here. To a newcomer like you that might not seem like much of a punishment, but I can assure you that we have quite the wondrous little system here. Being thrown out of Santa Mira IS punishment indeed. You see, the other prisons in the state of California aren't quite as....enjoyable, you might say. In fact they are downright nasty. It's likely they'll all come down with a digestive disease within a week. Horrible stuff." Corenswet gave his unnatural smile as he uttered the final sentence.

"But enough about them. Now that I've personally overseen a fitting punishment to your aggressors, word will go throughout the prison that you are under my protection. No one will have the will or desire to attack you. Fear of a reaction from me will assure that. I'd like you to keep winning those boxing matches for me. Does that seem like something you can accomplish?"

Murray didn't want to lose the opportunity to keep boxing, even if Corenswet was just using him.

"Yeah. I can do that."

"Good. I will have another set up later this week. Keep up the good work."

———

Corenswet's timetable was not something Murray was going to be able to rely on. The very next day, Mitchell led him from the FF back into the gymnasium.

"Who am I fighting?" Murray asked as they walked through the yard. Mitchell was silent.

"Hello? Paging Dr. Dragoon? Anyone there?" Murray's sarcasm was met with more silence. He wasn't going to get anything out of the guard.

Thirty minutes later, he was dressed and standing in the ring. A crowd was beginning to gather around the edges. This group was much different than his last audience. They stood casually talking to each other, sizing Murray up as he stretched. They reminded him of the first time he went into the training ring at Sam's gym against one of Sam's best boxers. The crowd continued to quietly study him as he warmed up, throwing jabs at an invisible opponent. Murray took heed of them. This group knew a thing or two about boxing.

Their gazes shifted when the doors of the locker room opened. Murray followed suit and saw his opponent exiting. He was slightly shorter than Murray, heavier set, and looked about forty years old. He met Murray's look and nodded to him. He approached the ring and slid under the ropes, with a little grunt in effort.

"Old bones ain't what they used to be," he casually said to Murray after standing. "Someday you'll know what I mean. You're Murray Bench. Gotta say, I'm honored to meet you."

The fighter put his gloved hand out to Murray who returned the gesture and bumped the top.

"I know you?" he asked.

The fighter shook his head.

"Name Joe Wasser, ring a bell? No? I didn't have much of a career. I fought out of Chino for about six months, but things didn't go as planned and ended up here," Joe said. "I know you though. Or of you, I should say. Guy I know from back in the day wrote me about you. Guess you know him as TuTone."

"You know TuTone?" Murray asked happily. "I love that guy. Small world."

"Yeah he used to write to me in here. Telling me about this boxer he knows. Gonna be the next biggest thing in the ring. 'Kid with the Golden Right'," he pointed to Murray's arm. "I was sad to learn what happened to you."

"Thanks. Man, that's crazy," Murray said still focused on TuTone. "Maybe we can talk some more about him…and you. If you'd be interested?"

"Absolutely. I'd like that a lot," Joe smiled again. "Unless you happen to knock my head off with that right of yours."

The sound of fists banging on glass came from overhead and Murray heard Corenswet yelling distantly from his viewing room. Murray glanced up and then down to the crowd who were getting restless as well.

"Shall we do this?" Joe asked.

Murray nodded then hit Joe's gloves one more time.

"Good luck," he said confidently. Joe's mouthpiece was already in and didn't respond.

The fighters separated and moved around the ring, searching the other opponent for a weakness. Murray approached first with a left that Joe blocked, then retreated. Murray tried again with the same result. *Okay, guess this is going to take a little longer*, he thought reflecting on the easy defeat of Marcus Cameron. His thoughts were cut off before he could make a plan, as Joe came at him with a flurry of blows around his midsection. Murray took the punishment, but used the opportunity to try an upper-cut from his right. Joe pulled back from the punch just in time. If it had connected, the fight would have been over but Joe was clever. As the fight went on, he kept avoiding the right. Over and over, Murray thought he had Joe where he wanted him but the older fighter was still agile enough to dodge or block the knockout punches.

What would have transpired as six rounds outside of Santa Mira's rules went by in a slow crawl for the fighters. What had started as decent-sized crowd had dispersed to other more eventful activities. Joe was smart, quick and lithe but his age was started to slow him down. While missing him repeatedly with the right, Murray was wearing him down with the left. He saw Joe falter a little. Once more, Murray came at him with the right, was blocked, but this time he followed with a cross from his left that caught Joe in the chin. This sent the larger man to the ground on one knee. The referee ran over to him and began his countdown. Joe waved him off; he'd had enough.

The fighters met in the middle of the ring and hugged.

"Good fight," Joe congratulated. "It was fun."

Murray was surprised by the even keel Joe refused to let give up. "You too, man. You good?"

"Yeah, just give me a while," Joe sat back down on the mat and leaned against one of the corners. "You go ahead without me. Just gonna take a breather."

Murray thanked him for the fight once more, said he'd meet up with him later and headed into the locker room.

———

"Bench, you've got a visitor," the guard shouted at Murray from the doorway of the recreation room. Murray turned to look at him and was waved over. He turned back to Mouse and Joe, then set his cards down. Murray had introduced Joe to Mouse and the three were getting along quite well. Cards had quickly became the go-to activity for their time together.

"I guess I'll have to remain undefeated," Murray said to his friends as he stood up.

"Saved by the bell, as they say," Joe replied.

"Rummy just isn't your thing. Nothing to be ashamed of," Murray jested.

"I think he's cheating," Mouse teased. "Got a deal with the warden or something to save his skin whenever we get close to beating him."

Murray shot Mouse a look of amused indignation and then turned from the table to meet the guard. He was led out of the cell block and across the yard to the visitors building. Inside he walked down the hall then into to the visiting area with a glass barrier where visitors could speak to inmates through a phone. He passed others talking to their wives, siblings or whoever was left in the outside world that still had faith in them.

He stopped when his saw his visitor. He was expecting to see Sam Davis making his third trip since Murray arrived. But the man on the other side of the glass wall was no friend.

Irvine Graves gestured Murray to sit down. Reluctantly, Murray obliged. He stared at Graves for a moment who already had the handset released and pressed to his ear. One eye stared back at Murray, its counterpart devoid of feature. Graves smiled. Murray relented and picked up the phone.

"What do you want, Graves?"

"Good to see you too," Graves said. "How's the food? More importantly, how are the showers? All exits still one way?"

Murray rolled his eyes.

"If you ever retire from being an A-1 piece of shit, you'd have a promising career as a comedian, Graves. And by comedian, I mean something your dad should have left in a sock, instead of your mother. How is your father, anyways? He ever come back from getting that pack of smokes thirty years ago?"

"I see your envy of my life still hasn't changed," Graves stated. "How's your daddy? Still fucking dead?"

"Get to it, Graves. What do you want?"

"Same thing I wanted two weeks ago. I want you to fight for me."

"Answer is still no. Besides, can't you see I'm not a free man anymore?"

"Let me tell you what I see," Graves answered. "I see a man stuck in prison who should be out fighting. I see a man who needs my help. I can make this all end for you, Bench. I can get you out of here today. I can help you get your life back. Would you like my help?"

"Faust made the same deal," Murray said. "It didn't work out for him."

"Faust made a deal with the devil. I'm not the devil that you think I am."

"Oh, so destroying a community and feeding on the lives of the weak makes you a saint, huh? I was told about you Graves. Guys know you in here. I know you aren't just a boxing enthusiast. You're a racketeer. I know what you tried to do to Davis Gym." Murray was already growing tired of being in the presence of the crime-lord. "Look, you're a low-life fuckwad. You're the filth that even dog-shit gets sick from. You're a reprobate who would fuck his sister, if only she could stop laughing at the size of your prick. Now you want more? Or are you ready to fuck off?"

"You love that community, huh? You think I'm ruining it? You haven't even seen ruin yet, you sniveling, spineless waste of meat. I can torch that whole neighborhood. The people you knew, their lives, their homes, gone! You fight for me or I'll watch Davis Gym burn to the ground in front of me."

Murray laughed. "Graves, you're booking a one-way ticket to federal prison. You make a move and the cops are going to come down on you like stink on shit."

"Oh but you are so wrong this time, Murray Bench. I'll stand there laughing as the cops won't be able to touch me. You see, I own the cops."

"Sure you do," Murray sarcastically replied. He was walking into a trap.

Graves leaned forward, his eyes burning with conquest.

"At 10:25pm on Friday, Officers Nate Johns and Louis Rodihan of the LAPD pulled over a vehicle on the suspicion of driving under the influence of alcohol. The vehicle was a blue sedan with California plates occupied by two adult males."

Murray almost dropped the phone. His heart began racing in his chest, fearing the words that Graves was going to say next.

"The passenger was Caucasian, mid-twenties, athletic build. The officers determined the individual to be heavily intoxicated and proceeded to administer a sobriety test on the driver, a male in his late twenties, heavy build, balding, of Slavic descent."

Murray's fist smashed into the window. The guards took notice.

"Yes, Murray. I had two of my officers take a special interest in your manager. You said you wouldn't fight for anyone else. So I had them send you a little message. Only you were too stupid to get it. Instead you pled guilty like a fucking idiot. But I would be happy to have them pay Sam Davis the same type of…call it a service to the community."

Murray was gone, only rage was left. He was on his feet, beating the quarter-inch acrylic glass with the phone. He'd struck the separator five times before the guards could pull him far enough away. The last blow cracked the glass and Graves snapped backwards in shock. The guards pulled at Murray, but he wouldn't let go of the phone. Not yet.

"You better hope they lock me away forever, Graves. I get out of here and the first thing I'm going to do is kill you. I'm going to find you and kill you, Graves! You hear me? I'm going to kill you!"

He was still screaming when the guards finally broke him away and removed him from the room.

CHAPTER 13

Darryl Whiteley stepped off the elevator of the fourth floor building and entered the hallway that led to Graves's private office in Los Angeles. He moved the hall that was adorned with modern art and photos of athletes that Graves had met or respected. Whiteley cracked a smile as he walked past a photo of Tito Pistelli standing over a defeated Alan Jords. Pistelli had once labeled him as "Graves's bitch boy" and Whiteley had loathed him ever since. He was only too happy when Murray Bench took that cocky asshole down. Whiteley was Graves's most trusted employee and the crime-lord's go-to man if he wanted something done right and none of his boss's boxers should ever disrespect him. Pistelli was lucky Whiteley hadn't buried him in the desert.

He nodded to the bodyguards standing at the end of the hall and they returned the gesture. The one on the right stepped forward and Whiteley put his arms out and spread his legs. The guard checked Whiteley for any weapons but found none. He'd already deposited the Walther 9mm in the guard's office downstairs. The frisk was routine but it still bothered him that Graves wouldn't trust him all the way and let him keep his piece on him at all times. Nevertheless, Irvine Graves hadn't got to his status in life by being careless. Suspicion at all times and with all people had been a long and powerful ally.

The guard finished his check and allowed Whiteley to enter the large office beyond the door. He stepped in. Graves's office was even more decorated than the hallway but carried one theme only: the visage of Irvine Graves. There were statues, commissioned paintings and more photos throughout, all bearing the image of his employer. It was a museum dedicated to just one man and it was no coincidence that Whiteley found the curator staring at a bust of himself. The bust was located at the end of the room, between a large set of windows that overlooked the street below and a large mirror. It was where Whiteley found Graves whenever his boss was angry about something. It was time to tread lightly for the enforcer. Good news first, then.

"The shipment arrived without any problems, sir," Darryl stated. "The occupants have been moved from the docks to the apartment and are being trained as we speak. They'll be ready to take clients by the end of the week. I've got Sweet moving the old ones out for this new line. I have to tell you, I saw the new girls. All young, all untouched."

Graves didn't respond. His gaze didn't break from the bust of himself. He was looking for answers that only he could find within himself. Whiteley tried again to break him from his rage.

"The track has paid out. Martinez didn't dodge us this time. The boy's time with his girlfriend must have brought him in line. I think we could apply the same tactic with Jennings the next time he tries to cheat us on the take from the H."

"And Davis?" Graves asked without breaking his fixation.

"Davis is a different type of problem. We need to acquire the land legally, you said so yourself."

"And your point?"

"We can't do so if he sells to us under duress. The underwriter won't ever sign off on the title transfer. I say we stick to driving the value of the property down. Make the surrounding area unsafe for clients. Drive it into the ground. He'll sell. With Bench out of the picture-"

At the mention of Murray Bench, Graves stood and turned to Whiteley. Any hope Darryl had of keeping his briefing cut-and-dried had dissipated by using Bench's name. He should have known better.

"Bench is NOT out of the picture!" Graves shouted in Whiteley's face. The employee tried to create some space between him and the infuriated employer but with each step backwards Graves matched it. "Bench IS the fucking picture!"

"I know, sir. I'm sorry," Whiteley cowered. "But sir, might I ask, just so we are all on the same page here, why now? Why the shift to Bench? He's no threat to your business."

"He's a threat to me and that makes him my business," Graves replied less aggressively but his eyes still burned with hatred.

Whiteley didn't understand, but it wasn't his job to. Yet he had to know what his boss wanted in order to keep his job and possibly his life. This wasn't the first time he'd witnessed his employer obsess over something that would at first appear to be trivial. What others would see as mania, Graves would see as strategy. Time and time again, Graves would prove his critics wrong. Whiteley trusted him as much as he feared him when he got this way. He had to play this carefully.

"I know that I don't have the same vision as you, sir. Your foresight in these matters is unmatched. You know I'm not on the same plane as you but you also know that I am no moron. If I can understand, then I can execute your wishes better. Without that understanding, I'll have to have you give specific orders on all matters, and I know how you hate that. You say you want me to act on your needs without being asked to do so. Well, I need to know what your motivations are with Bench."

Whiteley braced. He'd taken a risk, a gamble in his words. However, he had reached his position by doing just that. Without taking risks, he'd never have climbed out of the ghetto he was from to work for such an important man as Graves. Once again, he'd gambled and won. Graves didn't attack.

"He told me no. Twice," Graves said calmly. His mood had shifted once again, a shift that Whiteley had become familiar with but never accustomed to. "I refuse to accept no as an answer from anyone. It shows weakness, a lack of control over one's affairs. His rejection is enough to warrant my wish for his demise, yet there is something worse he's done. He threatened my life, Darryl. No one has ever done that before. Any threat to me was always dealt with before things came to that point. I didn't do that with Bench. I should have spotted him. I should have read him better. That is my mistake and one I intend to correct. I don't enjoy making mistakes, and so few have been made that I'm not accustomed to them. I find them insulting."

Whiteley nodded his agreement. Graves moved around the desk, opened a drawer and pulled out a bottle of bourbon with a rock glass. He gave himself a generous amount of the liquor, then turned his attention to the view out the window.

"No one can do that to you. I now share in your hatred for him," he said, telling his boss what he thought he would want to hear. Graves didn't take notice.

"I need this mistake, this aberration, to cease to exist," Graves said.

"What is it you would have me do sir?" Whiteley asked. Graves didn't respond immediately. He took a drink and continued to look outside. Whiteley knew that he was plotting. It was best to not say anything else for now.

Graves grit his teeth in anger. He was growing tired of failure around him.

"I can't have any more disappointments. If Johns had done as he was supposed to and just killed Brose, I wouldn't be in this situation. Instead, he arrests Bench. Fucking idiot."

"It was his partner Rodihan that filed the arrest, sir." Whiteley ventured.

"Really? Hmmm. I will have to make amends for that. If Bench hadn't been arrested, he would have had nowhere to turn to but me after the death of his manager. I could have been a support figure, guiding him into working for me. Instead, he gets arrested and made famous by those Keystone Cops. Thank god I have Simpson on the take."

"Why didn't you have Simpson let him go though? You could have then filled the support role and gotten Bench like you said before."

"Bench became a celebrity by then. If he'd been freed, there would have been a thousand other promoters wanting to get a hold of him. No, I needed him isolated. In a place where only I could get at him. A place where I had someone on the inside to keep him safe."

"You mean someone like Beckton?" Whiteley asked in reference to one of Grave's men serving time in California's penal system.

"No, not someone like Beckton." Graves grinned but not revealing more to his man. He squinted in a final thought as his plan had unfolded in his mind. "Where is Beckton currently?"

"Folsom."

Graves turned around and faced Whiteley. "Have Simpson order a transfer. Put Beckton into Santa Mira immediately. Have him put together a group. Then hit Bench."

"Clean or dirty?"

"Make it clean. Quick. Quiet. No message needs to be sent. I just want it done right."

"And Davis? Should I send someone to do the same with him?"

"No. Just Bench," Graves stated adamantly. "I want that gym on the up and up. Pay Davis another visit. Offer to buy the place again. Give him another 20% over our last offer."

"And if he refuses?"

"Tell him that he holds the key to save Bench's life. We'll pull the hit if he sells."

"Can I assume that is a lie?"

"It is. Bench dies."

Whiteley nodded, turned and left the office. Graves turned to the mirror, next to the bust of himself. He looked straight into his own eyes and said, "No one threatens me, right? No? That's what I thought."

CHAPTER 14

The sound of a commercial break coming from the speaker of a small television in the office was the only thing to be heard inside Davis Gym at 9:48pm. The last of the few members who still came and trained had left hours before. The punching bags were still, but the lights all remained on. Inside the little office in the corner, Sam Davis waited for 10 o'clock to come so that he could go home to his family. His daughter, Sofia, was turning 11 years old the next day and tonight he had plans to prep for the party with his wife of 14 years, Lucille. He still had to pick up supplies, balloons, hats, and the cake on his way home. He had the family's only car, so he had to be the one to do it.

There was a time when things weren't that way. They'd had to sell both of the newer cars and buy an older model just to pay off some of their credit card debt. With the gym not bringing in very much money, the Davises couldn't afford to continue paying the monthly fees and set aside funds for Sofia's college. Sacrifices had to be made. The night manager of the gym was laid off and Sam picked up the slack.

He sat each night until 10pm in case a late client needed to use the facility. No one ever did, anymore. Some time ago, someone did. Murray Bench would come in at 9:45pm and soak in a tub of ice after his fights. Brief though the fights were, the punishment on a boxer's body afterward was always heavy. After Murray defeated Greg Williams, Davis Gym saw an increase in customers, but it was all too fleeting. Unfortunately since the gym's most prolific fighter was gone now, fewer people came each day.

Sam was brought out of his memories by what he swore was a knock at the door. He sat up in his chair and turned his ear towards the entrance. *The door's open*, Sam thought. *Why would someone knock? Must be just the building shifting that I heard.*

The sound came again moments later and he clearly heard the rap of knuckles on the door. Sam left the office and walked along the wall that ran to the entrance. Looking through the window he saw familiar faces but they weren't the faces of any customers. He opened the door to the three men standing outside.

"The door is open," Sam stated flatly.

"Your sign says, 'Members only'. We are not members," the lead said. He was a man in his early 30s with short, black hair and a well-trimmed goatee. He wore a black leather jacket over a grey t-shirt. From the collar of his shirt hung sunglasses, despite the sun setting hours ago. His clothes were designer and it was clear that his appearance was important to him. His two partners did not have the same air about them. They were clearly hired muscle and looks were not important to them, except when it came to looking intimidating, at which they excelled.

"So then why are you here, Whiteley?" Sam asked as he walked away from the door. He knew why they were there but he still thought it'd be best to go through the motions of courtesy. These types were big on respect and being treated like normal people.

"We'd like to extend another offer to purchase this facility. Our employer is willing to increase his previous offer by 20%. I would recommend you consider his generosity. I'm afraid there won't be a better offer extended to you. Refusing it would make things...difficult for everyone involved."

"Well, you can tell your boss, once again, that I am not interested in selling the gym. Now if you will kindly leave, I'd like to close up," Sam motioned towards the door courteously.

"I'm afraid it's not that clear cut and simple, Mr. Davis." Darryl Whiteley held his position where he stood. "We've already acquired much of your neighbors' property. We own this area. We can do as we choose with it, because we own it. We know that your business is failing. We can make it even tougher on you."

Sam was losing his patience. "Well, bad news for you but this gym and the land it sits on belong to me outright. I don't owe a bank or have to make payments on it. If I wanted to, I could close the doors of this place and let it rot until the end of time and still not sell it to the mob or anyone else for that matter."

"I see your position is firm, Mr. Davis," The mobster's stance relaxed a little. He smiled at Sam. "I can respect that. But I promise you, we will acquire your property one way or another. I want you to know this, though. My employer does cares about you and your customers. Maybe you should consider Murray Bench's future."

Sam's laughed at the mobster's implication.

"Listen, you little shit weasel. Murray Bench is in a place where you can't touch him. You can take your thinly-veiled threat and shove it up your boss's ass."

"There's no 'veil' on my statement. Santa Mira is no safer for Bench than the streets of LA. If we want him dead, it will happen."

Sam's temper was starting to flare and he could feel his face flushed with heat.

"Go to hell and take your goons with you. You want to make threats? Here's one. I'll fucking burn this place to the ground and put the land back in the hands of the city of Los Angeles. You and your 'employer' will never get your fingers on it."

"Very well then, Mr. Davis." The trio turned and walked to the door. "You must do what you feel is right."

Nevertheless Sam wouldn't quit. He was too angry now and his rage boiled over. "You'll see. I've built a coalition to restore this neighborhood, you bastards! We're going to rebuild and take this neighborhood back from scum like you! We're forcing you out, not the other way around!"

Darryl Whiteley laughed as the two heavies walked out the door. The last turned and bowed to Sam and then closed the door behind him.

Sam cursed at them under his breath one last time and walked back to the office. It was now five minutes after ten and he just wanted to shut the place down and go home. Inside the office, the television was on and the local news was just starting. He hit the lights for the main section of the gym and the office, but as he did the words "Brose 4" caught his ear. He turned to the TV and saw the anchor with "Special Report" on the bottom third of the screen. Sam turned the volume up.

"-of this shocking report and allegations. We go to an interview recorded earlier today by KGGR's own Tom Jorman with the alleged victim. We must warn you though, the nature of the material is quite graphic. Parents with younger viewers may want to turn away."

Sam sat down in front of the television as the screen changed to the face of a woman in her late 20's. She wore a tank top that was worn along the edges and stitching. Her hair was pulled back from her face and it was clear that she was distraught. Tears had made a path through the dark makeup underneath the woman's eyes. She could have been considered pretty had it not been the miles of life that had taken too much of a toll. She was smoking a cigarette nervously as she talked. Behind her were plastic tubs of children's toys and stacks of magazines that were covered in dust. A broken bar-b-que grill sat just inside the frame. The woman was either poor or not much of a housekeeper. A large dog was barking in the background.

"I want justice. I want them to pay for what they did," she said between sobs.

Then the reporter came on the screen standing in front of an older house. "This is the home of Cindy Meyers. On a Tuesday night two weeks ago, she and her fiancé', George Martinez, were having a fight here when things got out of hand."

The shot changed back to Cindy. "I thought he was going to hit me with a wrench. He was chasing me around the house with it, yelling and screaming at me. He'd lost it."

The reporter continued, "That's when Cindy tricked him into going outside. She used the brief moments she had to phone the police."

"They came pulling up. Two officers, Johns and Rodihan, came to the door and George opened it up. He was calmer by that point and we were just talking then. I wasn't scared of him anymore."

"You'll remember Officers Nate Johns and Louis Rodihan as two members of the alleged 'Brose 4'," the reporter voiced over the images of police cars on screen and a picture of Anatoly. Sam's heart dropped at the image. "The subjects of a recent police brutality inquest into the death of Anatoly Brose, manager of the boxer, Murray Bench. Bench was sentenced to 10 years in Santa Mira for his involvement in the incident."

"One of our dogs, her name was Ginger, was barking real loud at the police at the door," Myers recalled. "We kept telling her to be quiet but she was protecting us real good."

The reporter interjected, while holding a photo of a black and white-spotted dog. "This wasn't the first time law officers had met with Ginger. In December of last year, Ginger attacked and killed a neighbor's dog when it came onto the property of Martinez and Myers. The police were called in by the owner of the deceased animal but no charges were filed against them."

"So Ginger was barking and jumping and I was like 'You stop it' you know? But Officer Johns, he hit Ginger in the head with his nightstick, and…," the tears started coming forth in Cindy's eyes again. "…and she died. He killed her right there. I loved that dog. She was my baby."

The voice of the reporter spoke from behind the camera, "I know this is hard but can you please tell them what you told me happened next?"

Cindy wiped the tears and collected herself as best she could. "I started hitting Officer Johns and screaming at him. I said I was going to kill him. I didn't mean it, but I was drunk and I was so angry."

The shot went back to the reporter outside the house. "Myers was arrested for assaulting a police officer, disturbing the peace, and obstruction of justice. She was placed inside the LAPD police cruiser."

"We pulled away and drove for just a bit, then they pulled over in a parking lot. And I was confused why they would need to stop, but I thought maybe they needed to check to make sure of something, I don't know. But Johns came to the back and opened the door and," Cindy choked as the tears began again. "He grabbed me and then put his hand down my shirt and he pulled my breasts out of my shirt. I was handcuffed and couldn't stop him. He was talking to the other and telling him to look at me. I yelled for help, but nobody did anything."

"Jesus, motherfuckers," Sam said out loud. Yet the report went on.

"Myers couldn't continue the interview but has given us a sworn statement that Officer Johns proceeded to rape her vaginally and that Rodihan masturbated over her and forced her to perform oral sex on him. She was then taken to jail and was put before a judge the next day and then released."

"I didn't want to say anything because I was scared they would come back and hurt me or my family again. But I can't live with the pain anymore. I need justice," Cindy Myers said as the shot faded to black on her.

The reporter came on the screen one last time, walking in front of the Los Angeles City Hall. "KGGR has sent the full interview and statement to the Los Angeles Police Department's Internal Affairs office as well as the commanding officers of those involved. At this hour, no charges have been filed and the only statement we've been given is that there is no evidence to support any charges or arrests in the allegation."

Sam had heard enough and turned the television off. It was an all too familiar scenario for him. He felt horrible for the woman. Those sons of bitches killed his friend and sent the other one to prison. Now that poor woman had to live the rest of her life with the emotional and physical damage that they caused her. Now he had two reasons to visit Murray: one, he had to share this news with him. It wouldn't do that poor Myers woman any good but maybe it'd help Murray forgive himself and realize he wasn't the one to blame for Anatoly's death. And two, he had to warn him about the threats Graves's men had delivered. Maybe he better call Murray tonight.

Sam shut the office door behind him and put his coat on to leave when he heard shouting from outside. There were many voices and they were angry. He listened for a moment until he heard the shattering of glass and cheers. Frightened but curious, Sam opened the door to Davis Gym and found himself in the heart of a riot. Cars were burning in the street. Masked people were throwing bricks through the windows of businesses. There were people running everywhere, yelling and screaming. He heard some of them yell out "Fuck the Brose Four" or "Fuck the police." It was mayhem. His poor neighborhood was falling apart enough as it was, and now the people that lived in it were tearing it down even further.

Sam ran back inside the gym and locked the wooden door behind. He reached into the umbrella stand next to him and pulled out a wooden baseball bat that he kept for emergencies. Ready for anything to come bursting through the door if the lock didn't hold, Sam cocked the bat back. He stood in this manner for what seemed like hours to him. Each time he thought he could relax, something would strike the door and he'd tense again.

He wasn't going to be making it home on time tonight. He'd have to wait until the violence around him subsided. He'd make it up to Sofia somehow, as long as he made it through the night in one piece.

CHAPTER 15

Murray exited the loading dock and hung the keys to the forklift in the lock box next to the door. The guard at the entrance into the FF told him good night and locked the box behind him. Murray was finding his job to be like a nine-to-fiver on the outside. It seemed so normal to him. Each day he'd do his work, then turn in the keys like he was punching a time clock. He half expected to hear a whistle blow each night when it was time to head to the dining hall for chow. He was going there next, followed by another battle with Joe and Mouse in their war of cards. He just had to checkout with Liu first.

He found Jan sitting at his usual work station, stitching a replacement piece onto a large rug that had been slightly damaged in an office fire. Murray had helped Liu earlier in the day with the dying process of the new piece. Already Liu was training him on some of his techniques. Murray found Liu's work to be strangely fascinating. Now he wanted to know more, and Liu was happy to have an apprentice.

"Hey I'm all done. I'm getting out of here. You good?" he asked Liu. He had learned to stop inviting Jan to his games; he wasn't interested. It was still a mystery to Murray what Liu did in the evenings but it wasn't his place to pry. Jan seemed to have secrets to be kept to himself.

"Mmmhmm," Liu replied without thought.

"Okay then…well, just want to let you know that the prison is rioting because a giant sea monster came out of the ocean and ate the warden. Good night."

Jan didn't budge. Murray shook his head and left the room, bound for the outer door and onto his evening of camaraderie and bad jokes. He walked along the outer wall to the opening in the wall that kept the main prison yard separate from the vocational buildings. He moved through the gate and proceeded towards the dining hall, when he heard his name called from behind him.

"Hey Bench! Graves says hi!"

Murray turned in time to see the thrown rock before it hit him in the forehead. Blood instantly poured out of the wound as Murray staggered from the blow. He shook off the haziness in front of his eyes as best as he could, but he couldn't see straight. He could count five men, but he couldn't tell who they were or if he'd ever seen them before. He waved at them in an attempt to fight them off but his depth perception was gone. He was fighting air.

"Oh look at the little boxer. Can't seem to land a punch? You should have gotten a better manager!" a voice shouted. Murray saw a figure coming that probably belonged to the voice but couldn't react before the attacker swung a bat into his knee. Murray screamed and dropped to the ground as he felt his joint give out. Another blow came across his middle and a different attacker shouted, "You think you're tough? You think you can beat anyone? You can't beat shit, asshole." Kicks were now coming as Murray did his best to tuck his legs in and use his arms to protect his head and neck. "This is for Graves" was the last he heard from his attackers when a new set of footsteps came. Then, without explanation, the attacks stopped. He heard the sound of someone else falling to the ground and then a series of grunts and screams from the attackers, followed by what sounded like soft meat hitting a hard object. Then silence. Murray lifted his arms off his head and opened his eyes to see the five men lying unconscious at the feet of an inmate who stood over them with two open palms in a cloud of dust.

"Come, Murray. Let's get you to the infirmary." Jan Liu said as he reached down to pick Murray up.

"They call him the Mannequin, but I would never do that if I were you. He hates it."

Mouse sat in a chair next to Murray's bed. Both were inside the prison infirmary trauma center. Mouse had come in and stayed with Murray after Jan Liu had brought him in a few of hours before. Murray had to know more about the apparently simple tapestry repairer.

"Why do they call him Mannequin?" Murray asked.

"Well, it could be the truth or it could be made-up. When it comes to stories around here there's not a whole lot of truth you can count on. From what I know, Liu is in here because he's Yakuza. Or was, I guess. He's got a life term; that much he's told me. The rest is just what I've heard around here."

Mouse told him that before Liu was convicted he'd been an assassin for the Yakuza. He started in Tokyo and then was moved to Los Angeles, where he became one of the best contract killers of the time. He was known for being able to take out any target in any location, specifically in public. Being able to strike at someone in broad daylight surrounded by a crowd is a very sought after skill for assassins. A successful public hit was next to impossible to hide. They were guaranteed to make a statement. Everyone could see right there, written in blood, to steer clear, or they'd be next.

Liu had a method that made him very successful and earned him the nickname The Mannequin. When Liu was hired to make a hit, he would follow the target for days, sometimes even weeks. He would study the way the target moved, how his security teams moved, where they went, what they would say, how people they talked to reacted and replied to conversation, how much they'd tip at restaurants, whether they were rude or friendly. He studied every detail he could about how the target and his team would interact with those around them until he could predict each one's reactions to any situation one might face in public. If someone bumped into them, what would happen? If someone spoke too loudly on their cell phone nearby, how would they react? If the waitress at a bar was attractive, would they make physical contact?

Liu could blend into any scenario so well that he was still able to reach his mark without any venue-based restrictions. One could call him a master of disguise, but disguises weren't really his thing. He could just get in and out of any situation without gaining anyone's attention. That's why they called him the Mannequin.

When the time to strike had come, Liu's weapon of choice was a Higonokami, a small folding knife that Liu could keep in his hand, only grasping it with a thumb. He would wait for the target to be seated, and then either casually walk or sneak behind them and deftly insert the blade into the back of the neck between the C3 and C4 vertebrae, severing the spinal cord and preventing the target from screaming or alerting his men. Very little blood accompanied the wound. The target would stay in the same seated position and quickly die as their organs shut down without anyone knowing. By the time it was discovered that the target was dead, Liu would be long gone.

"So I take it that's why he's here. He must have been discovered to be a Yakuza hitman," Murray interrupted.

"No. Liu isn't in here for being a hatchet man. He's here on conviction of murdering his wife and two daughters," Mouse responded with unease.

"What?" Murray was shocked. "That doesn't seem possible."

"Well just let me finish the story." Mouse ordered. He then continued his tale.

The Mannequin had become such a feared name that every boss was eager to attempt to bring him over to his faction. Yet Liu's loyalty to his *oyabun*, the head of the faction, was unwavering. Mouse said he'd always felt like the *oyabun* had something over Liu and was forcing his loyalty somehow, but that was just his own theory. Either way, Liu wouldn't budge. The *oyabun* protects the *kobun*, the child, and the *kobun* remains faithful. So the other bosses had only one choice. They couldn't keep letting the Mannequin kill them, but they could neither hire him nor kill him themselves. They had no idea who he was or who he worked for. Liu's *oyabun* had kept his employment and identity secret. When asked about the assassin, he treated the Mannequin like a myth, a tale told by the superstitious to justify their own cowardice.

So instead, a rival boss who was known for his clever plans made it look like Liu had betrayed his *oyabun*. He had one of Liu's faction bosses killed in the same manner that the Mannequin used. He even had one of his own men killed in the same fashion to throw others off his trail. It had appeared to all that Liu had been turned from his loyalty. The *oyabun* was crushed by the betrayal and had to take Liu out of the picture.

When Liu returned to his home one night, he walked into a nightmare. His wife and daughters had been murdered. Each bore the mark of the Mannequin: a small puncture at the top of the neck, severed spinal column, death within seconds. As Liu held the lifeless bodies of his family and cried, cursing those responsible, police swarmed into the house. They had received an anonymous tip regarding the location of a wanted killer. They found a blade on Liu, neatly hidden in a secret pocket of his coat sleeve. This blade matched the exact pattern of the fatal wounds that killed his family, as well as a series of murders perpetrated by a rogue Yakuza hitman.

On the day of Liu's sentencing to life in prison, the *oyabun* sat right behind Liu and whispered repeatedly, "No *kobun* betrays his *oyabun*".

"They say that Liu and the *oyabun* both had tears in their eyes as Liu was led away, never to see freedom again," Mouse finished.

"Well that's either the saddest thing I've ever heard or a total crock of shit," Murray said, nonplussed.

"Well no matter what happened before, he hates to hear 'The Mannequin' so there you go."

"I'll keep that in mind. It still doesn't explain how he took out five men in the blink of an eye though."

"*Daito-ryu*," Mouse said.

"I'm sorry? What is *daito-ryu*?" Murray asked.

"A martial art of some sort. He said he used to teach it in Japan. It's why the Yakuza recruited him, I think."

"Well I'm just glad he showed up when he did. Otherwise, you'd be talking to a corpse right now. What have you found out about the attack?"

"The leader is a guy named Sam Beckton. You'll remember him as the guy who took out your knee. He was transferred here two days ago. He's in for a home burglary that went wrong a few years back. Him and some boys broke into an estate in the Hills, found the owner wasn't on vacation like they were told, killed him, the wife and their eight-year-old son."

"Jesus," Murray grimaced.

"Yeah, he's a grade A, first class piece of garbage," Mouse concurred. "But that's not what is so interesting about him. Seems he wasn't working freelance. It was a contract job. Some sort of blackmail operation. He was supposed to get in, crack the guy's computer, and take some materials the owner didn't want getting out to the public. Let's just say that he and that sandwich selling guy would have got along."

"Child pornography. Guy got what he deserved then. Not his family though."

Mouse went on. "Anyways, Beckton was sent there by someone. I'll give you three guesses who."

"Irvine Graves." Murray sneered. "So Beckton is one of Graves's men?"

"That's my best guess. It gets a little clearer when you look at the transfer documents from Folsom, where Beckton came from. There's a note on them saying that Beckton can't be transferred out of Santa Mira without express written permission from the author."

"Who is that?"

"Judge Simpson. Same guy who sent you here."

"So you think Simpson is part of this too?"

"The note is just too weird. Simpson has to approve the transfer of an inmate he's never had any court cases for? The same inmate whose employer had your best friend murdered? Prompting the trial that got you sent here, presided over by the same judge whose signature is on the transfer of an inmate who just tried to kill you? Come on, Murray. It's clear as day."

"Well, when you put it that way," Murray affirmed. "So what the hell do I do now?"

"You do what the doctor tells you. Heal. You're just gonna have to stay here for now. However, I don't think today's attack will be the last time these guys try to come for you."

CHAPTER 16

Murray spent three more days in the infirmary until his knee was healed. In that time, Corenswet had moved Beckton to a different cell block, so Murray had at least one less problem he didn't need to worry about while he healed. Things were starting to look up when Mouse stopped in to visit with him on Murray's last day in the infirmary.

Mouse was especially anxious when he came in. Murray was napping and Mouse rustled him awake. Groggy, Murray shifted to face Mouse who sat down in the chair next to the bed.

"Is it lunchtime already?" Murray asked, confused about the time.

"No, much more important than that," Mouse effused. "You had a visitor come by today. One of the guards wanted me to let you know since he knew I'd be seeing you. They let me talk with him in your place."

"Really? Who was it?" Murray asked with anticipation.

"It was someone named Sam Davis."

Murray winced; he'd really wanted to see Sam. It had been weeks since the old guy had made the trip from LA. "Dammit. Bad timing. I guess the warden would never let him come here."

"Not a chance. I told him that you were out of visitation time. I didn't want your friends to know you were in the infirmary."

Murray paused and thought about how Sam would feel. He would worry himself too much about Murray's condition and feel completely helpless since there would be nothing he could do about it. Mouse had made the right decision.

"So what did he have to say?" Murray asked.

"Well, two things. First, he said that Graves's men visited him again." Mouse went on to tell him the recap of the night Sam had to spend at the gym. He told him of the threat to Murray's life that had been delivered, and Sam's response to Darryl Whiteley.

"That guy has got some brass ones on him, I'll give him that," Murray responded after hearing the tale. "Standing up to three mobsters all by himself isn't something many could do."

"You're right," Mouse confirmed. "My concern is that he was clearly rattled when I talked to him. He kept asking me if you were okay. I didn't dare tell him that the threat he'd been given was real and had already been attempted. He said he wanted to try and get you transferred."

Murray thought about this for a second. It didn't take him long to find the flaw in that plan, though.

"I don't think it'll work. Simpson can move Graves's hitmen wherever I go. I'd also lose any chance at boxing. I've got it pretty good with Corenswet and it'd be too big a loss over something that likely wouldn't matter. No, I need to stay here and keep my eyes open until the warden can take care of this situation."

"Don't believe it Murray," Mouse warned. "The warden thinks that he controls everything that happens here and for the most part he does, but you need to still watch your back."

Murray's forehead furrowed in recognition that the old man was right again. This wasn't just going to go away.

"Okay, well what was the other thing?" he asked, changing the subject from the previous dead end.

"It was about the dirty cops who put you in here. They were in the news again." Mouse went on to tell him the details about accusation against Johns and Rodihan and the subsequent riots in LA over the absence of charges against them.

"I really don't know how I feel about that," Murray mused once Mouse was finished. "I mean, what difference does it make here? Anatoly is still dead, I'm still in prison and Graves is still out to kill me. Nothing has changed."

"What about justice?" Mouse cried. "Those scumbags are still out there and getting away with whatever they want. There's no crime they can't get away with. Murray, they killed your friend and now innocent women are being violated and having their lives destroyed by these assholes."

Murray looked over at his new friend and calmly addressed him by his first name. "John, I'm lying in a bed in the infirmary. I just got my ass kicked for the first time since I was 8 years old. It won't be the last time either. There's an army of guards, forty foot walls and 500 miles between me and The Brose Four. There's not a lot I can do about them right now. All we can do is hope they get whatever is coming to them."

———

Understandably, Murray had trouble sleeping that night. Tomorrow he would be returning to the general population and leaving the safety of the closely guarded infirmary. He would be back out among the people who were being paid to kill him, not to mention the rest of the prison who wanted to knock him around just to make a statement.

The threat frightened him. Someone was trying to kill him. It was almost too foreign of a concept for him to understand. What choices had he made to bring him to this point? Postulating about what he could have done differently wasn't going to help. He'd made his own storm and now he couldn't be mad that it was raining.

Where to go from here, though? He had no plan. He was winging it. Not even that, he was letting everything happen. He had enemies and he was doing nothing against them. Graves was out there, the Brose Four were out there. They had all the power against him and he had none while trapped inside this prison. Maybe he should have pleaded differently. No! He'd done the right thing. He needed to deal with his problems instead of running from them. It was the only thing he knew he'd done right since the fight with Pistelli. How long ago that had been, it seemed…

Sleep finally came to him. In his dreams, Anatoly cheered from the corner of a boxing ring, while Murray fought Ivan Drago.

———

Murray woke up tired from his lack of sleep, had one final medical exam, then checked out of the infirmary and made his way to the FF. He knew that he had responsibilities and that Jan Liu would be waiting for him. He wasn't going to let his life be ruled by regret, only hope.

When he entered the textile department, Liu was nowhere to be found. This wasn't anything unusual so Murray went about his normal morning routine of cleaning up scraps and loose materials from the different stations from the previous day's work. Before he could finish picking up all the scraps from the first station, Liu appeared out of nowhere behind him.

"Not today," he said without any greeting. "Today and every day from now on, we are going to be adding to your tasks with a new set of skills to learn."

Murray had become used to this odd behavior from Liu so he kept working as he spoke. "Okay, so am I going to start working on building carpets? Am I done moving stuff around?"

"No, my friend. You will never be done with that," he replied as he led Murray to his tapestry area. "Today we teach you how to fight."

———

"That fucking moron!" Graves howled at such a volume that his bodyguards entered the office to check on his condition. Their concern was met with further yelling. "Get the fuck out of here!"

Darryl Whiteley shrugged at the guards, not knowing how to ease this situation. The guards glanced at each other and then made their exit.

"I sent him to steal a computer from an empty house. What does he do? He shoots a bunch of people. Then I send him to kill Bench and he fucks that up too? He had five men with him. How is that even possible?"

Whiteley had few details to share. He only knew that Beckton had failed and that another party had gotten involved. Whether Bench and this unknown had fought off Beckton and his men together or not was a mystery.

"I wish I could tell you sir, but the information we have isn't clear. All we know is that Bench was attacked, but it ended in all five of our men thrashed. The only good news I have is that Bench was struck in the knee and had to be taken to the infirmary. I have no idea if he's recovered from the injury or not."

Graves stewed on this information, his hands rubbing his temples.

"Goddammit," Graves said after a few moments of thought. "I didn't want to have to burn this card yet, but I guess now is the time."

"What do you mean, sir?" Whiteley asked.

"If you want something done right..." Graves quipped. "Get Judge Simpson on the phone. It's time to make the deal with the FBI."

Whiteley stammered. "But sir, there's gotta be another way."

"No way. Santa Mira is about to get a new inmate."

CHAPTER 17

"I'm pretty sure I know how to fight," Murray said with chagrin.

"You know how to play fight for people's entertainment and rules. You do not know how to protect yourself and others when there are no rules," Jan Liu said as he walked Murray to a crowded section of the FF. "You must learn how to use all of your body's instruments instead of just this one weapon you use," he continued, pointing to Murray's right arm.

"I've done all right with what I know," Murray said stubbornly.

"Oh you have, huh? Especially right here," Liu spoke as he quickly moved and poked the stitches on Murray's forehead, the remnants of his near-demise. He had moved so fast Murray felt the pain of the impact before his brain could process anything else.

"You cannot believe that your current abilities and training will be able to fight off those who would harm you. A day will come when you will face a challenge where mere boxing skills won't be enough. I will teach you how to use your environment as a weapon, to use your opponent's attacks against them, to take their weapons and turn them to your advantage. Besides, what else do you have going on?"

The last statement was meant in jest but it was just as truthful as any. Anything to keep Murray busy and out of the view of his fellow prison residents was welcome.

So Murray trained with Liu whenever they could. Each day, Murray would get up and go directly to the FF where he continued his work duties and then each evening he and Liu would train. Liu was a master in *Daito-ryu Aikijujutsu* and had trained in Tsukuba, Japan at the Sagawa School under Master Kimura. He told Murray that *Daito-ryu* was a blend of *Aikido* and *Jujitsu*, both having descended as separate branches from *Daito-ryu*. Murray would learn how to use his opponent's attacks against them and then strike in a manner that prevented further conflict.

At first things started slow with Liu teaching Murray meditation techniques with some stretching moves that Murray had never used or seen before. The stretching helped Murray immensely, considering he was lifting heavier rugs each day. He could tell that he was getting stronger in areas of his body that had never seen exercise in this manner before. He was now faster, more agile and had much more stamina than he had as just a boxer.

However, when it was finally time to move into learning how to defend himself, Murray was a slow student. The years of learning how to win in the boxing ring were now hindering his development. He relied far too much on what he had been taught and even as he tried to force himself to use Liu's methods, his muscle memory would fight his commands.

On one particular day, the pair were sparring in the small and cramped area that they had cleared of projects and tools. Liu came at Murray in an awkward and wild attack that Murray was unused to. Liu was schooling him on how to fight someone who was untrained but relentless. When one of Liu's blows struck Murray in the ribs, Murray took the blow and then swung out with his golden right in a heavy hook. Yet Liu deftly ducked this blow, striking Murray in the chest, knocking all the wind out of him. Murray jerked up in a desperate attempt to refill his lungs as Liu continued past him and gave him a parting elbow square in the middle of the back. The force of this put Murray face down on the ground.

"You strike predictably," Liu advised while Murray coughed his way back into respiration. "You rely on your knockout punch with every chance you get. You must learn patience. Bring your enemy down with a variety of tactics. Use your heavy weapon only when they cannot defend against it."

Murray was able to gather himself enough to sit on the ground, still panting. "Why draw things out when I can end each fight immediately with one punch?"

"It's true. When you land with your right, there is no one who could withstand it. But the key word here is 'land'. It is very easy to see coming, if you are smart enough to watch for it. You have learned to focus yourself into one blow; now you must learn to focus your energy elsewhere, making your entire body a weapon."

Murray pulled himself up onto a table and grabbed some water. "How do I do that?" he asked.

Liu came over to him and grabbed his right shoulder. "First, we must learn how you are able to make this such a force. Tell me, when did you first strike in such a manner?"

A scowl crept across Murray's face as his memory took him precisely to a place he didn't want to go. His eyes were pointed at the ground as he spoke but he was clearly seeing something else. "My father. My father was murdered. I see the face of the guy that did it each time I hit someone. Each time, I'm hitting that son of a bitch as hard as I can. I put every single ounce of anger I have into that one blow."

"Anger is a powerful ally. Yet turning your rage into a sense of peace within yourself is even stronger," Master Liu replied. "Anger is a hammer, whereas being calm and collected is the mastery of all tools. Come, let us continue."

———

When he wasn't working and training in the FF, sleeping in his cell or eating at chow time, Murray would enjoy sharing stories and chatting with Mouse. The two would often sit on the bleachers overlooking the prison yard where the other inmates would sometimes play baseball or just mill about.

Mouse would share news of the outside with Murray, as he was the only inmate in the entire prison who had internet access for the majority of the day. The other inmates had shared and limited access via one computer in the library, but Mouse's job at the prison vocational placement office allowed him the opportunity to keep a pulse on the events of the world outside Santa Mira. He gave Murray updates on The Brose Four and the public unrest about the excessive violence by police around the nation. Southern California wasn't the only place that was having problems. There were riots throughout the country, and it seemed like each week there was a new story about someone being beaten or shot by police, with heavy indications of racial motivations. Murray almost burst into tears when, just three months after Anatoly's death, two of The Brose Four were involved in the fatal shooting of two unarmed Bosnian teenage refugees. Both underwent a psychiatric evaluation and were found to have a deep hatred for Eastern Europeans, who they saw as little different from Muslim extremists and descendants of America's enemy in the Cold War. The officers were investigated, yet no charges were ever brought against them. This caused more protests, and Los Angeles was on the verge of erupting into another riot. Murray found it ironic that he felt that being inside the walls of Santa Mira was safer than being in the city he'd come to know as his home.

Murray would talk to Mouse about his time with Liu and his extensive training regimen. Mouse was not very surprised that Liu had taken Murray under his wing and showed encouragement of his training sessions. He had even found a book in the library called "The Techniques and Mastery of *Daito-ryu*" and gave it to Murray. Murray pored through the book, making mental notes, improving upon the techniques that Liu was teaching him. In just a few short weeks, Murray was employing his new knowledge with expertise.

———

Two months after starting his training, Murray was in the FF shadow boxing while Liu watched.

"Your technique is flawed. Your striking shoulder is too high, revealing your next move," Liu critiqued as he paced behind Murray.

"My position is where it should be. I am executing the *Shinyo-ryu* defense. My blocking arm must remain lower than my striking arm." Murray returned as he executed a block and throw against an imaginary attacker.

Liu's eyes lit up as he spoke, "Ah, you've been reading the book of *Daito-ryu* techniques. Mouse told me that he had shared it with you. It's clear you've been studying it thoroughly."

Murray was all too pleased that his teacher found him to be a good student. He replied "By using the opponent's momentum to redirect-" Before he could finish, Liu had moved to Murray's side and grabbed his striking arm, then struck him in the ribs while throwing Murray to the ground.

Murray's pride was the only injury as he lashed out in frustration at Liu. "That was not one of the techniques used in *Daito-ryu!*" he shouted as he pushed himself off the ground.

"Then it must be one of the techniques of a different path. Perhaps *Judo*? Or *Gwonbeop*?" Liu chuckled.

Murray rose and brought his stance back into a defensive stature. "I was unprepared for your attack. Try it again."

"Is that what you are going to say to your enemy? 'Oh, I'm sorry I was busy daydreaming. Could you please attack me again in a way that I would prefer?' You cannot learn *Daito-ryu Aikijujutsu* from a book." Liu instructed as he relaxed his posture and brought himself closer to Murray. "Your movements must become fluid and come without thinking. An attack could come from anywhere and anyone. You must learn to sense your surroundings, and instinct must dictate your movements. By channeling your energies you'll know how to move and strike without premeditation. You must be able to improvise."

"Like this?" Murray said as he brought his left leg up and quickly struck Liu's left ankle, causing Liu to drop to one knee. "I've noticed you tend to favor that leg."

"Very good. You've improved your ability to spot your target's weaknesses, even ones that are quite imperceptible. The wound is very old and one from my previous life that never healed right, even after 16 years."

"You've been here too long. Mouse told me about your family. I'm sorry."

With Murray's final word, Liu moved with incredible speed, bringing his forearm onto Murray's throat and pushing him back against a wall. Murray had completely relaxed his posture as Liu had spoken and he was paying for it.

Liu said, "You let your guard down, why? Tell me!"

"I was..."

"What? You pity me? My sad story?" Liu asked without relaxing his arm.

Murray couldn't tell if he was teaching him a lesson or truly angry. "Yes," was all he could say.

"You never have sympathy for your enemy! They are only prey and hunters can never bleed for their prey," Liu released his grip and stood back in his sparring stance, "Let us continue."

Prey and hunters. The simple categorization of people felt empty to Murray. Could he view another human only as prey? When it came down to it, he wasn't sure if this mindset was compatible with what his father had always taught him. If the time came when his life was on the line again, would he be able to be the hunter that Liu wanted?

The question burned deep into Murray. Beyond the walls of Santa Mira Prison, Murray's enemy had already made that decision. A hunter was coming.

CHAPTER 18

A black limousine pulled into the parking lot of Santa Mira and circled the walls until it reached the east side. It stopped at a small door along the wall that was surrounded by two guards armed with assault rifles. At a tower above, a lone sniper looked down the scope of his weapon, yet he never focused on the limo or its occupants. Instead he scanned the surrounding area, watchful for any possible targets in the lot. The vehicle sat still, blackened windows closed, until the small door opened.

Out of the limo stepped Irvine Graves. Away from the main entrance, out of view of cameras, news reporters, and the occupants of Santa Mira, he walked to the door. He was already attired in the light-blue jumpsuit worn by prisoners classified as "minimum risk". At the door, he was greeted by the guards who escorted him into the prison.

Beyond the door, Sam Beckton awaited. With him were Graves's other inside men, Kelsal, Pergent, Clark and Davison.

"Where's Whiteley?" Beckton asked.

"Just me. Whiteley will manage affairs in LA," Graves answered striding forward past his men, who followed in tow. "Where is Bench?"

"Gym. Its fight day."

"And his opponent?"

"I don't know him. But I heard he's huge. Bench should get his ass kicked."

"Don't underestimate him again. We will discuss your previous failure at another time," Graves advised as his team passed through the baseball field without paying mind to the inmates who were playing a game on the field. One of the players went to protest but another grabbed him by the arm, halting him before he could make a lethal mistake. No one else was fool enough to get in Irvine Graves's path.

Reaching the gymnasium, Clark and Pergent opened the doors for their boss and Graves strode inside, eager to face his enemy. No one would stop him. A proffer had been brokered with the FBI. Guards had been paid off. No one else would fail him again. Today would finally be the day when he would take Murray Bench's life.

———

Ten minutes into the fight, Murray was struggling against Marko. He couldn't know it, but Beckton had been right; a beating was exactly what he was taking, in front of a packed house, no less. Murray's fights were now the top event at Santa Mira and inmates would pack in deep to watch him. Normally that meant cheers for another quick victory. Today was a different matter.

From the moment he entered the ring, nothing had gone as planned. His opponent was a giant, but not the slow lumbering clods he was used to. This man had balance and a swiftness to him that didn't match the seven foot, three-hundred pound frame that supported his girth. This wasn't going to be David versus Goliath; this was Theseus versus Ares.

Once the fight began, Marko had come straight for Murray. The first punch was aimed at the smaller man's face and Murray dodged it. At the same time, Marko put one of his big fists into Murray's ribs. The first rib of the fight was cracked upon impact, it wouldn't be the last. The blow sent shivers of shock throughout Murray and he recoiled into the corner.

No one had ever hit him that hard.

The big man backed away to let Bench have a second. He didn't want to injure his opponent, he just wanted to win. Murray looked up and saw Corenswet in his version of a sky-box. The warden looked worried. Would this be the first time he'd lose on Murray? *Not yet*, Murray thought and rose back to his feet. He stretched his right arm to determine the effects on his abilities from the cracked rib. Good enough. The fight could go on.

The next ten minutes, Murray danced as best as was possible; nevertheless, his efforts were in vain. Marko was too quick and even a glancing blow from the beast was enough to knock Murray to his knees. Repeatedly the huge fists crashed down on him from above. His shoulders, his ribs, his chest and even his face were getting battered. Each time he'd try to protect a soft spot he'd open up to Marko a different one.

His attacks appeared equally futile. He couldn't jab at the man, as the only area he could reach was the giant's barrel-chest. Punching him in the mid-section was like putting your hand into dump truck--a dump truck that was coming at you at forty miles an hour. He lashed out with his right when he could. He'd let the power inside build and then strike into the side of his opponent. Nothing. Again. Nothing. Over and over, he tried to focus on one spot, delivering his deadly right into it. His only hope was to wear one part of him down and deal a fight-ending blow, however it was taking far too long for Marko to show any signs of damage.

Murray, however, was starting to show far too much.

Bruised, broken and bleeding Bench stumbled forward. His body was telling him to lay down, yet the thought of losing his first fight pushed his spirit to continue. One last time was all he wanted. One last solid right into the side of Marko. He dug down into himself, thought of the face of his father's killer and blasted his fist into his target.

His last ditch effort had opened him up once more. Marko struck him with a hook across the left temple. Murray Bench went down.

The ringing in his ears masked the sound of the referee counting over him. He couldn't hear the numbers being shouted. Had he blacked out? Beyond the ring, he heard a rumble from the fans and above pounding of some sort. Corenswet was losing his cool. Murray's head swam from side to side as he fought to clear his mind of the fog from his brain slapping into his own skull. The blow had surely caused a concussion. He looked for a way to climb back into reality, but only his right eye was open. His left was rapidly swelling shut. Through the gym, he caught the face of Mouse, concern lining his weathered face. Next to him, Joe Wasser was gesturing Murray to stay down. Maybe it was time for Murray to lose. No one can always win. At some point, all boxers go down, some need to stay there.

Then he caught sight of Irvine Graves. His enemy was there, in Santa Mira, dressed as an inmate. Graves saw him notice his presence and his mouth curved into a vile grin. He was watching the beginning of Murray Bench's defeat. He mouthed the words, "Fuck you" in victory.

This was all it took to bring Murray back.

He snapped back up and sprinted towards Marko. The giant stood straight, taking his face out of Murray's reach. Yet Murray had a new plan. It was time to end this. The nimble fighter slid under Marko's incoming knockout punch, leaped up and planted a foot onto the second rope around the ring. Like a bungee cord snapping, Murray launched himself up and brought his right into the neck of Marko. Both met the mat at the same time; Murray on his feet and Marko on his face. A ten-second count later, and the fight was over.

The crowd erupted at Murray's comeback. Mouse thought he was going to have a heart-attack. Joe just looked on with his mouth agape. Corenswet had jumped into Mitchell in jubilation. The grin had left Irvine Graves' face which was twisted in disgust.

Murray strode to the edge of the ring and faced Graves. He turned his hand to the villain, then twisted it and put his thumb down.

"You're next!" he shouted.

The taunt sent Graves into a fury. His disappointment at Bench's victory disappeared, and was replaced by unadulterated hatred. Whatever his original plan had been was now tossed aside in fury. Graves had lost control of himself and relented to his own mania. He broke from his men, pushed his way through the mass surrounding the ring and leaped inside.

Irvine Graves and Murray Bench stood facing each other, two opposites united in one moment of determined animosity.

Graves struck first. The blow caught Murray unexpectedly and was repeated by another. Graves knew what he was doing, something Murray hadn't foreseen. Back he retreated to find his defenses and then attack his nemesis. He reached stability in his footing, and brought his arms up to block the blows headed his direction. Two on each side came and then Murray sent his attack. Graves ducked the punch and brought a bare knuckle into Murray's stomach. Unpadded by gloves, it hurt like hell, knocked the air out of him and shivered his broken ribs. Another blow like that, and Murray was facing a punctured lung.

The next blow was halted, fortunately. Corenswet had yelled for his guards to come and break this circus up. Graves had power here, but Corenswet still reigned. He had an investment to protect and no one would defeat his prize, not without him having the opportunity to make some money, at least.

In the center of the ring, the two men were pulled away from each other. Both were livid. Both were screaming. Obscenities and threats spewed forth from them like two bulls fighting over the herd. The guards held them back while Corenswet and Mitchell descended the stairs from the viewing room. The crowd broke from the spectacle and parted to allow the warden to pass and enter the ring.

"Gentlemen, this is not the behavior I want to see in my prison, let alone my boxing ring. This isn't sportsmanlike," Corenswet lectured. "This is animal brutality. I like that in a fight, but we have rules here."

"This son of a bitch killed my best friend," Murray protested and pulling against the three guards that held him in place. "I'm going to fuck him up!"

The men holding Graves were having a much easier time as the gangster was beginning to resume his even temperament. His madness taking control and wanting to kill Bench, here and now in front of all, had faded, if only momentarily. He was satisfied to wait for another chance to end him. Humiliate Bench now, kill him privately later.

Corenswet unwittingly was about to give him another shot right now, with no repercussions, something Graves couldn't have planned better.

"I'd be happy to give you a try at him," the warden offered. "You know the rules, though. The only fights at Santa Mira must take place inside this ring."

"Fine," Murray spat. "Let's do this. Same time, same place, one week."

Corenswet shook his head. "No, that won't do. You owe me a fight today, Murray."

"What?" Murray stammered. "I just did that!"

"Aw, but that fight was forfeit. You broke the rules."

"What are you talking about, Corenswet?" Murray ventured forth. He was risking angering Mitchell but his temper blocked his reasoning.

"You used the ropes and I think some of your kung-fu garbage. You know you can't do that"

The color drained from Murray's face. Corenswet was right.

"You can't expect me to fight this man today," he shouted. "Look at me!"

"Rules are rules, Murray. I'm giving you the time it takes Graves to get dressed and gloved up. Then I expect a fair fight."

CHAPTER 19

Twenty minutes later and Murray was awaiting Graves inside the ring. He had Joe bandage his ribs, tape his wrists and apply Vaseline to the cut above Murray's eye. Lastly, he punctured the swollen arch above the eye to let blood escape, reducing the swelling and forcing the eye open. Murray looked like hammered shit, but he was going to fight. Joe had shared his thoughts on strategy in the locker room.

"He's got fifteen years on you," he pointed out. "He's in shape but you are in much better. He's going to try to do the same thing I did when we fought. He'll come at you hard, try to end it quick. Don't let him. You need to wear him down first. You're beat pretty bad but if you can protect yourself in the first five minutes, you'll have a chance at taking him down when he starts to slow."

Murray nodded and stretched his neck. Joe moved to restitch his gloves.

"Keep moving. Stay loose. You can do this."

It wasn't enough of a break, but the twenty minutes had helped. The work he and Liu had done over the last few weeks had made a great difference in Murray's stamina. He could do this. He could take Graves down.

Out of the locker room, Graves walked to the ring. Dressed and gloved up, the crime-boss stared down Murray as he approached. Behind him, his entourage of goons danced and threw taunts towards the man in the ring. Murray ignored them. He focused only on Graves and Graves on him.

The silver-haired, one-eyed man slid under the ropes and met Murray in the middle. The usual referee had been replaced for this match. Mitchell would have to oversee this fight, in case things turned ugly.

The two enemies stared each other down as Mitchell reminded them both of the procedures for this ring. No rounds, no kicking, no below the belt, fight ends when one is down for ten seconds.

And then it was on.

As expected, Graves came at Murray in a flurry. Each blow was blocked, Graves striking against Murray's forearms in futility. He bounced back giving Murray breathing room. Again another flurry came at him and again it was met with a solid defense. It was on the last strike that Murray noticed something was off with Graves's gloves. As the crime-boss released his blow, Murray felt something hard drag across his arm within his opponent's mitt.

It wasn't long before the mystery was solved. Murray caught Graves with left jab that stammered Graves. He followed it with a right hook that struck cleanly. Graves faltered backwards. He lashed out with a swing that Murray dodged, right into another blow from the other side. He felt the object inside the glove crash into bicep of his golden right. The arm went dead. Murray reeled back and inspected the impact area. A solid mark had dented into his skin. It was a set of brass knuckles.

Murray looked up at his opponent who drew his lips back in a snarl. This match was a fraud. Murray couldn't fight it, not with Graves cheating. One hard blow in the ribs and Murray would be done, possibly dead. He had to end this now.

He called out to Mitchell, but Graves was already on top of him. He was springing out in a full-on blitz, both arms thrusting out in search of contact, then kicks to Murray's knee. Now Mitchell knew something was wrong and had to stop it. The muscled guard climbed into the ring and grabbed Graves. No rules mattered to the maniac. He swung at Mitchell. The metal lining his knuckles caught the guard just above the ear and Mitchell fell to the ground.

The crowd gasped. This was no boxing match. It was a street fight.

Murray wasn't oblivious to what was happening, though. All the rules were off. Mitchell was unconscious on the ground. Corenswet was calling for backup to stop this madness. The big question was would they arrive in time. Murray couldn't take that chance. He put a lace of his glove in his mouth and pulled, then did the same for the other hand. Both gloves fell to the mat. The boxer was gone, the wielder of *Daito-Ryu* emerged.

Graves had removed his gloves as well. The metal of the rings glinted in the lights of the gymnasium, the weapon laid bare and uninhibited. Its owner came forward, unleashing his attack. Murray settled into his stance, preparing to redirect the attacker down and away. Graves brought blow after blow with a ferocity that Murray couldn't grasp. Even if he hadn't been hindered by the cracked ribs and now the battered arm, Graves would have been a challenge. He was fast, lithe like a cat and powerful like an ox. He was cunning, learning Murray's strategies in real-time and adjusting his attacks around them.

The pair battled it out, with each fighter putting forward their best counter-moves. Murray would gain a position and strike. He wanted to catch Graves in the throat. He wanted to crush the windpipe and let the murderer spend the final moments of his life grasping for life and looking up at the one who had bested him. Graves just wanted to split Murray's head open.

The fight was turning deadly. Blood splattered the mat and more was hurled onto it with every punishing impact. The sound of each blow had turned from hard slaps into wet splats. The crowd was no longer cheering. They were reeling in sickness.

Yet the two fighters went on. Blow by blow, each found a way to keep the blood bath going. Neither would relent. It was becoming clear that Murray was losing, though. The bandages around his ribs were shredded and slipping from his body. His right arm was limp and flopped at his side. He couldn't see out of his left eye at all, and his right eye stung with the flow of blood into it. He braced himself for another volley from his opponent. It failed. Graves broke through, sending crushing fist after fist down onto Murray, driving him to his knees.

Above, Corenswet screamed in horror. On the ground, Mouse covered his eyes. Joe turned away. Graves was going to kill Murray right there. It was all over.

Light flooded into the gym as the doors flung open and Corenswet's reinforcements poured through. They rushed into the ring and latched onto the fighters, pulling them away from each other and ending the fight. Murray watched from his pummeled face Graves being pulled away, cursing Murray and all around him in defeat. With nothing left, Murray slipped away into black.

CHAPTER 20

Eight days later, Murray was rattled from his coma. He felt as if hands had grabbed him and shaken him awake. He opened his eyes and found himself alone in a hospital bed. A heart-rate monitor next to him beeped regularly while IVs pumped fluids into his body. Confused, he looked around at his surroundings. He was in a room, but it was unlike any hospital room he'd ever been in. The walls were unadorned and were made of concrete blocks. There was no television and no bathroom. What equipment there was looked dated.

It was when he looked at the door that he realized his location. It was a metal door with a barred window at the top. He was in the infirmary of Santa Mira in one of the three private rooms reserved for critical condition patients. In his last stay, he'd only been out in an open recovery area of the prison's medical facility.

How long have I been in here? he asked himself. He looked himself over. His ribs were wrapped tight, inhibiting his movement, but they didn't hurt real badly. He felt his face and found stitches above his eye. His right bicep ached still but he had good movement coming from it. He lifted up his gown and found he was wearing a diaper. *Are you kidding me? What a mess I must have been.*

"Hello?" he yelled out. There was no answer.

Then he heard a rumble. Small and gentle but pronounced. The rumble stopped promptly. The IV bag above him swayed gently. *What the hell was that?*

Then it hit hard. The whole room shook violently. The wheeled bed slid to one side and medical tools spilled out of drawers. Murray braced himself as the shaking spun his bed around and then subsided again. Alarms sounded in the hallway, and Murray could hear yelling from beyond his room. The IV stand fell over, tightening the cord that connected to the needle in his arm. He pulled the needle out and blood spurted forward. He grabbed the end of the robe and tore off a section for a bandage.

A fucking earthquake. You've got to be kidding me.

He grabbed the sensors mounted to his chest and ripped them off. The heart monitor flat-lined in alarm but no one came to check on him. The screaming and yelling in the hallway had dissipated. He was alone. *I gotta get out of here.*

He shifted and swing his legs out when he felt something pulling on his crotch. He reached down and felt a tube where he wasn't happy to find one. *No bathroom needed in this room, I guess. This is going to suck pretty bad right here.*

He found the connection junction of two hoses just outside of his diaper and disconnected it. Then he pulled the diaper off with no mess. Now the hard part. He grabbed onto the hose that was still attached to him, took a deep breath and pulled.

The pain was immense.

He tossed the catheter against the wall and vomited on the floor. After he collected himself, he stood up. *Ok Graves. Pretty sure you can't do worse to me than that.* He searched the drawers of the cabinet and found a jumpsuit. He changed and looked out the door. He could see no signs of life, just more concrete walls and the spinning of an orange alarm light against them. He tried the door handle.

Locked. He breathed a sigh in anxiety and slumped to the floor. *Now what?*

The next second his question was answered in an outbreak of chaos and violence. The earthquake had finally warmed all the way up and was unleashing hell upon Santa Mira. The shaking was indescribable, and Murray felt like he was going to be vibrated apart. He clutched at the bed he'd slumbered in for over a week and put as much of his body underneath as he could and put the rest against the door. The place was coming apart. Mortar was loosening from the concrete and the floor above him began to sag down. Joists and wood frames were splitting and the walls were beginning to crumble. Still the quake went on. Murray held tight to the bed as pieces of debris started to rain down onto it. He could hardly breathe; the air was vibrating that hard.

When the quake finally subsided, daylight was pouring into the room and the sounds of panic reached him. He peeked out from behind the bed to see the outside wall of the room had collapsed and men were running everywhere beyond. The prison alarms were blasting in a disharmony to the air-raid siren of the town just past the fortress walls.

Holy shit, Murray thought. *There could be more walls down. The whole prison could escape!*

He got to his feet and slid out of the opening of the wall, hoping his timing wasn't off and another quake wasn't going to send the rest down on top of him. With his feet on the ground outside, he took a look at the damage of the earthquake. The walls of the infirmary had taken a heavy blow and the west wing had collapsed. Next door, the West Cell Block had an entire wall crumbled down. He could see inmates still in their cells staring out from the destruction to the ground below. There were inmates and guards everywhere. Some were badly injured and crying for help, debris having crushed their limbs. Others wandered aimlessly, confused at what had just happened. Some inmates tried to take advantage of the situation to attack guards. Scuffles were all around. Yet Murray could mostly hear only the screams of the injured and those suffering.

He ran out into the main yard and found a large group of inmates from the West Block standing in the baseball field. He scanned the congregation for any familiar face, but he specifically was looking for Mouse. There was no sign of the old man. With hope, he spotted Joe talking with a set of guards. Murray rushed over to him.

"Holy shit," Joe exclaimed and then put his arms around Murray. "You're awake! Did the earthquake do that?"

"It must have," Murray said in rush. "Are you ok?"

"I'm fine. I was already outside when it happened. Just a little shaky. How are you?"

"I'm just aces," Murray replied sarcastically. "Where's Mouse?"

Joe shook his head. "I don't know. Probably at work."

Murray didn't stick around to reply. He ran through the baseball field, past guards and inmates, past the fighting that was happening, past crumbled walls and injured men. He rounded the corner of the vocational wall and saw his fears realized. The small trailer that held Mouse's office had slipped off its foundation and had smashed into the walls of the building behind it. Part of the building's roof had fallen onto the trailer and there was debris everywhere.

Up the undamaged ramp Murray went and squeezed through the broken sliding door.

"Mouse! John, where are you?"

"I'm here."

Breathing a sigh of relief, Murray ran to the source of the answer. He found the old man, laying on his back underneath a section of roofing that had come down.

"My leg's trapped," Mouse grunted in pain.

"Okay. I'll get it off you. Hold on."

"Get help. It's too heavy," Mouse pleaded.

Murray nodded and ran back outside. He could see no one around. He was about to run back to the yard for help when he heard a strange and unfamiliar sound coming from the wall next to the San Francisco Bay. It sounded like horses running. The sound grew louder with each instant and then Murray saw water flowing over the walls. His eyes looked past them to find a large wave rushing towards the prison. The earthquake had caused a tsunami and it was about to hit Santa Mira. If the water reached Mouse, he'd drown. There was no time to get help.

He ran back inside and reached the old man. "LIFT!" he yelled. He squatted down and put all his strength into lifting the large wooden structure off of his friend.

"Come on, John! Push!"

The old man pushed against his captor. Murray's knee buckled and shook, yet he fought against the mass. The load began to budge and gave him a little leverage. Water was starting to rush into the office and flowed over Mouse. *Come on, Murray! Fight!* There was no more time. Mouse was going to drown. Time was rushing by and John Dormus was fading. *One more inch!*

Mouse filled his lungs with air as he slid out and knelt above the receding water. Murray let go of the pile of debris and it smashed back down next to him. The friends hugged and Mouse smiled up at him.

"I'm glad you decided to get your ass out of bed today," the old man beamed.

———

Santa Mira was in ruin. The water from the tsunami had flooded fifteen of the twenty buildings and the power was out. Walls of the buildings lay in smashed piles on the ground. Floors and ceilings split open throughout. It would take months to repair enough of the prison to operate at a minimum capacity, and years to bring it back fully.

The only good news for Santa Mira was that the outer walls had held up through the quake and then stood firm against the crushing waves of the tsunami. If it hadn't been for the prison's location, the entire town of Santa Mira, California would have been wiped off the map. With the outer walls holding firm, not one inmate had been able to use the disaster as a means for escape.

Yet, all inmates were escaping the prison, in a sense. Corenswet was forced to have his residents shipped to whatever other

California prisons could house them. The California Department of Corrections found new homes for each and every one of them, if only temporarily while the Santa Mira was repaired.

Mouse was sent to a low-security prison hospital. His ankle had been broken by the debris and he had suffered a bruised liver. Murray laughed that he would be spending the next chunk of his prison sentence getting sponge baths and watching daytime television.

Joe Wassar went to the minimum security section of Pleasant Valley State Prison. Three months later he would be released. Murray didn't get a chance to ever say goodbye and good luck. He hoped he would get to see him again, once he was a free man as well.

No one knew where Irvine Graves was or what happened to him. Corenswet had him locked away after he nearly killed Murray. All sign of him had vanished after the quake.

Murray and Liu were lucky enough to be sent to a new location together. Unfortunately, for both of them it was to Oroville Bay, a "supermax" and the worst place to be in all of California. The next six months of Murray's life would be the bleakest and hardest he'd ever faced.

CHAPTER 21

If one good thing could be said about Santa Mira Prison, it's that it wasn't Oroville Bay.

The moment Murray and Liu stepped off the transport bus that delivered them from their previous incarceration, they knew that things were going to get a hell of a lot tougher for both of them. The complex was huge, spanning two-hundred and seventy-five acres with half the grounds used for the general population. This section of the prison wasn't much different than Santa Mira. It had outside exercise courts, an assembly yard and even a library. It's where the pair from Santa Mira were expecting to spend their wait.

Instead, they were marched into the SHU, the Security Housing Unit. The building was much smaller and shaped in a cross, with each of its four wings storing some of the worst criminals in California.

"What is this? This isn't where we were supposed to be," Murray said to a staffer upon entrance. "There's gotta be a mistake."

"No mistake," the staffer answered. "General is full. Only room for you is here."

There was no registration process. Murray and Liu were just led through a hallway with cells lining both sides. Prisoners inside the cells called out to them as they passed, whistling and cursing their disdain and shouting threats at the new arrivals.

"Shut up!" screamed the guard leading them. The order was ineffective. One inmate pressed his face through the bars and made kissing sounds to Murray. The second guard leading them smacked him square in the face with a nightstick, sending the man to the ground. His face poured blood out and he screamed in pain. The guards didn't stop to check on him or call for medical help. They just kept leading Murray and Liu through the continual catcalls.

When they arrived at their empty cell, the pair were pushed inside. The cell door slide shut, the lock was engaged, and then they were told to stick their hands forward through the bars. After complying, their handcuffs were removed. The guards turned away.

"What? That's it?" Murray challenged. "You're not going to inspect us for weapons?"

The guard turned back and said only, "I don't give a shit if you got a grenade up your ass. Have a good time with it."

Then the guards left and Murray and Liu were alone with the rest of the maniacs.

———

No change in their environment came. They were stuck inside their cell. No visits to the outdoors. No recreational time. No sunlight. No books. No visitors. Only the cell.

Twice a day meals would arrive and slide under an opening at the floor. It was always disgusting. On good days, they would get served plain oatmeal. On bad ones, some meat stew. It gave Murray pause every time he took a bite of the unknown and unfamiliar meat. The only good part of the meals were the vitamins that were given, particularly vitamin D to avert deficiency from lack of sunshine. The pair would share the bottom bunk bed to eat as it was the only seating in the cell, unless you counted the toilet, if you could call it that. It was more of a tube that came out of the ground with a bicycle seat-sized platform at the top.

The whole place smelled like piss and shit and vomit. There were no showers. The only hygiene available was a sink that had surprisingly clean water, which doubled as their drinking fountain. No shampoo, no toothpaste, no deodorant. The latter wasn't as big of a problem as it could have been. Fortunately, the cell was too cold to sweat. Unfortunately, that meant they spent most nights shivering under the single wool blanket on their beds.

The temperature at night was just one of many problems that inhibited proper sleep. Sound carried throughout the cell hall, the endless coughing of disease, the shouting at inmates from their neighbors, the screams of hysteria, and the all-too-frequent sounds of flesh striking flesh. Then there were the rats.

It was hell on Earth.

Murray couldn't have been in better company for it. Liu went into work mode as soon as they walked into the cell that first day. He taught Murray meditation techniques to tune out the nightmarish cacophony. He coached him on focusing his mind on his current task and to eliminate all other things. Lastly, he trained Murray on how to find "a happy place". Murray laughed when Liu first told him this, but he soon realized the method truly worked, to a degree. In his mind, Murray entered into streets of West Hollywood, greeting the people he knew and enjoying the continuously gorgeous weather. He could even smell jasmine mixed with the scents of tortillerias from the local street vendors, if only temporarily.

Despite his best efforts Murray couldn't escape the horrific conditions he was living in. He missed his "home" and the life he'd lived at Santa Mira. There he at least had a purpose. Before he could work in the FF, learn new skills, box, and spend time with great people like Mouse and Joe. Here he was just meat in a cell.

Then there was Graves. The thought of Graves was what always broke his meditation. He would drift away in peace, walking the streets of his old neighborhood and then the image of Irvine Graves would creep into his mind. The buildings around him would crumble. The people he greeted would be beaten by thugs and there would be nothing he could do to stop it. Graves stung at him still, even though Murray had no idea where he was. He could have been in the next cell over, for all he knew. Someday he would have to face Graves again. He could only hope that when the day came he would know what to do to end this battle and avenge Anatoly.

Yet, here he was, trapped. Unable to do anything towards that goal. His frustrations at his time wasting away were just another vehicle for him to lose his focus and let the dread of his imprisonment creep into his thoughts.

The screams of his neighbors made him cringe as they slowly lost their minds from their isolation. Suicide was rampant. It was better to bash one's head against the wall than to go on in this hell. The guards and staff did nothing to prevent it, to stop the deaths. When one of the prisoners took their own life, they would just wheel the body out on a gurney the next day and then punish the other inmate in the cell block by beating them as a warning to the rest of the block.

Disease was everywhere.

Murray and Liu needed to build up their immune system as much as they could to stave it off. So when they weren't sleeping, meditating or eating, they were training. Murray spent eight hours every day exercising. He started by stretching, squatting, jumping and balancing. Then three hours of *taiji quan,* or shadow-boxing in the closest English translation. He would enter into stances, then let the energy flow through his limbs, guiding them, finding invisible targets, striking, and returning to form. He would blend the time with the meditation that Liu trained. He found a strength inside himself but a calmness to it. There was power inside him, yet he found peace in his training.

The pair would then spend the next four hours sparring around their cell. Murray would be put into a location of the room and Liu would attack from different angles repeatedly, sometimes just one attack all day until Murray had mastered the defense, without thought. His body guided his actions, not his mind. No attack could come from any angle that he could not defend.

Murray finished each day with weight training. There were no actual weights in the room so every exercise meant the weight had to come from his own body. The hardest each day was the handstand pushup. Then a fifteen minute cool-down and eight hours of sleep. The next day the routine began again.

When they finally left Oroville Murray was lean, strong, cut from wood.

———

For six months and twenty-three days, Murray and Liu were trapped in a cell at Oroville. In that entire time, they hadn't seen the outside or heard anything of the events of the world. Isolation had taken a toll on both of them, even with all the meditation and training. Murray and Liu had a hard time engaging in conversation, all the more obvious in small talk. They struggled to respond to any stimuli and couldn't find responses to common pleasantries like "How are you?" and "Thank you".

So when they awoke on their final day, to the sight of a large silhouette standing outside their cell, it was no surprise that they didn't know who or what it was. Murray thought the giant outside was a demon, finally here to end it all. In a sense, he wasn't wrong.

"Let's go," said the shadow. "Corenswet wants you both back, ASAP."

Murray blinked at the figure, trying to adjust his eyes to the harsh light behind it. He leapt off the top bunk and found Liu climbing out from his bed. The pair strode forward and in the proximity to the figure found a familiar and agreeable face.

"Mitchell," Murray breathed.

"Come with me," Mitchell replied.

The guard opened the cell door and Murray and Liu stepped out. Mitchell handcuffed both of them and led them through the hall. The inmates were catcalling, hissing and reaching through the bars trying to grab them. Mitchell ignored them. He walked in front of

Murray and Liu like a large plow through the extended arms, bashing his way through them. The force would slam the reaching inmates' arms against the bars and soon the jeering was replaced with howls of pain. Halfway through their march, the arms were no longer reaching out at them.

They strode through the block and out into the parking area. For the first time in half a year, they felt the sun on them. It was a contradictory feeling, the warmth sent chills in their flesh. It was like a cold shower of warmth, the rays of the sun shook loose the remnants of their isolation sickness.

Mitchell guided them to a white van with the words "Santa Mira State Prison" printed on the side. The sight of it gave Murray an odd and unexpected feeling. He laughed out loud, possibly too much.

"What is it?" Liu asked.

"I'm excited about going to a prison."

Liu just shook his head. He couldn't put into words how he felt. He was with Murray, though. Leaving Oroville could only be a good thing, whatever awaited them in Corenswet's fortress.

Murray must have been thinking the same thing as evidenced by his question to Mitchell.

"Are we going straight to Santa Mira?"

"Yes," Mitchell answered. He opened the back doors of the van and waited for Murray and Liu to climb in. He buckled them into a bench that ran along the side. Then he shut the doors and climbed into the driver's seat.

"Is the prison repaired?" Murray asked.

"Not all the way," Mitchell said as he started the van and drove towards the exit. "The South Block and the minimum security houses are still too damaged. The rest has been up and running for about three months now."

Three months? Murray remarked to himself perplexed. He looked at Liu who had the same look on his face.

"We've been in Oroville for almost seven months," Liu scoffed. "Why didn't you come get us earlier?"

"I know," Mitchell offered. "I'm sorry. The warden is sorry. Oroville didn't register you at all. You were lost in the system. You were never supposed to go there in the first place. You were supposed to be in Folsom. I spent three weeks there looking for you. The whole process was a mess. It was your friends Dormus and someone on the outside named Sam who tracked you down after daily calling each prison administration."

Murray and Liu smiled at each other at the mention of Mouse's name.

"Mouse is there?" Murray and Liu chorused at the same time.

"Is he good?" Murray added, still struggling with the correct language.

"He's fine," the guard answered. "He went where he was supposed to."

Murray's glee turned to doubt at the thought of who else may have returned.

"Graves?"

"Graves isn't at Santa Mira."

"Where is he?"

"Missing," was all that Mitchell could say.

CHAPTER 22

LAPD Officer Nate Johns entered the Wilshire Police Station on a Wednesday morning in time for his patrol shift to begin. He carried a brown paper bag with six doughnuts and a tray with two coffees from Bob's Coffee and Doughnuts: one black French roast, the other a whole bean espresso. The fancy coffee was the favorite of his partner, Louis Rodihan. Nate didn't ever buy coffee and donuts for his partner. His partner called him a mooch--he'd accept them from anyone else but would never offer to buy them in return, or even pitch in with a few dollars for the person of whose donuts he was eating. Today was different. Johns had heard a rumor that they were getting reassigned. It was worth celebrating.

Johns and Rodihan hadn't been assigned to Wilshire for long. They had been transferred from 77th Street in the South Bureau. The partners had fought against moving out of the South Bureau but the transfer was mandatory. They had been shown to have extreme anxiety and a propensity towards incident escalation when faced with situations involving members of the black community in the area. Fearing a possible event of police misconduct with the duo, their commanding officer requested they be moved to a division within the city where racial tensions weren't as high or as likely to rise due to their actions.

Not very many of the other officers at Wilshire liked Johns. They found him to be rude and overly vulgar, regardless of the situation. Just a couple of weeks beforehand, Johns had refused to stop swearing and using racial slurs at a community outreach event where a woman had asked about the increase in crime in their district. It had made the department look bad to the community they were trying to earn the trust of, and Johns's fellow officers had let him know their feelings towards him during the weeks since.

So when Johns yelled out, "Where's fucking Louis?" as he walked into the men's locker room, the dirty looks and silence he received in reply angered but didn't surprise him. "Hey don't anybody answer me or anything, you faggot assholes," he set the donuts and coffee down on the bench in front of his locker and changed into his uniform. He had just finished tying his shoes when the watch commander came in and told him to report to the captain's office immediately.

"Perfect. I can tell the prick to kiss my ass," he muttered to himself as he picked up the donuts and coffee.

"Leave 'em," the watch commander ordered sternly. "Follow me now, please"

"Fine. Jesus."

Johns followed the officer through the station and up the stairs to the captain's office. Along the way, they passed other officers who looked at Johns and spoke low enough that he couldn't hear what they said, but he knew they were talking about him. This wasn't the first time he'd been brought into a captain's office and one thing he knew about working in a police station, word spread like fire, often before those involved knew anything.

Johns opened the door to the captain's office and before him sat Captain Perez at his desk. Behind him stood two men in suits, both with very serious faces. He knew exactly who they were without meeting them or knowing their names; this wasn't the first time he'd met with Internal Affairs. This didn't feel like a meeting about transferring elsewhere.

"Officer Johns, please take a seat," the captain said as he gestured to the chairs in front of his desk.

"What's this all about? Why is IA here?" Johns asked as he sat down.

"This is Detective Holmes and Detective Rice," Perez said. "They're here because of a very serious situation, Nate."

"We'll handle it, captain, thank you," Detective Rice cut in. "Officer Nate Johns. You are being placed under arrest for sexual misconduct and sexual assault."

"What the fuck?" Johns burst out.

"Out of respect for your service to the department, we're giving you an opportunity to come one hundred percent clean with us about your actions and your conduct."

"My conduct?" Johns exploded, shifting in his chair. "What the fuck is this? Where's Louis? What did you tell these guys, Perez?"

Detective Holmes spoke at Johns, "I urge you to remain calm here. We need to be clear with you. We have enough evidence and information already to make an arrest. Three other officers, including your partner, Officer Louis Rodihan, have already been arrested. When we are done here we'll read you your rights and then place you in handcuffs. We'll then take you to a private cell where you will await an arraignment. We will have further questions for you during that time and you may choose to have an attorney present."

Johns wasn't having it. "This is bullshit. This is some hack job on me for doing my job."

Rice spoke again ignoring John's remark, "This meeting is strictly off the record. We want to give you a fair chance to know what we are arresting you for and to add anything or make your own statement to us and your commanding officer before we begin the official process.

"Nate, we're just cops too. Movies always make it seem like IA is out to get you guys. We aren't. We're on your side. All we do is what we have to do to keep the public and the bureaucrats away from you so that you can do your jobs. Sometimes cops screw up, sometimes they get arrested and we're the guys that have to do that unpleasant business. But we understand. Hell, both Detective Holmes and I were patrol officers just like you. I was a beat cop for fifteen years. I've had my fair share of mistakes too. So just tell us what we want to know so that we can do our best to help you."

Johns looked at Captain Perez questioningly. The captain nodded his head, encouraging Johns to cooperate.

"Well, what's this all about? What the fuck did I do?" Johns asked. "Is this about that drunk woman who went on the news and lied about me and Louis? You guys know that was bullshit right?"

Holmes and Rice looked at each other and then Rice spoke, "Not directly. Another victim has accused you and three others of the same thing, though. She claims that you and Rodihan raped her after you pulled her over under suspicion of DUI on May 16th, one week ago today."

Johns knew exactly what Rice was talking about. Still, that was supposed to go away. The evidence had been destroyed, he'd thought. He left Greem to take care of that. Had Greem stabbed him in the back? Had he betrayed him and his fellow officers?

"I'm not saying anything else to you. You think you pieces of shit can intimidate me? You got nothing. I'm not buying this *I'm your friend* bullshit. You want to arrest me, motherfucker?" Johns stood up and put his arms out for handcuffs.

Holmes shouted to someone outside the door, "Officers!" and two policemen came in.

Johns was livid now. "You go right ahead and arrest me but you be ready!" he shouted as the officers put the handcuffs on him. "Because when you find out you have nothing on me, I'm coming for you. You and your whole fucking faggot office is going to know that you can't fuck with Nate Johns!" He was still screaming at them as he was led through the hallway and down the stairs to the jail.

"Well, that could have gone better," Holmes remarked.

———

The second trial of The Brose Four lasted from November until January and was the second most watched trial in America, second only to the OJ Simpson proceedings. The Four were on the cover of every major magazine and covered by every major news channel and internet media outlet. Talk show hosts lambasted them nightly, and social media spread memes of their faces with scathing comments over them. They were all anyone talked about. Even the violence across the nation came to a halt as the people of the United States watched the events and testimonies of the trial unfold before them. Twice the Brose Four stood accused of misconduct. Twice they had escaped without punishment or justice. Now they stood in front of the entire nation on trial for a horrible crime.

The trial wasn't segregated from the denizens of Santa Mira Prison. Corenswet allowed the inmates to watch the trial on the news each day. He found it a great distraction for them. His wards would gather in circles and talk about the trial just like people at an office gathering around a water cooler. It gave them something to focus on and unite towards. There wasn't a single man in Santa Mira who didn't think The Brose Four were guilty, and all wanted to see them face the maximum sentence. All except one.

Murray Bench watched the case unfold just like the rest of his neighbors, but used it as a distraction from the lingering aches from his time at Oroville. The trial was a replacement of the hurt he felt with an obsession: justice for Anatoly's death and against the people who caused it. He stayed updated with the news on the inmate television in his block, reports that Mouse found on the internet, and by reading the *San Francisco Chronicle* in the prison library. Murray was the one voice that wasn't out for blood on the Four. He wanted justice and that was what the court would decide, not him. While he kept a moderate view on the trial, he also learned everything he could about it.

By the time the jury was deliberating, Murray had a pretty good picture of what happened. Another woman, Mishel Armis, testified that she was pulled over at 10:35pm on May 16th at the corner of Venice Boulevard and Normandie Ave. She was celebrating with friends after finishing her last class of the semester at USC. Officers Greem and Crockett pulled her over and said that she improperly yielded when entering Normandie from the one-way road that fed into it. She explained that she was pulling over to park and therefore didn't need to yield since she was not entering the road. Officer Crockett asked how much she had to drink and she explained that she had a couple of beers but switched to water an hour before leaving. He asked her to exit the vehicle and then conducted a field sobriety test.

It was then that another police car arrived with Officers Johns and Rodihan. Crockett finished the test and asked her to stand by his car while he talked to the other three officers. She couldn't hear the conversation but when they returned Rodihan told her she was under arrest for suspicion of DUI. Johns handcuffed her and walked her to his car. She pleaded that she was sober and they were violating her rights. They told her she was going to be taken back to the station and given a breathalyzer test. If she was under the legal limit for blood/alcohol level they would drive her back to her car. She refused, and asked to speak to her attorney first. They were violating her constitutional rights and had no legal power to force her to go with them.

Johns kept telling her to shut up or she'd be in real trouble, but she refused and shouted at them repeatedly. Rodihan pulled the car over and Johns yanked Armis out of the car. He slapped her across the face and Rodihan hit her in the back of the head with his nightstick. At that time, Greem and Crockett, who were following, pulled over as well. The woman was disoriented from the blow to her head and lost focus of the events as she faded in and out of consciousness. She recalled waking briefly and hearing yelling. She was on the hood of the car and knew she was being raped. Her pleas for help were unanswered, then she fell unconscious again. She woke in the hospital emergency room with a concussion and three bruised ribs. Confused, she asked what happened and was told she had been brought in by the police. They had found her in an alleyway after being attacked by a homeless person. The police said they found her with her skirt ripped and no undergarments.

The hospital had given her a rape test but found no evidence of semen. Armis was released the next day and contacted her attorney immediately.

The defense claimed there was no evidence of any of those events happening, an elaborate fabrication by a college student who protested against the LAPD. There was no record of the officers pulling over anyone matching her name. Officers Rodihan and Johns were not even on duty at the reported time of the attack. Police department and dispatch records showed Greem and Crockett were on patrol in the area, but had not reported in between 10:25 pm and 11:31pm, with their last report having been taking their evening break for dinner. The officers were equipped with body cameras and the vehicles had dash cameras, yet there was nothing unusual in the video. With no DNA found to test and no records or video footage of Armis' alleged arrest, the prosecution had only the victim's testimony as evidence. Things were starting to look like The Brose Four were going to walk again. Law enforcement agencies nationwide braced themselves and prepared for the almost-guaranteed riots that were coming. The country sat on the precipice of self-destruction.

Sometimes guilt can be overpowering, though. Sometimes, just one man can make a difference to the entire world. Officer Cyrus Greem's guilt was too much to live with after he heard the tearful testimony of Ms. Armis. On the second to last day of the evidence phase of the trial, Greem came forward as a witness for the prosecution. He confessed that everything Armis had said was true. Johns and Rodihan protested, but their attorney made them sit quietly. He told them that he would handle it. When the defense asked Greem if it was all true, then what about the video evidence that proved otherwise. Greem said that he was supposed to destroy the evidence. Johns had put him in charge of it. He said it was simple but he screwed it all up.

The LAPD were one of the first departments in the country to incorporate video camera technology; that also meant the system was now out of date. Instead of immediately uploading the footage to a cloud-based storage system, the video was stored on a hard-drive within the police cruiser itself and then uploaded to the station's video storage system when the vehicle returned. Since none of the officers had returned that night, the video was still on the hard drives. To access it, one had to have a special key and password to remove the storage device. Only captains, commanders and sergeants had this access. Greem had been a sergeant at his last position before moving to LA. The keys were universal and no one had ever removed his password. He only had to drive to the station, check into the evidence room and then replicate the camera footage of a night almost 30 days prior. Footage was only stored for 30 days, so no one would miss the video. He returned to others with the new footage and loaded storage device back into the car. He told them everything was taken care of and he would destroy the old storage devices. He had lied to them about that, as he had no idea how to destroy the devices without leaving evidence somewhere. He thought it was best to just hide them. He put them in a box in his garage and there they sat until today.

The footage was never released to the public, but the media had a field day with the court records that documented the events that transpired. The reports Murray read stated that the video from Greem's and Crockett's body cameras did indeed show exactly what Ms. Armis stated up until the time she lost consciousness. What she nor anyone else except The Brose Four knew was what happened after she had been struck across the back of her head. The car's dash cam showed Johns slamming her face down onto the hood of the car while Rodihan reached down to her legs with another set of handcuffs. It was believed that their early intention was to hogtie her so that her feet and hands were bound together in a very uncomfortable manner. Greem and Crockett protested this assault. At that point, Johns told them to back off and that things were under control. He kicked Rodihan aside before he could fasten the handcuffs, and told him to hold her down for a second. Rodihan complied and kept her pinned against the hood. She was still clearly unconscious.

The next thing Johns did was unthinkable. He pulled a condom from out of his pocket and unwrapped it. Greem and Crockett told him to stop and attempted to grab him. Officer Johns shrugged them off and pulled his gun out and stuck the barrel against Ms. Armis' head. He said that he would shoot her here and now if they tried to stop him. The other officers backed off and Johns unzipped his trousers and applied the condom. Crockett and Greem had to watch the entire thing and were helpless to do anything to stop it. Johns had all the power. They couldn't risk him shooting this poor woman.

The rest was as Ms. Armis remembered. The Four drove her to the hospital and dumped her there with a false report about her attack. They didn't leave their names and drove away before anyone could ask any further questions.

When the jury gave their verdict, they did so after spending only 25 minutes deliberating over it. The verdict was guilty across the board. Justice had finally come to The Brose Four.

———

A week after hearing the verdict, Murray awaited news of their sentencing. The bombshell came to Murray when he opened the new issue of the Chronicle and saw the headline "BROSE 4 SENTENCED". His eyes skimmed to the section of the article where the periods of imprisonment were listed. Nate Johns received 11 years for the rape of Mishel Armis, along with numerous accounts of police misconduct. Louis Rodihan received 8 years for accessory to a felony, Cyrus Greem and Matt Crockett received 6 years for complicity to a felony. It wasn't until he read the last line of the paragraph that his heart sank. The Brose Four were being sent to serve their time at Santa Mira.

CHAPTER 23

The day The Brose Four came to Santa Mira was the quietest day Murray ever had while he was imprisoned. The FF was completely deserted except for Liu and himself. Every other inmate that wasn't in the infirmary, on some work detail, or in solitary was out at the entrance to the prison where the bus would come in to drop off The Four. The inmates lined the fences along the parking area and looked out from windows of the east cell block to get a glimpse. The bus pulled along the roadway that led around the prison on its way to the double doors, the same entrance that had greeted Murray as he surrendered his freedom to the California justice system.

Murray had decided he wanted no part of seeing the arrival of the men who had killed his best friend. He felt they wouldn't last long enough in Santa Mira for him to have to worry about it. Their imprisonment here could have just been another PR stunt by Corenswet to garner more attention (and more public funding). Whether The Brose Four were here for days or years didn't matter.

If they were killed inside the walls, then Corenswet could say he needed more men to keep things under control. If they survived their sentence, then Corenswet would be shown to be doing his job well and thus deserved more funding than his counterparts. It seemed that the inmates had their own plans though, and a long stay at the fortress wasn't part of it. The prisoners of Santa Mira were all too ready to receive four former LAPD officers who had sent many of them to be confined within its walls.

However, as the bus pulled into view and drove down the one-way lane to its destination, the residents of the prison were silent. They crammed around the walls to get a view of their new neighbors, but only a slight murmur of discontent could be heard from them. Perhaps this wasn't the bus that held The Four after all. Perhaps it was just a different delivery that they hadn't heard about. Why waste their anger on some bus load of transfers returning from Folsom or Salinas Valley prisons? They would wait until they knew for sure that the bus contained the four men whose faces they had seen for weeks in the news.

When the bus stopped and its reverse lights illuminated, the tension began to grow. As the white California Department of Corrections transport bus began to back up, the audience started to push against each other to try and get a view of the passengers it was unloading. Shouting began to be heard as men smashed together and tempers flared up. Some of the more agile inmates began climbing the fences to get out from the crowd and gain a better vantage point. Guards yelled at them to climb back down and the replies snapped back from the inmates caused even more retaliation from those on the ground. Soon the place was in a frenzy. The pushing and shoving became too much for some, and blows were thrown. The guards had to choose to ignore those on the fences to try to quell the unrest from those who were now fighting. Billy clubs were struck against the instigators. Blood was being spilled on the ground and the bus hadn't even parked yet.

The violence went on when finally the doors of the bus opened and out stepped The Brose Four. The fighting ceased immediately and all anger and hatred was instantly diverted to the former law enforcement officers. From booing to vulgarities to threats, every insult imaginable was hurled at them. The Four marched sullenly forward to the admittance building, their heads down and their hearts pumping with fear. It was only Cyrus Greem who looked at his surroundings and the faces of the men who were out to humiliate, wound, cripple and even kill them.

"What hell have we been brought to?" he asked aloud as he stopped to look at his situation. His question was only answered by a shove from the guard escorting him. He and the three others passed through the entrance of Santa Mira and left the anarchy of their arrival outside.

———

Johns, Rodihan, Crockett and Greem spent the next four days of their lives in quarantine. After entering through processing, Corenswet had Mitchell and three other guards escort them directly to a group of four cells within Cell Block D, the block where Solitary Confinement was housed. They were each tossed into individual cells and told to wait until someone came for them.

It was twelve hours before their first visit. A member of the medical staff gave each a physical and drew blood. Fifteen minutes after the nurse left, a meal was finally delivered to them. They hadn't eaten since the day before and the four men were completely famished. The meal consisted of a cup of salad without dressing, a cup of chicken and dumpling soup, a half cup of canned apricots, a cup of milk and a cup of coffee. It was sparse and tasted bland but he Brose Four didn't care. Each tore through the meal in a matter of minutes. When the next guard came thirty minutes later to take the plastic tray and utensils left from the meal, the men had licked the items clean. Each was then given a liter bottle of water and were told to make it last until the following day.

Another 12 hours passed. Isolation was beginning to show effects on the condition of the men. Their bodies started to ache and their joints were stiff. Greem and Rodihan spent most of the time sleeping. Crockett talked to himself and recounted stories from his days in the military. Johns did nothing but stare at the door and quietly cursed the people who had put him in such a position.

Mitchell was their next visitor. He delivered another meal of toast, scrambled eggs, oatmeal, and coffee. He replaced their water supply. He told each of the four men that they had all passed their physicals and blood tests, but the warden had them locked away for their own safety. The prison was still in a state of unrest and he wanted to wait until he felt sure that the four former cops could enter into the population with minimal threat of violence.

The rest of their time in solitary proceeded with the same schedule. Twelve hours alone, a visit with a meal, then 12 hours alone again before a visit from a nurse and another meal came. The men continued to suffer in their cells, alone both physically and emotionally. It was Crockett who broke first. When Matt came back from his third tour of duty in the Middle East, he was diagnosed with a mild case of PTSD, a fact covered up by the LAPD. In fact, it was a serious case. Now in isolation, the horrors were taking an amplified effect.

While all of the men were continuing to experience increasing pain in their limbs and back, Crockett began experiencing hallucinations. At first there were floating spots of light moving around the room in vivid blue and green, accompanied by an unpleasant smell. He chose not to say anything to the nurse who came to check on them at first, but after the second day things grew worse. Matt thought he saw a woman looking down on him when he closed his eyes. When he opened them again she was gone, but he would close his eyes and he could feel her staring at him from somewhere above. On the third day, he felt something or someone was touching his arms. He started hearing a repetitive clicking sound and a tapping from the floor, like something hard crawling across it. Matt told the nurse about his visitors and was frightened by them. He begged for someone to come get him and to get rid of the pests in his room. The nurse told him that it wouldn't be much longer and to just be patient, but by the fourth day he was clawing at his skin to remove imaginary bugs that were trying to get in his lungs. When the nurse came on that day and found Crockett with bleeding streaks from the cuts up and down his arms, he was finally removed and put in the infirmary under heavy sedation.

The other three were also finally moved on the fourth day, just hours after Crockett. They were sent into the West Cell Block and put into a four man cell specifically meant for them. When Greem entered the cell and the former officers were reunited, Cyrus was disappointed to see his partner not among them. Their isolation nightmare was over and he only hoped Crockett was doing okay. He knew about Matt's PTSD and it made him worried for his friend's mental health.

When Nate Johns entered the cell, there was no joy. Rodihan was the first to greet him and say that he was glad to see Johns. When Johns didn't respond and sat on one of the bunks, Greem asked how he was feeling.

"I feel hate," was Johns's response.

———

Greem and Rodihan left Johns alone after that. Johns didn't speak again until the following day when Corenswet visited their cell with Mitchell and his personal bodyguards in tow. The warden had chosen to bring his coffee mug with him and one of the guards carried a thermos to refill it when needed. After the warden introduced himself in his contrived and overly formal manner, he spoke to them about their stay at Santa Mira.

"I'm sure you're aware of the type of system that I run here?" he asked. Greem and Rodihan nodded, while Johns just stared at the ground from his position on his bed.

"Good. Then I won't have to waste any time with explaining to you how the rules work. This here is my man, Mitchell. You may hear him called 'Dragoon' by the other inmates. I find the moniker distasteful, but it seems to have stuck. He will be overseeing a special guard duty assigned to offer you four protection. Now, if you feel you are ready-"

"Protection from what?" Johns interrupted without breaking his gaze from whatever he found so interesting on the ground.

Mitchell moved to Johns in a flash and put both of his hands on the sides of the former officer's head and then pulled him up to his feet. Johns groaned in pain. Greem and Rodihan reeled in shock as the giant guard continued his assault.

"Mitchell, that is quite enough," Corenswet commanded. The guard released his grip and Johns crumbled back to the bed below him. "Now that was a good demonstration for you all to witness. I will remind you that interrupting me while I speak is not only rude, but strictly not considered a wise decision in this confine. You'll do well to remember that. As I was saying, I am having you released into a special population of the community under close supervision. You will be paired together; let's just go with the same partners you had when you were on the right side of the law and each pair will have their own private guard...at least until this whole affair blows over and you can join in the general population."

Corenswet paused to catch his breath and take a sip from his coffee mug.

"So to answer your question about protection, I am frankly surprised that you aren't aware of your circumstances. There are many men here who would love the chance to do horrible things to you three, plus your little friend with the mental situation. There is one particular guest that has a special relationship with the four of you."

After Corenswet finished his sentence, he raised his eyebrows in an expression of expectation. It was Greem who got brave enough to respond.

"Who would that be?" he asked.

"Don't you know?" Corenswet replied. It was clear that he wanted to gloat over them. His demeanor and prepared statements made it hard to remain calm, but Greem did his best to play along.

"Know what?"

"Why, the very man with whom you earned your national celebrity status is here! It was his dear friend who gave you your nickname, The Brose Four. I must say that it makes you all seem like some group in the Old West."

They had all remembered that Murray was an inmate at Santa Mira. The day he was sentenced was the day their nightmare began. It was the day that Greem and Crockett found themselves suddenly lumped together with the scumbags, Johns and Rodihan, probably until the end of time. Greem kept the charade going with the warden. *Let him have his fun*, he thought. *I don't want to do anything to piss off Dragoon.*

"Murray Bench is here, huh? That'll make things interesting."

Corenswet continued. "Now I have a very special interest in Murray Bench. I will have no trouble from the four of you with him at all. Is that understood?"

The three nodded.

"Good," Corenswet said as he exited the cell and Mitchell closed the door behind them. Corenswet turned and spoke through the bars of the cell.

"Last but not least is the topic of your final member, Matt Crockett. I have heard from the medical examiner and I'm pleased to report that Mr. Crockett's condition is improving. He should be ready to join you all within a couple of days."

Greem smiled, nodding his approval at the news while Johns and Rodihan showed no emotional response.

"And with that I must return to much more important matters," Corenswet said and then turned and left without a gesture.

It wasn't in a couple of days, but nearly a week later when Matt Crockett was brought to them. It all started with the three being separated as Corenswet had told; Johns and Rodihan in one cell, Greem in another next door. An hour later, two medical orderlies arrived with Crockett. They were carrying him by his shoulders as his feet dragged behind him. His mouth was open and his eyes were lifeless. The sight of the once proud man in this state brought tears to Greem's face. The orderlies had Greem's cell door opened and they brought Matt inside, laying him down on the bed. They left the cell and when the door closed behind them, one spoke to Cyrus.

"He is going to be coming off his Thorazine in a few hours. He'll have some withdrawal symptoms that you will have to help him deal with." With that, the orderlies left Crockett in the concerned care of Cyrus Greem.

That night, no one in the cell block was able to sleep much. The wailing of Matt Crockett woke the inmates at 1:12am. He was feverish and delusional. He was suffering from extreme nausea and he was crying out in pain. His cellmate did his best to try and keep Crockett quiet and comfortable, but it was to no avail. The other inmates, including his former colleague and current neighbor, Johns, yelled at him to shut up, not understanding that Crockett wasn't conscious enough to understand. Rodihan just pulled his pillow over his head, trying to mute the moans from next door. Matt's withdrawal symptoms from the antipsychotic sedative was something no one could stop without another prescription for the drug.

For the Brose Four, their nightmare at Santa Mira Prison had only just begun.

CHAPTER 24

Things didn't take long to return to normal, or at least the Santa Mira version of it. The Brose Four had been locked away ever since their arrival and the prison eventually forgot about them. The discussions in the yard and at chow time went back to sports, women and stories of days before the inmates were locked away. For Murray, normal meant working in the FF, training with Liu and enjoying his free time chatting with Mouse.

On one such ordinary day, Murray and Mouse were sitting on the baseball field bleachers. No one was playing baseball, but it was a nice enough day out and this spot, albeit bleak and dirty to a free man, was one of the nicest places to sit and visit within the prison confines. The pair were discussing topics of complete triviality, as they often did. No one can have heavy and life-changing discussions all the time; often Murray and Mouse liked talking about nothing important. Today they were discussing whether American sports cars could ever compete with European. Neither really had any vested interest in the outcome but Murray was on the side of the powerful and heavy American cars of the 70's while Mouse argued for the lightweight and zippy roadsters of 60's Europe. The two were so deep into their conversation that they lost themselves in it and didn't notice that they had visitors.

"My dad had a '72 Corvette Stingray," came the voice behind them. Turning to follow it, they saw Cyrus Greem standing next to Matt Crockett and their personal Santa Mira security guard. Corenswet had finally let them into the general population. Cyrus was smiling, while Matt looked pained but alert.

"He said it was bulky and slow, and steered like sticking your dick in a bowl of mashed potatoes, but when you saw him in it you could tell he didn't care about any of that. He just liked how it made him feel."

Murray turned back around without response and looked out at the baseball field. It could have been a sewage dump in front of him, but he would have rather focused his gaze there.

Mouse was still facing Greem and replied, "That's nice. Does he still have it?"

"Haven't seen him since I was 8. He drove that car out of the garage one day and never came back. Guess it offered him a better way of life or something."

Murray spoke without turning back in a hollow and vindictive tone, "If you don't mind, I was having a conversation with someone that I actually care about."

Greem tried to speak, "Murray, I-"

Murray wasn't interested in letting Greem finish. He stood up and faced the former police officer.

"You two come up here, thinking you can just set me up for Graves? Is that it?"

Greem and Crockett looked at each other in confusion.

"Graves?" Matt ventured.

"We just wanted to talk," Cyrus added.

"Look, I said I don't care. I don't care if you become king of the world or if you just fall over and die. I just don't want you doing it here."

"Come on, Cy. Let's just leave him be," Crockett said and pulled Cyrus Greem with him. The two walked away in silence along with their protection. After they were out of sight, Murray sat back down next to Mouse.

"Jesus, Murray. I understand you have room to be pissed but I've never seen you like that before," Mouse said, more than a little worried about his friend's temperament.

"Look, just forget about it. I don't want to talk about it. In fact, I don't want to talk about anything," Murray spoke in frustration as he stood back up. "I'll see you later."

Mouse sat on the bleachers dumbfounded at his friend's anger as he watched Murray walk away.

———

Just a little while later, Murray was in the FF with Liu for his evening training, sparring in the little training area Liu used for such sessions. While Liu had spent months training Murray to work from the defensive position and turn his opponents attack into a weapon, today things were going differently. Murray had come straight into the fight on the offense. He was rapidly attacking Liu from all angles and with a ferocity that Liu hadn't seen from his usually cool-headed student.

Left and right, Murray threw blows at Liu, who had little trouble deflecting the force or dodging the attacks that Murray was practically shouting out beforehand. Liu let the attacks come without word. He wanted to see if his pupil would relent first, or if Liu would have to force him to stop. After the fifth time Murray tried to strike with a forward jab from his right, Liu caught the blow and carried Murray's weight forward with him, pushing the student's clenched fist into a wall. The force of the impact bruised Murray's knuckles but he hadn't time to react to the pain, for in the next second Liu had kicked his legs out from under him and he landed hard on the ground.

"What is wrong with you today?" Liu asked. "You fight like a rabid dog. All bite, no conscience, no plan, and no thought behind your intents."

Rubbing his hand and getting to his knees, Murray replied, "Nothing. There's nothing wrong with me. I'm fine."

"Wrong answer. You are not concentrating."

"I said, I'm fine. Now can we do this or-"

Murray couldn't finish. Liu had struck him across the chest with a kick that knocked him back into the wall.

"There is your 'I'm fine'," Liu said sarcastically. "That attack should have been caught by you and redirected. I taught you that on your first session months and months ago. You are distracted. Until we can 'undistract' you then you are in no condition to continue training. I wish you luck in life. Now please leave me to my work."

Liu turned and walked away from Murray.

"All right, all right!" Murray shouted. "I get it. You don't have to go all Yoda on me."

Murray sat down on a box of thread at the edge of their makeshift arena.

"I saw them today." Murray saw the look of confusion in Liu's eyes. "You know? THEM."

"The policemen. I see. You are angry at them still."

"Well yeah, but no. Shit, I don't know." Murray couldn't fully explain how he felt. He'd spent so much time since he arrived at Santa Mira trying to forget, to move on. He'd been so focused on Graves as the centerpiece for his contempt that he'd subconsciously tucked away his anger at the Four. In the back of his mind, he knew he'd have to face the tragedy of that fateful day, the day that The Brose Four took his best friend and freedom, but he wasn't prepared for it to happen so soon. Seeing them brought back so many memories and pain that he wanted to lash out at something, anything.

"I want to hurt them," he finally said.

"Well you're certainly capable of doing that!" Liu quipped. "What's stopping you?"

"I know it's not right. It's not what you have taught me. It's not what my father would have wanted. Hell, I don't even think it's what 'Toly would have wanted. I know all this and I keep telling myself that over and over again but I can't help it. I want them to feel loss like I've felt."

Liu listened quietly to his troubled friend from across the room. He reached behind him and from the workbench he was leaning against, collected a pick for stitching fringe onto the ends of Oriental rugs. He tossed the pick up in the air and held it out to Murray.

"You see this. It's a pick," he said.

"I know what it is," Murray replied gruffly.

"And you know what it does. It is the last tool you use to finish a piece of work. The last tool in the last step."

"Yeah I know, it punches holes on the edge so fringe can be sewn onto the rug. Are you training me on a new technique or something?" Murray was agitated but knew to listen to Liu when it came to his job at the FF.

"New technique...yes. That is what I'm doing," Liu said and walked over to Murray.

"When it is used, every step in the process of the work before it does not matter. That work is gone, done. All this little pick can do is do its job, which is to end the project."

Murray was getting lost, but still remained quiet. Master Liu's voice had calmed him down and his anger was vanishing. Whether that was the former assassin's intention or not was unclear.

"Yet the tool does not get to say when the work is finished. The master who guides it is the one that makes the decision. It is the master who says what is done and what is not."

"I get it. The master is in charge. What's your point?" Murray finally asked completely confused.

"You have not finished your work, Murray," Liu said as he put his hand on his pupil's shoulder. "You have the tools, you have the knowledge on how to use them. You must end this thing that is keeping you from moving forward onto the next project. That is life; a series of challenges where when one is finished, the next takes its place. You must finish this challenge so that you can move to the next."

Murray watched as his mentor set the pick next to Murray and walked back to his work.

"I said, 'Don't go all Yoda'!" The Master of Daito-Ryu only smiled enigmatically in response.

———

"Finish this challenge."

The words from his mentor came to Murray again as he lay in his bunk that night. It was close to midnight and Murray had been staring out into the darkness of the cell block. He couldn't sleep. His mind was too focused on what Liu had said earlier in the day. His cryptic advice, what it meant and how it connected to The Brose Four had been on his mind since that afternoon.

After Liu spoke to him, Murray put away his work for the day and took a walk around the prison. He usually didn't risk wandering around alone. It wasn't that he was worried about injuries or another fun-filled week in the infirmary. No, with Graves and his men gone, his days of getting his ass kicked at Santa Mira were over. He just hated feeling alone. Solitude made him feel even further away from his previous life. He needed companionship to feel normal. Today, he just didn't care. Alone was preferable to being lectured about his anger.

His walk led him around the back of the Furniture Factory and around the print shop building, where other inmates learned about graphic design and sign printing for local businesses. He wondered if the print shop also had someone like Liu working inside. He laughed at the thought. He imagined that, right in that very moment, some dumbfounded idiot was sitting on a crate and being told by a facsimile of Liu that "The poster does not say when it is finished. Only the printer can say that." He imagined Liu and the print shop kung fu master being locked in combat, Liu holding a thread and needle and the other holding a computer mouse.

He walked past the library and education building. He knew that Mouse would be inside at this point in the evening. He was now teaching computer classes every Tuesday and Thursday in the library. It was a good hobby for the old guy. He liked teaching and had learned a lot about computers in his time at the vocational office. He was a natural fit for the job. It also helped Mouse build relationships with some of the inmates. A guy like him needed all the friends he could get here and it made Murray feel happy for him. The old guy had been saddened by Joe Wassar's release--the pair had become close. Any path to making new friends was good for Mouse. Murray wouldn't always be there.

He thought about stopping in and seeing if Mouse could help him figure out what Liu was saying, but he didn't want to be a distraction. It was getting late anyway and was time to be heading to his cell.

Once inside his cell, Murray laid down and reflected more deeply. He was no longer agitated about seeing Greem and Crockett, but still couldn't get them off his mind. How was he supposed to serve the rest of his sentence without facing them or coming to some confrontation? It wasn't possible. Try as he might, you couldn't avoid someone forever at Santa Mira and he hadn't even dealt with Johns or Rodihan. Johns...Nate Johns... The name made the hair on his neck stand up and his blood pump.

He stopped his thoughts. Just the thought of Johns made him get worked up again, undoing everything his walk had done. He needed to clear his head of them. He employed the meditation technique from Daito-Ryu he'd learned at Oroville to purge his mind of distractions. In and out he breathed slowly while focusing on an imaginary point in his mind. The harder he concentrated on the focal point, the farther the other thoughts went away. In and out, he continued. In and out.

And then his eyes opened.

That was it. So obvious that he could not even believe it. He needed to finish the challenge of the Brose Four. He needed to end this standoff with them. Then he could move on with his life. He was the master and only he could say when it was over, and he clearly hadn't been able to do that yet.

But if he was the master, what were the tools? The other three of the Four? Maybe Liu was saying that they couldn't take full blame, they were just being used by Johns. He was guiding them and they were doing what he said. No, that wouldn't make sense because Johns would have to be the master for that scenario to work. If Murray was the master, the tool had to be...*Daito-Ryu*. Liu was telling Murray to use his training to end the challenge of his anger about Anatoly's death!

Tomorrow morning, Murray Bench was going to take the Brose Four down.

CHAPTER 25

The instant the lights came on and his cell door opened in the morning, Murray went looking for the Brose Four.

He checked their cells and found them empty. He checked the yard. There was no sign of them. The gym was empty. They were not in the library. *Maybe they'd been assigned work? Better check with Mouse.*

"I haven't assigned them to anything," Mouse stated when Murray found him pulling book requests inside the library. "I haven't assigned anyone to anything, actually. There are no new vocational jobs until Santa Mira is back to full operations. My office isn't even fixed yet and from what I hear, it's pretty low on Corenswet's priority list."

Murray thanked Mouse and departed. His next stop was Corenswet's office. Maybe he could pull some leverage on the warden to give up their location. He'd still have to find a way to deal with the private guards that were escorting them. It didn't seem very likely that Corenswet would be up for granting a favor of this magnitude, yet he had to try.

He never got the chance to ask.

On the way to the administration building, he spotted the Four entering the cafeteria. Johns was holding the door open and ushering the others inside. They were being cautious in their movements with Johns standing lookout at the doorway. They hadn't spotted Murray. He ducked against the wall next to him to prevent being seen. *It's not chow time, yet*, Murray thought. *Why are they going in there?* He also didn't see any guards with them. They were alone.

After the door closed and they were all inside, Murray rushed across the grounds, ignoring any inmates that greeted him along the way. Now he had two missions. Find out what the hell these guys were secretly up to, and finally demand some answers for Anatoly.

Reaching the building, he pulled the door open as slowly as he could until it was cracked enough to peek inside. He couldn't see them but he could hear them just fine. They couldn't have been more than fifteen feet away from him and despite their hushed tones, he picked up their discussion clearly.

"You need to fall in line. There's a job to be done here and you two are a part of it," Johns was saying. "Louis and I are in. There's no other option. We need to finish what we started."

"What you started," Greem chimed in. "We didn't sign up for this and you know it."

Johns' voice was getting louder and angrier. "Bullshit! When you decided to fuck up the only job you had, you became part of it. You were supposed to get rid of all the evidence but instead you put yourself on the stand and cried like a little bitch!"

"Shhh…we don't want anyone hearing us," Rodihan cautioned. "If they don't want to help, then let's just get rid of them too."

"Get rid of us?" Crockett questioned. Murray heard the motion of someone sliding their chair away as they stood. "You brought us here! We're here because of your stupidity and behavior. Our time with you should have ended after that Ukrainian guy. If not for you, we'd be still free men. But no, you just had to keep pushing, keep seeing what you could get away with and you took me and Cyrus down because of it, you rapist piece of shit!"

The situation was blowing up and Murray didn't know what to do. It sounded like they were going to kill each other right there and then. Should he let it happen? No, he needed answers and that was going to happen now, before any guards heard the argument from the cafeteria and decided to take a look. Murray wouldn't have any chance with them if that happened. He swung the door wide and walked inside.

Rodihan spotted him first.

"Fuck me," he said and rolled his eyes. The others turned to see Murray coming.

"What the hell do you want?" Johns groaned. "This is a private conversation. You're not-"

"Shut up," Murray said forcefully. "You guys can finish your little circle jerk after I am done with you."

Cyrus walked up to Murray calmly and put his hand out. Murray ignored it.

"Murray, if you want to talk I'm willing. Now just isn't a great time."

"I should kick your ass right here and now for trying that with me. You're in here talking about killing my best friend because of some job you all are part of. Well, my job is to get some justice for him and I say that starts with the closest one of you assholes."

"I'm not going to fight you," Cyrus declared. "I have no beef with you."

"Me either," Matt confirmed and walked up to his partner. "We just want to talk to you."

"Bullshit," Murray barked. "I know you are working with Graves. I know he brought you in here because he thinks you can get to me. He thinks he'll just bait me into letting my guard down so you fuckers can finish the job he couldn't."

"I think you have some bad information," Cyrus explained. "We don't work for anybody."

"I've never even heard of someone named Graves," Matt echoed.

"I have."

Johns leaned against the table with his arms crossed. The makings of a knowing smile began to form on his face.

"I'll be glad to admit it, dipshit."

"Nate," Rodihan warned but Johns swatted his caution away. He walked away from the table and straight to Murray.

"Graves helps me and Louis out. He's like a client of ours and we're couple of freelancers."

He was now face to face with Murray and leering at the boxer audaciously. Murray held his ground despite the proximity and apparent threat.

"One night he called us about a guy that was standing in his way. Some clown told him no and this fella needed to be taught a lesson. So me and Louis here killed his manager. Put his brains on the concrete."

Murray felt the anger rising within him and he started to shake. His fists clenched. He needed to hit this guy. He was going to hit this guy until he stopped breathing.

He was too slow. Matt Crockett had already beat him to it. The former cop had tackled Johns to the ground and was hitting him.

"You did this! You started all of this! And you did it for money?"

Before Murray could react, Rodihan had pulled him off his partner and slammed Matt's head into the table. Matt fell to the ground, unconscious. Greem ran at Rodihan, but failed to avoid Johns grabbing his leg. Cyrus went to the ground and Rodihan kicked him in the face. Blood shot out of Greem's mouth and then he also passed out from the blow. Johns rose and turned towards Murray with his partner.

Murray had watched all this go down in surprise. When he walked in here, he thought they were going to tear each other apart yet he had guessed they would all turn on him first. He wasn't expecting Greem and Crockett to attack their colleagues before then. He had to admit though, it had been fun to watch.

Now he needed to focus. Johns and Rodihan had done him a favor. Now there were only two instead of four and Murray liked those odds. When he thought he was going to have to fight them all, he was confident he could do it, but it would be tough and he'd take a lot of punishment. Now he wasn't just confident, he was eager. This was going to be a pleasure.

He set his stance low, lined up towards Rodihan with his body facing Johns. His left hand stretched forward, his right braced in defense against his chest. One slow and long breath came out.

"Try me," he calmly taunted his opponents.

Rodihan came at him first. He struck out with the punch aimed at Murray's face. Murray caught the blow, twisted Rodihan's arm around his back and forced him to the ground. He finished it with a strike to the base of Rodihan's skull. The former officer was out cold before his head hit the ground.

"You ready?" Murray asked Johns facing him for the attack.

Light flooded into the cafeteria with the opening of its doors. *Shit, too late,* he thought expecting to see guards rush in. Johns backed away, and Murray turned to see Irvine Graves alongside Mitchell.

"Stand down!" Graves shouted. Johns obeyed. "These men are under my protection, Bench."

"Fuck your protection. It's good you're here, shitwad. Now I can whip your ass too!"

Mitchell lunged and caught Murray before he could strike Graves.

"Not now," he whispered. Murray fought against him with Graves just out of reach.

"Let me go, Dragoon!"

Mitchell's grip didn't release. "No, now is not the time."

"Fine," Murray said and relaxed. Mitchell softened his grip but didn't release it. Graves just smiled.

"It's good to see you again old friend. It's been a while. It took me too long to find my way back to you. Back to Santa Mira."

"Not long enough," Murray spat. Behind him Cyrus and Matt were waking up. "Your goons aren't going to do any better than you did."

"We'll see," Graves sneered. "Now if you'll excuse me, these men need medical attention."

"Come on Bench," Mitchell ordered. "Time to go."

Murray grudgingly walked out of the cafeteria having failed once again. He hadn't found any justice for Anatoly. He hadn't received the answers he wanted. Now Graves was back, and Murray found himself with more enemies than ever before inside Santa Mira.

CHAPTER 26

Rodihan awoke that night on the bottom bunk in his cell when he heard movement. He opened his eyes but could see nothing but the blackness of the shutdown cell block. The sound came again.

He sat up fast and called out quietly, "Nate? Nate, you ok buddy?"

The response came, not in the form of words from above, but from the flickering of a lit cigarette lighter in the corner. The lighter closed and the ember of a cigarette blazed, showing the face of the smoker. Louis had never seen him before. He was an inmate. In the low light, Louis could barely see the collar of the light blue jumpsuit worn by prisoners classified as "minimum risk". He was middle-aged and Caucasian. His face had no distinguishing scars or tattoos, which meant he hadn't been a gang member on the outside. In the dark, the only thing that Louis could focus on were his eyes, or in this case, his eye. Gazing at him was just one. The other was just a white ball of glass, with no detailing to create a perception of a real

167

eyeball. Without any point of reference, Louis couldn't tell if the glass eye moved or not. Prosthetic or authentic, both eyes of the man showed intelligence and determination that held back a layer of pure, unadulterated rage and hatred. The light from the cigarette faded as the man removed it from his mouth and the eyes disappeared, an all too welcome change for Louis. He'd only had a brief glimpse at his face, which the once fearless Rodihan found to be terrifying.

His eyes adjusted to the dark around him. He noticed that there were three other men in the cell with him. One stood behind the smoking man and two were on either side of Louis. All three wore the dark crimson jumper specifically given to inmates designated as condemned; these men were on death-row. How could they move freely through the block at this time of night? Why would they be involved with someone who wasn't condemned like them? Worse, why were they here and what did they plan to do with him and his partner?

"Nate?" he asked.

"Shh shhh shh," whispered a voice from the corner. Another puff of the cigarette brought those terrifying eyes back and Rodihan shuddered. "You needn't worry about your cell mate. He's not here. I need you to be quiet. You promise to be quiet?"

Louis saw the glint of something metal next to his face. He knew it had to be a knife of some sort.

"Yes," he whispered in reply. "Please don't hurt me."

"Shh, shhh, shhh. Do you know who I am?"

"No."

"I'm Irvine Graves. We've not met, although I saw you earlier today. You were...sleeping. It's good to finally put a face to the name of the man who has worked for me for so long. It's a shame your partner never thought you worthy of meeting me."

Graves took another drag of the cigarette. Louis turned away to avoid his gaze.

"These men around you, they are sentenced to die. But die they will not. Not without my permission. As long as I'm alive and they do what I ask, they stay alive. And a man's basic will to survive will make him do some very nasty things."

"What do you want with me?" Louis pleaded.

"An apology."

"For what? I've never done anything to you. Johns set up all the jobs and I just went with him. We did everything you asked of us."

"I know what you've done, Louis. I know I once sent you on an easy job. Just a simple hit on a boxing manager. Quick, clean and simple. No witnesses. Do you remember that?"

"Anatoly Brose. We did that. He's dead."

"Dead? Yes. Yet not how I instructed. He had a friend with him. A friend who kicked your ass earlier today. A witness and a man of great importance to me."

"Bench. So what? We left him alive for you."

"YOU ARRESTED HIM!" Graves raged risking the shout to demonstrate his anger, then took a drag. His tone returned to the previous hushed level. "I needed him a free man. If he was not here, he'd either be working for me or he'd be buried in the desert and I could wipe my hands clean of the task. Instead, I've had to put myself in prison just to chase him around. If I didn't have a judge in my pocket, my whole plan would have been ruined because of your incompetence."

"You've got all these guys," Louis stated, trying his best to gain an advantage. "Why don't you just take them and kill Bench tonight?"

"The warden put Bench away in a place I can't get to. Your little altercation earlier didn't go unpunished. Fighting is against the rules, see? You're lucky you got knocked out before Mitchell saw you, or you'd be locked up too."

The villain paused briefly. "Actually I guess that makes you unlucky."

"What about Johns?" Rodihan was beginning to panic. "He was there that night Brose died too. Did you kill him?"

"No, I still have use for Officer Nate Johns. You, though…"

Louis searched the room in the little amount of light his eyes had adjusted to. He tried to stand, but the men on his sides pushed him back down. There had to be something he could use to protect himself. Maybe he could try to call for help but the flash of light from the knife now came from right next to his eye.

"I don't know what you want me to say. You want Bench dead? I'll do it myself. Please," Louis was frantic.

Graves laughed. "Yeah I saw how things went for you even when you had help against him. You are no match for Murray Bench."

"Okay, okay. I'm sorry. Please, I'm sorry." Louis begged. "It was Nate who did it, not me. I tried to stop him but he wouldn't listen. He was the one that killed Brose in front of Bench."

"Shh, shh. You were the one that proved to be a poor asset, Louis. Maybe we should help you understand. Just a little."

A hand clasped over his mouth firmly and then he felt another grasp his hand. The pain of his ring and pinky finger breaking shot up through his arm and down his spine. He screamed in agony, but the hand held his mouth shut tight, making his cries no louder than the snoring of the sleeping inmates outside.

When the sound he made died to only a whimper, the hand let off his mouth. He opened his eyes and saw that Graves was kneeling in front of him.

"Shhh, shhh, shhhh. I need to hear you apologize, Louis. I need to hear you say, 'I'm sorry for failing you'. Tell me you're sorry. We can do this all night if you want, Louis."

"What are you going to do with me if I say it?" Louis was crying now.

"I'm going to kill you either way. I'm going to kill you. You don't get to leave here. You don't get to get out of this. You fucked me over. But you see, I'm a very forgiving man. You tell me you're sorry for what you've done and I won't go out and have your family killed. I know you don't care for ol' mom and dad but I know you care about your little brother. Jimmy, right? I guess he goes by James, now that he's 18. Just about to start school at USC, isn't he? Go Trojans, right?"

"Yes. He's a good boy. He's better than me. Please don't hurt him."

Graves reached around and grabbed the back of Rodihan's head and pulled him to his own. "I promise, I won't hurt him, Louis. I'll make sure no one else hurts him either. He'll grow up and be just fine. I'll see that he finds a new family in mine. We'll protect him. All you gotta do is say that you're sorry for what you did."

Rodihan swallowed his tears and nodded. "I'm sorry for failing you." Those were the last words he ever spoke.

———

The body of Louis Rodihan was found in the cell the next morning. Cyrus Greem awoke to the sound of shouts from other prisoners.

"He's dead!"

"Fucking disgusting!"

"Motherfucker got what was coming!"

Greem looked at the cell next to him and fell backwards into his bed in shock. The sight made him recoil in terror. His still sleeping bunkmate above him stirred but remained snoring in his slumber.

"Matt," Cyrus called. "Matt! Wake up!"

"What the fuck you want, Cy?" Crockett sleepily asked.

"Look!"

Crockett looked at the cell next to them. Guards had just reached the door and were unlocking it. Inside, the corpse hung from the bunk with bedsheets tied to the wrists. Rodihan was nude and horribly mutilated. He had been flayed open from his chest to his abdomen. His entrails were pulled out of the wound and stretched down to the ground. His genitals had been cut off and stuffed into his mouth. His nose, ears, scalp and most of his face were gone. His eyes remained; he would have witnessed his own torture.

No one in the cell block had heard a thing, or at least weren't willing to say if they had. A toxicology report of the victim revealed that he had been given a dosage of pancuronium bromide. Pancuronium is a paralytic, that when administered renders the subject completely paralyzed except for involuntary functions, like respiration and blood circulation. The former officer would have been conscious and aware of what was happening to him but completely unable to do anything about it. It didn't take long for investigators to know where the agent came from--pancuronium was one of three compounds used in the prison's lethal injection process.

No one except for the men within the cell that night would ever fully know what had happened and by whom. The case was quietly swept under the rug by Corenswet and the prison investigation team. No one mourned the death of a former LAPD officer who'd put a big black stain on the reputation of the already embattled police system, including his estranged family. The media found nothing but dead ends in reporting on the fate of Rodihan, and within a week had moved on to more sensational stories. The murder went unsolved.

When the news came to Murray about the death, it was Mouse who delivered the details. He found Murray in the FF, freed from his night in solitary, working diligently on moving new inventory into the warehouse. The small man asked Murray if he could take a break.

"Sure thing," Murray answered and set down the large bundle of rug materials he had over his shoulder. "What's up?"

"Not here. Can we go outside?" Mouse asked.

Murray turned and yelled to another worker, "I'm going outside for a minute. Can you see that this stuff is still here when I get back?"

The worker nodded, giving leave to Murray and Mouse to continue their discussion elsewhere. The pair exited through the loading dock of the warehouse and Mouse led him around the side of the building into an alley that ran between it and the Furniture Factory. Mouse checked around both sides of the alley and behind the dumpster for any listening ears.

"What's with all the secrecy?" Murray asked. "We're in a prison. There's no need for being surreptitious."

"What? Where'd you learn that word?" Mouse asked, but continued on before Murray could answer. "Listen, Louis Rodihan is dead. They found him this morning in his cell. He'd been tortured and mutilated."

"Jesus Christ"

"It gets worse. Corenswet had assigned Johns to the same cell but he was not in it last night. I looked at the residence logs this morning and his entry was blank. He wasn't assigned to a cell at all."

"So someone screwed up?"

"No, the logs had been changed. Someone had deleted the location for him but had forgot to delete the record of their login from the system. It was Corenswet himself that had done it."

"Holy shit. He had Rodihan murdered?"

"I don't know. I don't think so. It would stand to reason, though that the other three aren't the safest people in Santa Mira."

"You mean Johns, Greem and Crockett?" Murray asked and turned away. "You think the same person is going to have them killed."

"Absolutely. This was a vengeance killing. You only torture someone for two reasons: to get information from them or because you're a sick bastard who enjoys hurting people."

"Why didn't they just kill them at the same time?"

"I'm guessing cutting a man open and playing with his guts without anyone noticing takes some time. Probably didn't have enough to do the others. I think you need to help them before they come to finish the job."

"What? What are you talking about? Why would I help them? They're the reason I'm in here!"

"They don't deserve to die like that, Murray. From what I understand, Johns and Rodihan were the scumbags. Greem and Crockett were put in a bad situation and didn't do anything about it. Did they do the wrong thing? Absolutely. Do they deserve to be in here? Absolutely. On the other hand do they deserve to be cut up and have their own dicks stuffed into their faces while they're forced to watch it all? Hell no. No one deserves that. That's not justice, that's...I don't know what that is. Evil, I guess."

"What did you just say?" Murray turned back and walked to his friend. Mouse had triggered something buried deep in Murray's memory.

"I said it's not justice. It's evil."

Murray leaned against the wall of the warehouse and slumped down. He put his hands on his knees and looked withdrawn. Mouse walked over to him and sat down on the ground beside him.

"What is it?"

"You just reminded me of something my dad once said. *Revenge isn't justice. It's just hatred.* I've been hating these guys and wanting revenge for Anatoly this whole time. That's not what my father would have wanted. I think he'd be disappointed in what I did in the cafeteria. Letting my anger take over like that."

Mouse saw Murray struggling and let him think for a little bit. He sat down next to his younger friend who was silent in thought.

What the hell would have happened if I'd gone through with hurting or even killing one of the Four? I'd be in here for life. That's not what Liu was trying to tell me. He wouldn't ever suggest an action that would lead to that. I misunderstood his advice, clearly. And why was I looking for it anyways? Once again, I should have just listened to my own father. He wouldn't have wanted me on a path of vengeance. He'd want me to be a protector. A protector of life and justice. No more revenge, Murray. Anatoly wouldn't want me to avenge him. He'd want me to save them.

"What do you want to do?" Mouse asked. "Go to the warden?"

Murray furrowed his brow. "No. The warden may be compromised. Get a message to Johns. Make sure it's for his eyes only. Tell him we need to talk."

———

Johns turned off the TV in his new cell when he saw Graves standing at the doorway. His employer smiled and knocked casually on the door. Johns sat up.

"Come in."

"Relax," Graves gestured his hand to sit back down. "As you were, soldier. I just came by to see how you were enjoying your new home. Little better than sharing a cell in the main block, right?"

"Oh, yes it is Mr. Graves," Johns agreed. "Thank you very much for letting me have it."

"That's what being a valuable member of society is all about, Nathan. I'm glad you like it. As long as you do right by me, I'll do right by you. Unfortunately, I had to dispose of someone you knew who did not do right by me last night. I'm assuming you heard?"

Johns's expression dulled. He broke eye contact with Graves and looked down at the floor in a mixture of shame and sadness. He hadn't loved Rodihan but he was the closest thing to family he had. Still, his boss knew what he was doing. If he said something had to be done, well then, he would support it.

"I did. I'm glad you did. We don't have any room for traitors. We should weed all of them out. Kill them all, you know."

"I appreciate your eagerness to please, but Rodihan was the only one that needed dealt with," Graves said and then his expression shifted to suspicion. "Unless you have something to tell me about, Nathan."

"Oh no, Mr. Graves. I'm your man."

"Good. I'd like to have you stay that way. I've got a position open for a good man in Santa Mira. Are you interested in increasing your role in our little game?"

"Yes sir. Whatever you need. I'm ready."

"Good. I like the spirit and energy. This won't be an easy job. If you fail, well, I think you know what will happen."

Johns shook his head. "I won't fail."

"Don't be so sure," Graves replied. He'd underestimated his adversary time and again. Bench was more of a match then he'd thought when he put himself in prison. This war was taking longer, much longer than he'd originally planned. It was time to use all the tools he had at his disposal. He eyed Johns, determining if he could actually succeed in the task.

"Your sole job is to kill Murray Bench."

CHAPTER 27

With the wind blowing in from the bay, Murray leaned against the railing behind the library. Dust was flying into his face from the breeze, but it felt good on his skin against the hot sun of the Californian summer. Liu squatted down next to him. They'd already been waiting for twenty minutes. It was beginning to appear that Johns wasn't going to show.

"This was a bad idea," Liu finally spoke up. "Johns isn't going to want to meet with us. Why would he? He has no reason to trust you."

"I know," Murray answered. He picked up a rock and threw it at some garbage cans across the way. "What am I supposed to do though? Just let him be murdered?"

"Don't you think he's already suspicious of that? His partner was butchered in the same cell they shared."

"I would hope so. Graves is tricky though. He's got a way of guiding people into thinking he's on their side. Johns may be an asshole, but he's not smart enough to pick up on Graves's manipulation."

"Didn't you just yesterday want to kick this guy's ass?"

"Yup," Murray confirmed. He tossed another rock. This one thrown with more velocity. It pinged off the garbage can, denting the side. "Still kinda do. I'd rather kick Graves's ass. Maybe I'll get to do both. Either way, I'm not going to let Graves murder someone else. Anyone else."

"Gonna save the town by dancing huh?"

"What?"

"*Footloose*? Bonnie Tyler? 'I need a hero!'" Liu sang out.

"Just when you think you know someone," Murray muttered. "Hey, knock it off. He's coming."

Nate Johns turned the corner and walked towards Murray. His face was void, but Murray smiled in greeting. It was best to start this out as cordially as he could. That didn't last long. Just paces behind him, Irvine Graves followed. At the sight of him, Liu stood up and Murray tensed.

"Shit," was all Murray could muster. The plan had backfired.

"Hello boys!" Graves announced. "Glad we could all get together like this. It's great that you invited a friend, Bench. You must be The Mannequin."

"My name is Jan Liu," he replied. His tone was gracious, but Murray could see that the name made him uncomfortable.

"Yes, yes. The famed assassin who murdered his own family," Graves mocked. Johns just grinned behind him. "It's good to finally put a face to the name."

Murray had to change the subject quickly or risk Graves distracting Liu emotionally. He spoke out to Johns, hoping it wasn't too late.

"This guy is trying to kill you, Johns. He's not your friend."

Graves laughed and patted Johns on the back. It made Johns smile even more.

"I'm not going to kill him," Graves chuckled. "No, not at all. That wouldn't be very good planning on my part since he and I are here to kill you."

The joking was over. Murray could see it in their eyes that they meant business. He went into his defensive stance, and Liu joined him.

"Don't do this, Johns."

"I let you live once before, Bench," Johns countered. "Not now."

Murray had been wrong. It was too late. The fight was on. Johns rushed at Murray with full force, quicker than he expected. Murray's attempt to block and redirect failed. Instead, Johns caught Murray in the chest and drove him to the ground. The impact was enough to send both men in a tumble backwards. When the momentum finally stopped, Murray pushed Johns off and got to his feet. Just in time. Another attack from the trained officer was coming. Murray caught this attack, spinning Johns in air, then driving him downward. Johns wasn't going down that easily, though. He reacted by putting his feet underneath him, leaving Murray unable to finish the move.

Where did this guy learn to fight like this? Murray asked himself, caught off-guard by Johns's technique. It was clear the former cop had been trained in close-quarter-combat.

Johns spun around in the dirt so he could face Murray and then twisted Bench's grip with his own in a reversal. The pair danced, trying to gain leverage on each other, their feet kicking up dust. The cloud continued to thicken after Murray broke from the grasp by sweeping John's legs out with a sweeping kick. Again they went to the ground and again the dust flew up.

Murray had made a serious mistake. By letting Johns twist as they fell, he pulled Murray's right awkwardly, popping it out of joint. It wasn't a critical injury to the arm, but it meant he couldn't put his full punch into Johns. He was going to have to rely on other means of ending this battle.

When they picked themselves up they could barely see each other. There was no sign of Liu or Graves anywhere. Murray had lost track of them from the moment Johns attacked. Behind Johns, Murray could just spot a stairwell leading up to the second story of the library building, so he knew that they were at least in the same alleyway the fight had started in. Liu couldn't be too far away. He couldn't be counted on to help Murray deal with Johns though. There would be no way for him to find them. Murray was alone in this.

They circled each other, looking for opportunities in the other's defenses. Johns squatted down, compacting his body to eliminate openings. Murray stayed upright, hoping to use his reach on the shorter opponent. When Murray's back was turned to the railing, Johns sprung forward. *Perfect.* Murray grabbed the railing and swung his momentum, hurling his leg into Johns' neck. The cop went down again, dazed. Murray sprung on to him. Left, right, left, right. He struck at him over and over again. Blood shot out of Johns's mouth with each punch, and his face was quickly becoming a lump of dough. When teeth started to follow the blood, Murray stopped. Johns was done. He was conscious, barely. There would be no more fight in him today.

Murray's victory was short-lived. A cry from above him traveled through the wind. It was a cry for help.

Jan!

Leaving Johns in a bleeding mess, Murray latched onto the railing and leaped up to the second story of the library. Above the dust cloud, he could see the rest of the prison, yet there was no sight of his mentor.

"Liu!" he called out.

"Up here."

Next to him, Murray spotted a ladder leading up to the roof of the building. He climbed it with haste. On the roof he could see a turret of some kind with a hose attached to it leading to a water tank. Stacked around it were crates and boxes, yet aside from that, there was no sign of any life.

"I can't see you!" he yelled.

"Over here."

Murray turned behind him and spotted a metal overhang leading away from the roof. Carefully, he climbed out onto it. The metal shook with his weight but he balanced himself and cautiously moved forward. At the end of the overhang, he spotted fingers clutching against gravity. Diving down, Murray slid forward and caught the wrist of Master Liu.

"I got you," he said and began hauling the light-weight man up. Once he was safe, they crawled back to the rooftop of the library and collapsed in exhaustion.

"What the hell happened?" Murray asked once he'd caught his breath.

"Oh, you know. The usual," Liu responded casually. "Little this, little that."

"Seriously," Murray grunted. "Where's Graves?"

It was then that Murray noticed the blood along Liu's arm.

"Look at your arm! Are you alright?"

"Fine," Liu responded, then stood and walked over to the water turret. He turned a knob and let water flow over the wound in his hand. Cleaned, he tore the sleeve off his shirt and wrapped it around the laceration.

"I cut my hand on the roof when I slid. Graves and I fought on the ground next to you someplace until the dust got too awful. I couldn't see a damn thing so I tried to get to a better vantage point. Graves chased me up here. We fought on the roof. He's no slouch, Murray. He can fight. It took all I had against him. He knocked me off the side and we both slid down the roof. I don't think he cared that he was putting himself over the edge either. The man is suicidal. I grabbed on and that's where you found me."

"Where did Graves go?" Murray asked.

"No idea. I thought he would be on the ground in a pile of dead, but when you pulled me up I looked for him. He wasn't there."

CHAPTER 28

"So where is Graves now?" Mouse asked.

No response could come from Murray or Liu. The three of them sat within Liu's work room in the FF. The tables had been moved aside opening a meeting area. Murray had found two wingback chairs that were deemed "beyond repair" by the furniture team. He and Mouse found them to work well enough to use for this makeshift conference. Liu preferred to stand.

"The guy has an uncanny knack of making himself vanish before we can do anything about it," Murray replied after giving some thought to Graves's actions over the past year. "The reverse holds true. If we don't know where he is, he doesn't know where we are."

"You can't assume that," Mouse corrected.

"No, no I can't. Dammit!" Murray shouted and slammed his fist in frustration into the arm of the chair. The old wood creaked in reply. "We had him. We could have ended it. If I hadn't dinked around with Johns…"

"Johns isn't exactly a novice in the violence department," Liu chimed in. "I saw how he fought. This wasn't the first time he was ready to kill his opponent. It's a testament to your training that you handled him in the manner that you did. I'm proud of you."

Murray smiled briefly in recognition of his mentor's approval. "At least we know where Johns is. The infirmary should have him for a while. That's one less problem to deal with for now."

Mouse shook his head.

"I wish I could say that I felt good about our odds, but I don't. More of Graves's men are either returning to Santa Mira or coming in fresh. I just got word that his five top guys arrived this morning."

"Top guys? You mean he has better guys?" Murray asked.

"Well, you'll remember Sam Beckton, of course."

Murray nodded.

"He's with them. The other four aren't new to you either. They were here before. You might have seen them with Graves when you fought him in the ring."

"I didn't exactly pay attention to anyone else but that one-eyed bastard, to be honest."

"Probably a good call," Liu joked.

"Well, they noticed you. Here's what I could find out about them." Mouse went on. "Frank Pergent used to be a loan shark. He had to quit that when he sent some leg-breakers to collect on the wrong customer. That guy? Irvine Graves. Pergent's men never reported back and to this day are missing. My best guess is they are tied to some concrete at the bottom of San Pedro Bay. Since then Pergent has been working as Graves's money launderer. Don't let that fool you, though. He's a grade-A monster. He's in for first-degree murder of a casino manager. Beat the guy to death. Coroner had to use dental records to identify the body. That's how they caught Pergent. He broke his hands hitting the guy so many times that he had to go to the hospital to get them fixed. Two DNA swabs later and the cops had him.

"Steven Kelsal is Graves's driver. You can spot him by his bald head and long beard. He goes with him on every job. Delivery of drugs, weapons, human slaves, you name it, Kelsal has sat in on all of them. Rumor has it that a deal went wrong with the Russians once and Graves had to get away. Kelsal not only kept Graves safe in the back of the car but killed seven guys using the vehicle as a weapon. Another two he killed hand-to-hand inside of the car, while he was driving it. So he's killing men while killing men. Tough.

"Tony Clark is a straight-up hitman. Used to be a contractor. Now he just works for Graves."

"I know of Clark," Liu interrupted. "His name came to me when I moved to LA from Tokyo. Lots of confirmed target eliminations. Messy. He always would get his target but he cared nothing about killing others to do it. Yakuza refused to work with him."

"Yeah, not a 'one-shot, one-kill' kinda assassin," Mouse nodded and continued. "Remember that bombing at the Century City mall three years ago? Blew up an entire department store. Twenty-eight dead? That's Clark. Just to get one guy."

"Last but not least is Ryan Davison. This guy is the pick of the litter. I have no idea what he does for Graves, but you want to name a violent crime, well he'll have done it. Clever too. He's broken out of each prison that's ever tried to keep him. Last time he got out, he used the warden as a hostage with a pipe-gun he built from random crap around the prison. The fun thing is he didn't ever use it. He walked the warden right out the front gate and then over to the edge of the cliff the prison was built on. Pushed him right off. Sixty foot drop, splat. Then he turned to the guards and surrendered himself. The whole thing was just to let the warden know that he could leave whenever he wanted to before he killed him."

"Okay..." Murray responded sheepishly. "Well, then I'd say we're in a pretty deep mess here. Graves will want to hit us now, while we're weak. My shoulder is still screwed and Liu's hand is fucked. I want you guys to be careful. Keep sharp. Stay in places where guards will be. Don't trust anyone. Keep your distance from other inmates. We'll have stay vigilant until I can come up with a way to end Graves."

"Maybe it's time we enlisted some help?" Mouse offered.

Murray shook his head.

"There is no one else."

Liu stood up straight and walked over to Murray. He put his hand on his shoulder to comfort his pupil.

"You know there is. Graves will be coming after them as well. Either to kill them or add them to his force."

Murray shrugged his hand off and stood up. "No. I don't want their help. What I tried to do for Johns backfired in my face. I'm not going to make the same mistake with Greem and Crockett. I'll help them but we just can't trust them. We'll figure someone else out. I have to go; it's late and I'm hungry," he said and left the room.

Liu looked at Mouse and shrugged. "He'll come around. Give him time. He'll learn that he needs Greem and Crockett as much as they need him."

"I'm afraid that you and I do too," Mouse pointed out.

———

Murray didn't have much time before he was forced to make a choice on the remaining two members of The Brose Four. That evening at chow time, his decision was made for him. There wasn't even time for him to think about his actions, he only had time to react.

Just nine hours after the discovery of Rodihan's grisly death and four hours after the battle in the dust, another attempt on Murray's life happened. With Mouse, he stood in the food line. Cyrus Greem and Matt Crockett were also in line, only feet away from them. Greem saw him and smiled, and then time seemed to slow down for a few seconds. Murray noticed a prisoner in the line adjacent to Crockett who was eying them and moving from side to side nervously. He held something in his right hand underneath his tray. Mouse spotted him too.

"Davison," he said quietly to Murray, identifying Graves's man.

The line of men moved forward and Davison made his move. His tray dropped and Murray saw the shank, the sharpened end of a hair brush. The inmate lunged at Mouse, but by then Murray had already arched his arm back and swung his food tray at full velocity, striking the would-be executioner across the bridge of the nose. This halted his attack, but Murray didn't let up. He dove onto him and struck him across the open wound three times, rendering him unconscious.

When Murray got to his feet, he saw Mouse, Greem and Crockett were still near but the sudden violence and the thwarting of the assassination had caused the mess hall to erupt in violence. People were pushing and shoving each other as three others, presumably the rest of Graves's new army, tried to get at Mouse and Murray to finish the job. The guards around the edge were piled into by the crowd. They couldn't do anything to stop the attacks on Murray and Mouse. The riot was their priority. This was planned, organized. Eliminating the guards from the equation meant Murray and Mouse were on their own to stay alive.

Murray had his own hands full. After he reached his feet, he was met by another assailant who was running wildly at him. He quickly ducked and his attacker dove over his head. Trays were being thrown from every direction and Murray used his own to deflect their trajectory. Underneath the tangle of clashing inmates, Murray spotted Mouse, trying to stay out of the fray and failing. His arms were up over his head trying to block any incoming damage, but the poor old guy was getting pushed around and beaten. Murray pushed his way through the crowd, kicking the knee out from anyone who blocked his progression. He grabbed the old-timer and pulled him away from the fracas, guiding him underneath one of the dining tables.

"You just stay here and keep your head down," Murray said. Mouse nodded, but his expression of gratitude turned to fright as he looked behind Murray.

"Look out!"

Murray turned and saw the sharp edge of an improvised blade come at his face from a bald and bearded inmate. *Kelsal.* Murray was finished, there was no time to block the jab. His best option was to try and catch the blade or the attacker's arm somehow. He put his hand up to grab whatever he could, but the blow never came. Kelsal dropped to his knees, his face twisting in pain, and then a tray hit him against his temple. The inmate went to the ground in a lump. Murray watched his failed killer go down and then turned his eyes to the man standing above the comatose figure. Cyrus Greem stood, dinner tray in hand. Greem returned Murray's gaze and nodded his head in acknowledgment. Next to him, Matt Crockett reached down and helped Murray stand. In that moment, knowingly or not, Cyrus and Matt had become part of the team.

Guards dressed in riot gear stormed into the dining hall and broke up the remaining fights. Order was restored and those uninjured were escorted out of the dining hall and into the general assembly area outside. The injured went straight to the infirmary. The entire brawl and failed murder had only lasted a couple of minutes, but more transpired between Murray and the remaining Brose Four in that small window of time than any words could have done.

———

Murray walked around the edge of the administration building and headed towards the green gazebo that sat in the courtyard at the front of the prison. The courtyard looked like something outside of a business park. He could imagine people in suits and dresses sitting on the benches, drinking Starbucks and tapping obsessively on their smartphones.

Despite the serenity of the courtyard, it was left unused by the residents of Santa Mira. The emptiness of the courtyard could have been due to its proximity to the administration building. Whatever transpired in the courtyard, Corenswet would have a view of it if he so chose. Few inmates were willing to knowingly let the warden and his staff witness their activities.

Fear of the warden's watchful eye didn't stop Murray from entering the area for his meeting. Inside the gazebo, he could see that the other party was already waiting for him. As Murray stepped inside, Cyrus Greem stood up.

"Hey. Thanks for meeting me," he said.

"Yeah, well it took some convincing but I guess it's time we talked," Murray said as he sat down across from Cyrus. "I want to say thanks for what you did yesterday in the mess."

"Funny they call it a 'mess' because that's exactly what yesterday was."

"Where's Crockett?"

Cyrus looked up at the administration building behind him. "Matt's up with the warden, I guess. I have a feeling Corenswet is trying to find work for us that will keep us away from the more dangerous members of the community, or he's trying to come up with a way to exploit Matt and me somehow."

"I see you're familiar with how the warden does things, then."

"Yeah. He's got this attitude of 'I'm so much smarter and cleverer than you' but he's kind of predictable, you know."

"It could be that he's talking to him about Rodihan. I heard you guys saw what happened, or the aftermath anyway. Maybe he thinks Crockett's got some baggage about it."

Greem shrugged. "What happened to him was seriously fucked up, and Matt's struggled with PTSD, so maybe? He and I have had to deal with a lot of bad shit when we were on the force, but Matt served in Afghanistan before he joined up. He's told me some pretty awful stories."

"I didn't know that," Murray replied.

"Yeah, that little tidbit didn't really come out during the trial. Not too many people want to hear about a veteran with issues getting sentenced to prison."

Murray nodded in silence.

"Believe it or not, Matt's a good guy. I can't say that Louis got what he deserved but he and Johns were going to end up in a place like this at some point. It was inevitable."

"And what about you and your partner?" Murray's voice had lost the friendliness it'd started with. "It seems like whatever those two assholes were involved in, there you and Crockett were too."

"Yup," Greem confirmed, begrudgingly. "Yes, we were. I'm angry that I'm in here. I don't feel that it's fair or right or justified, but it doesn't surprise me at all. If there's such a thing as destiny, then I was destined to follow those sick bastards to their grave. Just so I could try to contain any of their madness."

"Look I don't need to hear you defend your actions. That's not why I'm here. I came here because I think what happened in the cafeteria isn't going to end. I'm asking for your help and to make sure the same thing that happened to Rodihan doesn't happen to you. Not because I like you or give a crap about you, but because I don't think it's right to let you get murdered and I don't want you and Matt to get turned like Johns did. I still want you to pay for your crimes."

"Are you talking about the crime we were sentenced for, or what happened to Anatoly?"

Murray sighed at the mention of his best friend's name.

"Look, you two did what you did, but you did it because of me. I don't blame you for what happened. Irvine Graves killed Anatoly."

Cyrus shook his head. "That's not true at all, Murray. Graves didn't kill Anatoly. Hatred killed Anatoly Brose."

Murray didn't understand. He looked at Cyrus in confusion. "What's that mean?" he asked.

"It's a bit of a story but I guess we have time."

Cyrus went on to tell Murray about Johns and Rodihan and the night Anatoly died. Nate Johns and Louis Rodihan had earned a reputation for their xenophobia and nationalism. While racism was a common factor in police forces across the nation, Johns and Rodihan had a different view on things. They didn't hate anyone living in America based on the color of their skin. They hated them for their national heritage, and no group of people were hated by them more than those that had once been under the sovereignty of the Soviet Union. Both of their fathers had fought in the Vietnam War, watching their friends die and committing horrible acts against humanity under the flag of freedom. When Johns's father came home and found out he hadn't been fighting a war against oppression but a metaphorical war against the Soviet threat, his hatred had focus. Every word of aggression he ever said fell right into the young ears of his son, who soaked it up like a dry sponge. When Johns reached adulthood, he joined the police force as his way of continuing to fight the Cold War he knew had never ended. When he was partnered with the easily-influenced Rodihan, it didn't take long for his rage to pollute the mind of his eager new ally.

No one they worked with wanted anything to do with them. They would often shout their hate speech at anyone within earshot. They blamed the entire era of terrorism squarely on the Russians and any country that had been part of the USSR. The pair were particularly awful to refugees from the former Soviet Union. They saw refugees as not only a burden to the American people, but scum who had come to the country to pollute it and find ways to reduce its defenses against the Red Army, who in their minds were going to attack at any moment. While their rhetoric was fierce and disgusting, they were not breaking any policies. The First Amendment applied to members of the police department as well the citizens of the United States, after all. The duo had a clean track record in their service, so no action was taken against them.

It was no small wonder that when Graves asked them to kill someone, they didn't think twice when they found out who the target was. They were all too happy to have an excuse to do harm to the Ukrainian refugee. Now they were getting paid for it.

"It was Nate and Louis who beat Brose," Cyrus explained to Murray, who sat listening and choking back tears. "It was Johns's nightstick that shattered his skull. Matt and I needed to secure you so that we could try and stop them. I was the one that knocked you out. After you went down, we ran over to stop Nate and Louis but it was already too late. We called an ambulance, but by the time it arrived Brose was already gone. I'm so sorry, Murray."

Murray couldn't hold back the tears anymore and sobbed into his hands.

Cyrus continued, "It wasn't our fault at all. It was unchecked hatred, fear and a sense of absolute power that killed Anatoly. Those fucking assholes were two time bombs that were going to get more and more people hurt and killed. All we could do was try and minimize the collateral damage. We did our best but it wasn't enough and now we're here."

Cyrus gave Murray a little bit to collect himself. Murray wiped his face and looked up. "Thank you," he said. "Thank you for telling me this."

"So you want our help against Johns and Graves?" Cyrus asked. "Well, you've fucking got it."

CHAPTER 29

That night Matt and Cyrus were paid a visit in their cells by Irvine Graves. It was before lights-out so the pair were awake playing cards with a deck gifted to them by Mouse for helping him in the cafeteria. When Graves showed up outside their open cell door, the pair nervously set the cards down and stood.

"Please, stay as you were," Graves motioned. "I'm here as a friend."

The cellmates didn't budge. He could be here to finish the job he'd started with Rodihan. Better to be cautious and rude than trusting and dead.

"Really," Graves added. "If I was here to harm you I wouldn't be alone, would I? I'd have some help, right? It'd be pretty foolish of me to think that I could do anything to you guys by myself. Two against one in a cramped space as this. Please, you would have me in a heartbeat."

Cyrus checked his partner's face for assurance, found it and the pair sat back down.

"May I?" Graves gestured to sit on the bunk next to them.

"Go ahead," Crockett said.

Graves sat down on the bottom bunk and put his hands together in front of his face. Unbeknownst to Cyrus and Matt, this was the exact look he had the night he met Murray. He was wearing his sales face.

"I'd like to help you two. I'm a man of power. Great influence. I can make things happen around here that even the warden would struggle to accomplish. Just with the wave of my hand. If I want something to happen, it happens."

Graves looked around the cell.

"Your accommodations here are less than stellar. Lumpy beds, no view, no privacy. A man needs privacy, don't you agree?"

Cyrus and Matt remained mute.

"There's a whole set of rooms here that are empty. Waiting to be filled by men that I find I can trust. Good men. The kind of men that know what needs to be done. I'd like to think you two are those types of people."

Cyrus gave a half-smile. "Listen, I-"

"Hear me out," Graves interrupted. "It's not just comfort I can offer. I know people on the outside. People of influence. Important people. Politicians, LAPD, the mayor even. Specific to you two though, I know certain judges that can help as well. Judges that can take some time off your incarceration. How about cutting your sentence in half?"

Matt raised an eyebrow and looked at Cyrus. He could see that this offer had caught his partner's attention.

"Not enough? Okay," Graves went on. "How about the fourth piece on Maslow's list?"

The partners looked blankly at Graves.

"Abraham Maslow? Psychologist? Hierarchy of Needs? Fine. I'm offering safety. Protection."

"Protection from what?" Matt asked.

"You do know where you are, right? You're a couple of cops sent to the pokie. You're surrounded by people that aren't big fans of you. Hell, I bet there's a whole cadre of villains that you specifically sent here. You think they don't want to watch you bleed out? Oh, but that's not where things start. See, when prisoners have you, they don't just shank you like you see on TV. First, they rape the fuck out of you. They stand in line to wait. Dozens of men, pent up with rage, one after the other. Tearing your insides apart. If you weren't going to die after they were done, you'd be so filled with syphilis you'd go crazy in a month and then die. Then comes the torture…"

"All right, we get it. You can stop," Cyrus grimaced.

"Yeah, please," Matt agreed. "What is it you want from us?"

Graves face lit up in surprise. "What do you think I want? I want you to kill Murray Bench."

"Oh no," Matt stopped him. "That's not us."

"But it IS you. He likes you. He is bringing you into his little clan of miscreants. He needs you. It's just him, some old man and a washed-up Jap. You get in close. Make him trust you. Then when he's not looking…well, I'll let you handle that part. I want it clean. Looks like an accident."

"And if we say no?" Cyrus ventured.

"The Rodihan treatment," Graves said poker-faced. He stood up and walked to the cell door.

"If you do not do as I ask, I will have Murray killed tomorrow night. It'll be messy, so I prefer you do your job. If you fail I'll have him killed anyway, but I'll also see you two dead. I suggest you get to work."

———

Mitchell walked Murray along the hallway of the top floor of the Administration Building. Predictably, the massive prison guard with the disfigured face remained reticent as he escorted the prisoner. Yet the hallway was far from silent. Even through the closed wooden doors at the end of the hallway, Corenswet's voice echoed in anger. Murray couldn't distinguish what he was so unhappy about or at whom his frustrations were aimed, but the message was clear enough. Someone had messed up and the warden was letting them have it.

Despite the activities inside their destination, the pair continued down the hall. By the time they reached the office, the yelling had ceased and all was quiet in the hallway. Mitchell sat Murray down on a bench outside of the double doors, but just as Murray took a seat the doors flew open and down the hallway walked two very dejected and humiliated men, wearing shirts with the words "Santa Mira Investigation Services" embroidered on the breast. The pair didn't look at Murray or speak, but walked as fast as they could away from the verbal assault they had just faced.

Mitchell disappeared inside the office for a second and then grabbed Murray and led him in. The warden stood over his desk with both hands on top, palms down. His head was slumped and he was taking deep breaths to calm his obvious anxiety. On the third one, he raised his head and smiled at Murray.

"I'm sorry about that. Sometimes the only way to reach someone intelligently is to punch through their own ineptitude," The warden gestured across the desk. "Please sit."

Murray nodded and sat down in one of the chairs across from the desk.

"I understand you wanted to see me about something?" the warden asked as he sat down in his leather desk chair.

"I do. Irvine Graves killed Louis Rodihan. He tried to kill Jan Liu. He enlisted Nate Johns to kill me. He organized a riot in the cafeteria that almost got me and Mouse killed. If it hadn't been for Cyrus Greem and Matt Crockett, he would have succeeded. Now, I'm told that Graves is threatening to kill them too. I want better protection for Matt Crockett and Cyrus Greem. Same for Mouse and Liu. I want guards on them at all times until you can find out how to get rid of Graves, and I want guards that aren't on someone else's payroll. Good, honest men that can't be bought off. If you don't have anyone like that then I think it would be best to move them to a low risk facility instead of Santa Mira where they won't be in danger of getting killed. Until that happens I think Mitchell and three of his best men should stay on Mouse, Liu, Greem and Crockett."

The warden listened patiently, focusing on Murray's words with his hands together. When Murray finished, Corenswet didn't move or speak immediately. He sat in the same position, looking at Murray as if he was still talking. It made Murray very nervous and he wondered if the warden was waiting for him to continue. Murray was about to ask him if he had heard him when the Corenswet finally spoke.

"I heard about the scuffle in the cafeteria," he said calmly as he leaned back in his chair. "You're quite the fighter, I hear. You used a cafeteria tray as a shield and weapon? Not just some boxer anymore, are you?"

"I did what I had to do to protect lives. That's why they need more. I can't be watching them every second of the day."

"That's right, you can't. Nor will you worry about them at all. I can assure you that they are in no danger. My men will make sure they are safe, the same as they do for all of the residents here."

"But the fight in the cafeteria-"

"Was nothing more than a misunderstanding. And a situation that is not your concern, Murray. Your fight is in the ring, not in the cafeteria. You need to stay focused on your matches and your job. I'm the warden. I'll worry about the safety of my inmates."

"But Graves-"

"-Is someone you are accusing without any shred of evidence. I have no reason to believe anything you just said about him. Irvine Graves is a pain in the ass. He cheats at boxing, sure, but he's not who you say he is. He's connected. Hell, he's a federal witness. He's only in here as part of a proffer with the FBI. The fucking FBI. Your accusations could be considered as threatening a federal witness, which I hope you know will make your stay at Santa Mira quite indefinite. I'd be all for that, so go ahead and continue digging yourself into a hole you can't climb out of."

The warden stood up and nodded to Mitchell. The burly guard lifted Murray to his feet as Murray simply gazed at the warden in astonishment. How could he just brush this off?

"I thank you for being concerned with the well-being of those that reside here but I can fully assure you that we are doing what needs to be done to keep everyone safe and sound. Lastly —," he broke off and got right in Murray's face "the next time you come in here and tell me how to run my prison will be the last time you open your mouth. I will not tolerate insubordination from those that are benefiting from my decisions. Consider this a warning. Now fuck off."

Murray was still dumbstruck about how poorly his meeting went as Mitchell pulled him through the doors of the warden's office and down the hall to the elevator. Mitchell pushed him inside and hit the button for the first floor. Murray watched the doors close, while at the opposite end of the hall the warden walked around his desk and closed his office door.

——

Mouse and Liu were already waiting for Murray when he walked into the training area of the FF. Mouse was sitting in one of the wing-backs by the entrance and Liu leaned against a wall in the corner. Both were silent when Murray walked in, but Liu stood straight when he saw the two men who followed him.

"So it's five of us now?" he asked. "You changed your mind about the extra support? Good."

"We've talked. I think we understand each other now," Murray replied, looking to Cyrus for confirmation. Greem and Crockett nodded their approval in return.

"We're here because we want to help," Cyrus said.

"We also need you," Matt added, humbly.

"That's why I've set up this little get together," Murray confirmed.

"Good of you to join us," Liu stepped in front of Matt and Cyrus and extended his hand. "My name is Jan Liu. It is a great honor to finally meet you both."

Cyrus and Matt shook the waiting hand.

"It's mutual," Matt replied.

Mouse smiled in greeting at them then looked at Murray. "Can I talk to you for just a minute?"

"Sure thing," Murray replied. "Give us just a second, guys."

Greem nodded and took a seat near one of the stitching machines. Crockett followed suit and sat across from him.

"Murray, are you sure this is what you want to do? We all have to be on the same team here. There can't be any bad blood between you and them." Mouse advised.

Murray shook his head and spoke softly to his friend.

"I appreciate your concern but I'm fine. We're all on the same side now. Okay?"

"Okay," Mouse said. "All I needed to hear." He returned to his chair.

Murray walked over to the middle of the group but didn't take a seat. Instead, he addressed the four inmates while standing.

"We all know that Louis Rodihan was murdered two nights ago in his cell. He died because he became an enemy of Irvine Graves and now we are all are in danger of the same fate. Matt and Cyrus have told me that Graves plans to have me killed tonight. He came by to warn them last night. Guess he didn't want them standing in the way. Guess he misjudged." He nodded in thanks to Matt and Cyrus.

"You said you were going to speak to the warden. Can't he do something?" Matt Crockett asked.

"The warden is either unwilling or unable to help. We're on our own," Murray answered.

"How are we supposed to prevent this? Even with their help?" Mouse interjected. "There's just five of us against Graves and his men."

"It's not just Graves and his men," Liu finally spoke up. "It's the whole prison. I've heard that Graves is reaching out to all the gang leaders. He's forming an army as we speak. It'll be easy for him to get their aid. What gang wouldn't want to take part in the murder of a famous boxer who has been beating the piss out of them one by one since he arrived, two former LAPD, and two old guys that won't pose any problems to them? No offense, John."

"None taken."

Murray sighed. "Great. We're outnumbered, outflanked, and frankly out of options. However, Graves only wants me dead. I'm the target. The rest of you are just in the way. As long as Greem and Crockett don't interfere or get caught up in this, then Graves will leave them be."

Matt and Cyrus shifted in their chairs. They said nothing about Graves's threat on their lives.

"That leaves, Mouse. I don't think he was part of the hit in the cafeteria. I think he was just in the way. Proximity to me. So the same goes for him. John, you stay clear and Graves will ignore you if this goes south for me."

"Not a chance. I'm with you all the way," Mouse affirmed. "What about Liu?"

"I'm in the same boat as Murray on this now," Liu said. "Graves and I have fought. He knows I'm involved with Murray and he knows that I can handle myself. He'll see me as a threat. He'll also think of me as weakened by my hand. He'll want to take me out now."

"Correct," Murray confirmed. "Jan and I are the ones that Graves will be coming for. Tonight."

"Okay, what about tonight?" Crockett asked. "You can't just go back to your cells and sit and wait for the Graves to come visit you."

"Matt's right, Murray," Cyrus added. "He's got the guards in his pocket. You can't fight them all off. All he has to do is inject you with that panco stuff. It'd be all over before it began."

"No, I agree. We can't go back to our cells tonight," Murray said as he rubbed his chin in thought. "We've only got one option."

"Where are you thinking?" Mouse asked. Liu answered before Murray could.

"Solitary confinement."

"That's right," Murray replied. "It's the only place where we can be locked up that Graves can't get us. The cells are sealed with electronic key-codes. He'd have to have the warden's access to open the door locks."

"How do you know he doesn't?" Mouse asked. "Remember it was the warden's log on the guard roster that he forged. He could have the key-codes as well."

"We have to take that risk," Murray explained. "It's the only option."

"You're wrong. There's another place," Crockett volunteered. "You could stay in the infirmary."

"The infirmary?" Liu asked. "That building is no more secure than our cells. Graves could just waltz right in there."

"No, he can't," Mouse stated. "I completely forgot about it. When the earthquake tore it apart Corenswet had the infirmary completely remodeled. The security system he added is top notch. Seriously. First, you need a key-code to enter the front door. Fine. Then inside you need to be verified by a two guard system, one checks your badge, the one that only staffers have; the other scans you for weapons through a metal detector. Then if you are staying in the new private rooms, you need a combo of all three: key-code, badge and thumbprint scanner. He set it up so that each visit to patients could be tracked as an added level of documentation, I guess. There's no way Graves could get in there."

"I had to stay there when I came in," Matt said, then quietly added, "I had some problems with solitary."

"So how do we get you in there?" Mouse asked.

"Well, it's wouldn't be that easy," Murray cautioned. "We could injure ourselves, but without any broken bones or major lacerations, they will just send us back to our cells. Anything more would be too permanent."

The room fell quiet as the five conspirators tried to come up with a solution. It was Cyrus who finally spoke up.

"There'd be only one way in there that wouldn't involve permanent injury," he said to the group, then looked directly at Matt. "Poison."

"Too risky," Liu said.

"What do you mean, poison, Cy?" Murray asked.

"You'd drink bleach. I'm sure you've got some here for cleaning purposes. You'd get real sick. I mean *really* sick. However, the bleach won't be enough for you to have to spend a few nights in the infirmary. They'll just give you some intravenous fluids or pump your stomach and be back out in an hour. You'll need to add something else after you drink the bleach."

"Ammonia," Matt said in recognition of what his partner was suggesting.

"Bleach or ammonia on their own won't do enough but combined they'll cause a chemical reaction inside your stomach that will create chloramine gas. It will rise up out of your esophagus. You'll cough the gas out and then breathe it right back in. That will then poison your lungs as well. You'll be your own chemical weapon."

"Holy shit," Mouse cursed. "How do you know about this?"

"We saw it used in gangland assassinations," Cyrus said. "Every household's got those chemicals laying around. You feed it to one junkie and send them in. They belch it all over, spreading the gas throughout the house. Lots of bodies, not a single bullet fired."

"It's too risky, Murray. They'll be lucky to save either one of us," Liu advised again.

"I'm with Jan on this," Mouse added. "You could die without Graves having to lift a finger. I say we go back to the solitary plan."

Crockett shook his head in disgust. "There's gotta be another way. You said yourself that Graves could break in there!"

"No, I said we can't know that he doesn't have the ability," Mouse retorted. "I can see if I can change the key-codes for that night. The warden doesn't realize how much access I have to the prison systems."

"Why can't you just stay here? In the FF?" Cyrus asked.

"Even if we could disappear and stay here, we could only hide for so long," Murray answered. "Maybe just one night. We need more time to come up with a permanent solution for the Graves problem. I'm sorry guys, but the poison route is too dangerous. It risks too much, including the lives of the medical staff trying to treat us and everyone around. It's gotta be solitary."

A look of disappointment between the former LAPD officers went unnoticed by the others.

"How do we do it, Murray?" Mouse asked. "How do we get you put into solitary?"

"We'll have to pick a fight with each other," Murray answered, turning to Liu. "It'll be a fake fight, but we'll need to make it look real. Vicious. Unable to be contained. It's gotta be right in front of the guards too."

"They'll break you guys up and stick you both in solitary until the warden authorizes your release again," Mouse added.

"It'll be at least a few days," Murray said. "He's already on edge about things and he'll want to further ensure things will be kosher when we come back out."

"Once the guards come in, they aren't just going to push you away from each other and then walk you off to safety," Mouse added. "You're probably going to be beaten by them. Your fight might be fake, but they won't be. Just be prepared."

"Yeah, we can do it," Liu concurred.

"One last thing, guys. We can't help much while were in there. You'll have to be on your own," Murray went on. "You still might be in danger from the other inmates. Graves may not have motivation to harm you but the other inmates sure do. If you're attacked, you'll need to defend yourselves from multiple sources. When the blows come, try to absorb them. Don't flinch or tense up. Let the momentum carry you. Flow with it."

"Thanks Murray. That's some real zen stuff right there," Greem jested sarcastically. "I'm afraid not all of us can be martial artists."

Murray smiled.

"Yes you can, because as soon as we get out, that's exactly what I'm going to teach you."

Greem and Crockett nervously looked at each other. After how this meeting went, it looked like they were going to be up to their necks in danger.

CHAPTER 30

Murray stirred his plastic spoon into the soggy bowl of corn flakes. In the food tray's indentation next to the bowl were the remnants of his biscuits and gravy. He'd torn through them, but his mind began to wander when it came to eating the cereal. The pile of grapes, pineapple and cherries would go uneaten even if he didn't have so much on his mind. He sat in a locked cell alone, playing with his breakfast and thinking about Liu.

The plan had worked, sort of. When they had gone to their cell for the night, they began screaming at each other outside the door. Guards at the end of the hall yelled at them to stop and go to sleep. As planned they didn't stop; they instead escalated their argument. Murray called him "Charlie" and said that illegal immigrants weren't welcome in the US, that they should all be sent back to where they came from instead of coming to America to commit crimes. Liu called him a fascist and the two dove on top of each other, throwing punches that softened when they hit their mark but looked real enough.

The guards at the end of the hall ran at them to pry them off each other. It was Liu's elbow that hit the guard in the face as he pulled back to throw another fake punch. It was a calculated blow that ensured they both landed in solitary. He'd broken the hapless guard's nose, who then lay bleeding as more guards piled on the pair. As predicted, they were beaten with nightsticks. When they finally had them separated, Liu was put in solitary.

Murray had failed to count on Corenswet's need for him. The warden put Murray in a private cell. Through the window of the metal door, he could see a solo guard standing with his back to him. It was better than nothing. The guard was one of Mitchell's most trusted, the warden had told him. Still, Murray would have preferred a location more isolated.

So now Liu was safe and secure and Murray was loose among the monsters. Corenswet's guard duty would only last for two nights at best, and then he was back in the same dangerous position as he was yesterday. Graves would be coming and now he was down a man, his best one. They needed a better plan, and fast.

His first thought was to try Corenswet again. Maybe he could convince him now. Maybe he'd listen. On the other hand what if the warden was in on the whole thing? Murray quickly dumped that thought. If the warden was in bed with Graves, Murray wouldn't be alive right now. Corenswet would simply hand Murray over on a silver tray. No, the warden wasn't part of the conspiracy. That didn't mean that he would care one way or another though. Would he even talk to Murray? Their last meeting wasn't exactly cordial. Even if Murray could get through to him, Corenswet still wouldn't believe him about Graves.

Say they acquired irrefutable proof of Graves's involvement in the death of Rodihan: maybe then Corenswet would see the killer put away in a place where he couldn't hurt anyone else. But where would that be? He was already in prison and his network of connections had to extend beyond the walls of Santa Mira. Even if Corenswet had the killer moved to a different prison he'd just find a way back as he did before. In the meantime, he'd still have his underlings here who could get at them. There was also the chance that other inmates would remain loyal to this powerful figure and would follow out his orders to kill them, even orders issued posthumously. It wouldn't end. As long as Murray Bench remained in prison, he and his friends wouldn't be safe. That meant Murray had two paths open to him: get out of prison or somehow become untouchable. However, any escape he made wouldn't help anyone else and he'd be on the run for the rest of his life. No, the only way Murray was going to survive was if he stayed and found a way to keep them out of Graves's reach.

How could he make them untouchable?

His thoughts were broken when the slot at the bottom of the door slid open and something was tossed into his cell. The opening slid shut and the room fell silent again. Murray looked at the window of the door and saw the guard still standing there, his back turned and no sign of change in his position. Had he passed something in? Murray stood up from his breakfast and looked down to find a white envelope sitting by the door. His name was written on the outside.

Dammit, he thought. *Is it a trap? Poison? Anthrax in the mail?*

He stared at the envelope for a moment then looked up at the guard. No change. Cursing in fear under his breath he resolved to open the delivery. He grabbed the envelope and sat on his bed. Inside was a single piece of paper with a message, handwritten to him in block lettering.

I know you are correct about Graves. He's an evil, murdering sociopath. There's no time to tell you how I know this right now. I need you to stop him.

He has consolidated power. He's offered up territory on the outside to the other gangs in exchange for your death and the death of your friends. They will be coming for you.

PS3537.E654 S-1 E-22

I will be wanting a favor in return.

"What the hell?" Murray asked aloud.

Who could have sent this? Was it real? How did this person know that he was involved with Graves? Maybe it was unrelated. What if it was some sort of trap? Maybe even this note was poisoned somehow and swallowing it would have killed him. There were too many possibilities and questions to ponder over without even decoding what the message meant. Those numbers looked familiar to him. A code of some sort?

If the note was truthful it meant he was trapped by his own failed plan. Graves was out there, making himself stronger and a bigger than ever threat to Murray. What could he do to prevent it? He was stuck in a box for another thirty-six hours. At least he'd have plenty of time to think about the note and come up with a solution.

———

At 5:33pm the next day, Murray strolled into the little room that he and Liu worked in. His personal escort from the isolation cell, Cyrus Greem, walked in behind him. No sign of trouble. When the team heard that Corenswet was letting Murray out, they thought it best to send Cyrus to guard him while he made his way to the FF. Graves must have either not heard about Murray leaving or had something else planned in the works. Conversing in the pair of wingback chairs, Mouse and Matt stood at his arrival and greeted him. Jan Liu was absent, still safely tucked away in solitary.

"Hey! It's The Kid with the Golden Right!" Matt joked. "Hope you guys didn't hurt each other too much."

"Murray, it's good to see you again," Mouse said.

"You too, guys," Murray nodded his appreciation for their care. "Unfortunately, we have a lot of work to do so we need to cut the celebration short. Liu is still locked away, so we need to end this Graves problem as soon as possible so we can get him out of there."

"It's good to have you out," Cyrus said. "Don't get me wrong for saying this though--isn't it better that Liu is in solitary? He's safe there. Isn't that where we should be trying to get you?"

"Yeah, I mean Graves is still hunting you. Maybe we should consider having you stay in the infirmary for a little while. There's still the poison," Cyrus added. Whether his concern was for Murray or for himself couldn't be told. Since Murray had been in isolation Matt and Cyrus had heard nothing from Graves or seen any manifestation of his threat of violence to them. With Murray free, Cyrus felt the shadow of the threat on their lives would only become real once again.

"There's no need. I think we have a plan," Murray said. He found a desk chair and spun it around, sitting with the back against his chest. "Mouse, I think it's time we told them. I'll let you handle it."

Mouse stood up from the wingback and walked to the head of the room. He would have preferred to continue sitting, yet this was too important to relax for. He needed to lead this meeting and that required keeping everyone's attention, even his own. Age had started to make his mind wander if he got too relaxed. Best to stand.

"When Murray was in isolation, someone slipped him this," he announced and held up the note. "In it was a message that said Graves has consolidated the gangs of this prison in a...confederacy of murder. All under the flag of killing Murray and his allies."

"Fuck me," Matt said. "So now the entire prison is against us? We have to go to the warden. The corrections department. The press. We have to get out of here."

"Who sent the note?" Cyrus asked.

"I don't know," Murray answered. "It came through a slot in the door. No way to tell."

"Any guess?"

"None whatsoever."

"Gentlemen," Mouse interrupted. "If I may continue?"

Seeing no objections, Mouse continued to tell his report.

"The note also carried a cryptic message at the bottom. PS3537.E654 S-1 E-22. Murray didn't know what it was so he wanted to get the message to me and see if I could find an answer.

He was savvy enough to get the note out through a return library book he had in his cell. The guard delivered it with the note inside and I found it when checking the book back in. Good work there."

Murray winked. "And? Were you able to decipher it?"

"Didn't need to. I could read it, plain as day."

"Huh?" Murray's face scrunched in disbelief. "Well what did the code say?"

"It's not code at all," Mouse laughed. "The irony of you sending it to the library is lost on you."

"Mouse…" Murray cautioned sternly. "Not all the time in the world for jokes and mystery, pal."

Mouse composed himself. "Wasn't that funny anyways. It's not code, it's Dewey Decimal."

Murray knew it had seemed familiar. "So it points to a book?"

"Not quite," Mouse said. "It points to an author--actually not even an author. A television producer. Rod Serling."

"'The Twilight Zone' guy?" Cyrus asked.

"That's the one. It was pointing to a particular episode of 'The Twilight Zone'. That's what S-1 E-22 is. Season 1, Episode 22 - *The Monsters Are Due on Maple Street.*"

"So how does that help us kill Irvine Graves?" Murray asked. He was starting to feel like the note had just been some sort of prank. Maybe even Graves sent it himself to waste their time.

"I wouldn't say it helps us kill Graves, Murray," Mouse answered vaguely. "I watched the episode this morning and I think it will help keep us alive, though."

Mouse went on to explain the episode. On Maple Street in Anytown, USA, the people of the neighborhood were greeted to the sounds of a flying object and flashing lights overhead. Almost immediately afterward all the electronics and machines in town quit working. No one knew what could have caused it. The suggestion from a small boy that it was aliens was dismissed as being ridiculous.

While the townsfolk tried to determine the cause, one neighbor's car started completely on its own. The rest of the group found this suspicious and thought that the man and his family may be hiding the truth. He emphatically denied this accusation, but few believe him.

More people get blamed by each of their once-happy neighbors. A man who stared up at the sky some nights was accused of looking for something. Another got blamed for working on something late at night in his basement. As night came, someone shot at a figure walking toward them. They found it to be another neighbor, which cast suspicion on the shooter. *Why were you so quick to fire the gun?* The shooter's house lights unexpectedly turned on without warning, only casting more doubt on his loyalties. In defense he accused the small boy of being an alien, simply for suggesting aliens previously.

In a panic, the town tears itself apart. Chaos reigned while the citizens destroyed their beloved community. On a hilltop in the distance, two aliens observed the events below, congratulating each other how easy it would be to conquer mankind without ever firing a single shot.

"I get what you're saying, Mouse," Murray smiled. "I like it. It seems that whomever sent the note gave us just the weapon to use against Graves."

Cyrus shook his head. "I'm sorry. I'm not getting it."

"You see, the townsfolk are the inmates and gangs-," Mouse began.

"No, I get that. We make them tear themselves apart. Distrust each other. I'm asking *how*?"

Murray straightened up and walked around to the front of the room where he could be seen by all.

"By using the same tools and strengths Graves has in his favor. We make ourselves so feared that no one will come near us. We make it so the rest of the prison sees us as protected and can't be gotten to. We make it so that people move out of our way as we approach. We will be so above them that no one will come near us out of fear and respect."

Cyrus showed the same expression from before and was about to speak but Murray stopped him.

"How, you ask? Well, by myths and legends. We're going to create a pretend gang that doesn't exist. And we'll all be part of it."

Mouse finally chimed in, "Murray, that's the dumbest thing I've ever heard of. There's only five of us, and only two that can fight at all and one of you is in solitary!"

"Hey, we can hold our own!" defended Matt.

"Against an entire prison? I don't think so."

"I think you missed the operative word here," Murray interrupted. "Pretend. Made up. Fake. Not real. This gang doesn't need to be real, just believable. We're going to prey on the fears and superstitions that the rest of the inmates carry in here. It's going to take work, but if we can convince them that this gang is real and we're all a part of it, no one will be out to kill us anymore. They'll be too afraid of the consequences."

"We're left with no choice," Mouse said. "Good plan, bad plan, it doesn't matter. This is our plan and if we execute it, it will work."

Murray smiled and nodded at his friend, then looked at the others. It was Cyrus who voiced his agreement first.

"Okay. If this is it, let's make sure we do it perfectly." Cyrus said.

Matt shifted his weight, the last to agree. Rolling his eyes, he smirked, "All right gangbangers, where do we start?"

CHAPTER 31

And so they went to work.

For the next three weeks the team spread rumor after rumor about their phony gang. They called it The Night's Ghost, a metaphor for their inspiration. Mouse printed fake infirmary admittance records for people that had been injured or killed by the secretive and alarming new gang. It was easy. He just looked up an inmate at another prison outside of California and used their identity to create someone that no one in Santa Mira knew, but could believe existed.

Murray asked to speak with Corenswet. When he, as predicted, was denied by Mitchell, he let it slip to the big guard that he had heard of a new gang that was so feared that the other factions wouldn't even talk about them. Murray knew that Mitchell would tell the warden and the other guards. He would do Murray's work for him.

The stories they spread were small and relatively mundane at first; mundane for a prison, at least. Just a story here about someone crossing the Night's Ghost and getting their legs broken or that the warden wouldn't do anything about them because he feared them. They laid the foundation for the rumors and they spread through the prison like wildfire. Then the stories they told grew larger and even took a mystical turn. They said that the Night's Ghost sold his soul for the power to influence and control men. The members were elite killers who had pledged their allegiance and their lives to the Ghost. They could get into any room in the prison, even inmates' cells. They would have members sit in as plants in other gangs and sabotage them from within. They were everywhere, and no one could be trusted.

They sprayed graffiti on the walls of the prison with paint they "borrowed" from the FF. The markings were in calligraphy so vague and ornate that it looked like a plausible message but was really just garbage text. The inmates saw these messages and took them to be warnings from the Night's Ghost. They believed they were written in the language of Hell.

Mouse was a master conspirator. It was his idea to plant "proof" of membership. He would have a random inmate's rations increased for no obvious reasons. Then he would issue new shoes to the same inmate. Already under suspicion of preferential treatment, he would lastly drain the commissary accounts of another random group of inmates. When they would go to make a phone call or order an extra ration of biscuits, they would find they had no money and no ability to pay their debts to other more powerful inmates. Someone was stealing from them, which by itself was a major crime, yet the added fear of repercussions from late payments was enough to send these inmates into a fury.

By the end of the week, people were telling Murray about the things they'd heard about the Ghost. He heard that the Night's Ghost was the name of the leader and that he couldn't be harmed. He drank blood with his top lieutenants each night in a satanic ritual. He once had his men switch the soap in the bathroom so that when a rival gang used them they all were inflicted with a flesh-eating bacteria. Murray almost laughed out loud when he heard it but kept himself in check.

———

It didn't take long for the gangs of Santa Mira to begin fighting amongst themselves. Accusations of treachery were flying. At best, a member would be exiled from the gang, left to fend for themselves against the other inmates. At worst, their bodies would be found lying in an empty shower and stabbed repeatedly or within their cells, strung up by their own bed sheets.

The effect of the Night's Ghost was more than Murray and his team had expected. The entire prison was chaos for any member of a gang. For the rest of the inmates it was peaceful, if one could call a prison sentence that. The superstitious and inherently mistrusting gang members were so busy with their infighting that unaffiliated prisoners went unfettered in their affairs. Murray, Cyrus, Matt and Mouse watched from the sidelines, just outside of the radius of fallout.

In his cell, Irvine Graves was fuming. He was losing power to a myth and his prey was slipping out of his reach. All of the effort and progress he had made toward turning the prison against Murray Bench had been for nothing. He tried to meet with the leaders of the gangs to talk some sense into them but no one would meet with him. They were all too busy trying to control the havoc within their ranks or investigating whether any of their boys had been turned.

His circle of control had diminished to just the six men he'd started with. Six men who had already failed to kill Murray Bench: Beckton, Kelsal, Pergent, Davis, Clarkson and Johns. Johns, his best fighter, the one that had had the best success, was still laying in a bed in the infirmary.

He still had the hope that Greem and Crockett would come through. Yet those two were either slower at getting things done than his men were or they weren't cooperating with Graves's threats. He'd have to give them more time to get in tight with Bench and then strike. Their time and his patience was running out though.

Worst of all, Warden Corenswet had found fit to assign a permanent chaperon to him. A new guard, Corenswet's cousin, large and loyal. Graves couldn't take a piss by himself, let alone murder Bench. He wasn't even allowed within twenty feet of the warden's prized boxer.

Irvine Graves had never lost confidence in anything he'd faced in life. For the first time, he was beginning to doubt himself.

He'd sentenced himself to prison, made a deal with the FBI, offered territory up in trade, wasted eight months of his life while Santa Mira was rebuilt, and had absolutely nothing to show for it. Yet inside him his rage still burned. The face of Murray Bench haunted him in his sleep. He'd never failed, never quit. The cost had been high already but there would be no cost too high to finish what he set out to do. He'd been through tough times before, moments when he wasn't sure he could go on. Times when he was a no one, working at low levels and doing despicable things, embarrassing himself all so he could move up and up in the ranks. Gain power. Dominance. If he let this situation dominate him, then it wasn't just the last year of his life he would have wasted, it would have been his whole life. No, Murray Bench still needed to die. If not for Graves's reputation, then for his own pride.

There had to be a way to take down this "Night's Ghost", a way to use the chaos of the prison against Bench and an idea was coming to him on how to do just that. It would take time, patience and sacrifice, yet for Irvine Graves there was nothing he wouldn't do to see his revenge made manifest.

———

Without Liu around, work had begun to pile up for Murray. He was the only one who had any experience in the tapestry department of the FF, the only one that could step into Jan's role. They were big shoes to fill and despite his best efforts, Murray could not handle the extra load. He struggled to keep pace with his own work, and stepping into Liu's role only furthered the problem. Repairing tapestries was something he only had a fraction of the needed knowledge and skill required to keep up with the demand. His nights within the FF became longer and longer as the work stacked up around him. Corenswet gave him special privileges to stay late, with a guard posted just outside. The warden had too much money on the line to let the tasks be delayed, so Murray found himself once again working past 10PM this night.

Alone.

The Night's Ghost had been a success, yet Murray was still at unease. Each time the old building shifted and creaked, he had to close his eyes and breathe slowly to keep from panicking. The needlepoint work he was doing would have been a disaster if he jumped whenever he heard a sound. *It's just noises. Nothing to worry about*, he would tell himself repeatedly. *Just focus on the task.*

Movement on his left.

That's not the building. Someone is in here.

He set the needle down gently, yet maintained his posture. If he was going to defend against an attack, he wanted to know the location it would be coming from. His ears sharpened, he slowed his breathing, his eyes widened. Still, quiet, he searched for any sign of threat.

There!

From the storage room above, a shadow dropped to the ground. Murray spotted the attacker land behind the large spools of thread ten paces off. He leaped from the workbench, cleared the distance and threw his weight into the spools. He planned to pin the intruder to the wall, then get some answers.

The answers didn't come. His attacker had twisted through a gap between the thread and Murray's knees. Murray was thrown to the ground and instinctively closed his eyes and brought his hands up in defense. He'd been beaten that fast.

Nothing happened. No fists or kicks were brought down on him. The room was quiet. Confused he opened his eyes, looking at a man standing over him with his hands on his hips.

"I've taught you well, Luke. But you are not a Jedi, yet," Master Jan Liu said through a giant smile.

CHAPTER 32

The bell sounded and the fight was on. Murray came out of his corner and put his fist close to his face. He moved cautiously ahead as a fighter came up on his left and another came up on his right. He was fighting in another of Corenswet's high stakes matches where Murray always was handicapped.

A month had passed since the Night's Ghost made its first appearance and the prison gangs were still too distracted to reinvest themselves with Graves's alliance. Inmates were on edge, fearful, suspicious. Any chance one could take as a diversion from the turmoil was welcome. Murray's fights fit the bill.

Today the gym was packed. The fights had been drawing a large crowd for weeks. Each time, Corenswet sought to profit more and more so the fights kept getting more elaborate and unique, even themed. Today was Three-Way Thursday.

This wasn't the first time he'd fought two men in the ring. In fact, this was a pretty common thing with the warden. Murray preferred these matches; he got hit less. One might think that with two opponents throwing punches at him, he'd be hit twice as much. Not for Murray. Corenswet always pitted him against the same type of fighters: large, imposing, muscular heavyweights that moved about as fast as LA traffic. It just wasn't enough for Corenswet's rubes to bet on two men over Murray--they'd heard about him and how he could defeat two men with ease. So they would come to the prison with betting on Murray in mind until they saw the bruisers he was pitted against. No way could he take on two of those monsters, let alone even one.

Murray's advantage was in his speed. He could be wherever he wanted in the blink of an eye and dodged the heavy punches with ease. Still the real trick was that he would shift his opponents' positions so that one would get behind the other, just as one would throw a punch. If the one on the right punched, Murray would move left. If the one on the left punched, he'd go right. The blow would miss Murray completely, but would often strike the other opponent as the heavy bruisers tried to adjust their swing after it was too late. His opponents would often punch each other out and be too tired to take Murray on directly after the other fell. Then it was just up to him to clean things up.

"It looks completely stupid," Mouse said to Cyrus and Matt. "But it works."

The three of them sat in the new bleachers that lined the wall of the gym, a donation to the prison by Sam Davis after visiting a few weeks back. There was even a rumor that he would be adding training ring, as well as all new training equipment. The prison and Murray's influence was the perfect way to recruit new talent for Davis Gym, not to mention giving newly released convicts an avenue to a fresh start. It gave Murray hope for some of his new friends to have Sam making their lives better on the outside, including Joe Wassar, who was Sam's newest trainer.

The new bleachers were well made and sturdy, but the mob of angry spectators were making them bounce up and down quite a bit, which made Cyrus a little uneasy. His fellow viewers of Murray's fighting style were furious at him for just dancing around the ring. They wanted to see someone get hit and hit hard, not the glancing blows that were tiring the two heavyweights out.

"It's like this every time," Mouse shouted over the booing. "Just wait, though. It'll happen any minute."

A few rows of bleachers further up sat another collective of inmates who were watching Murray intently. Around Irvine Graves sat his usual six goons, Kelsal, Pergent, Beckton, Clark, Davison and his new right hand man, Nate Johns. Johns had been released from the infirmary weeks before, yet his face still showed the punishment Murray had inflicted on it, a swollen eye and jagged grin. He wanted Bench to lose more than anyone, an eye for an eye, yet he remained silent as the fight was waged. His mind was too busy thinking of new fresh horrors to commit on Bench to cheer.

Graves's other men watched Murray and yelled with the rest of the viewers. Beckton called Murray a pussy. Clark yelled out that Murray was a dancing faggot. Pergent and Davison just yelled "Kill him!" However, not all eyes were on Murray in the group. Irvine Graves instead watched the only three men cheering for Murray. He saw Mouse, Greem and Crockett quietly speak back and forth without yelling at the ring. They were watching the match, analyzing it, judging the champion's performance. It seemed Murray Bench had some fans, two men Graves had tasked with murder. Yet here they were cheering for him. It made Graves only hate them all even more.

"If three guys that size attacked Bench, then he couldn't use his little dance maneuver," Davison claimed one level below Graves. "There'd still be one guy left to take him out when he tried to dodge the others."

"So what?" Beckton asked. "You think we can take him? I've been ready to kick that punk's ass."

"Yeah, I heard how good you did last time," said Pergent.

"Fuck you," Beckton sneered.

Clark spoke up, "I say we should do it. There's six of us and only one of him now."

The others nodded and shouted their agreement but their eagerness was cut short by the voice of their leader.

"You think you're the first to come up with this plan? I congratulate you all. You're the cleverest band of fools in Santa Mira. Bench has been attacked by groups of eight men before and come out on top. Each time he escapes injury and instead his attackers end up in the infirmary. So go ahead. Add yourselves to the list of idiots who let their own egomania dictate their actions against that pugilistic affliction."

Graves' goons looked at each other and then Beckton asked, "So that's a no?"

Nevertheless, Graves's mind had moved on from their conversation. He focused his thoughts internally since his comrades, while quite useful at completing the tasks he assigned them, were no great thinkers on their own. He watched Murray move. There was something new to his movements since he'd last fought him. He could see training in him, a fluidity to his actions that could only be taught and then practiced repeatedly by an able learner. There was something familiar to his new fighting style, but he couldn't place it. Maybe there was something more he wasn't seeing.

In the ring, Murray bounced left and the man on his right threw a roundhouse that misfired and caught his partner in the ear. The struck man staggered for a second and Murray threw his first punch of the fight, a solid uppercut to the jaw. The reeling man's eyes went white and his body shook when the force of the blow broke his feet from gravity's tether. He was unconscious before he started to come back to Earth and fell into a pile on the mat.

Murray stepped over him and faced his remaining opponent directly. He wasn't even sweating yet. The other man was red in the face and blood dripped down from a cut above his ear, the remnants of another failed attack by the man on the ground. His sluggish movements were eclipsed by Murray's speed, as his jab only grazed Murray's forearm, passing it aside. Another roundhouse was thrown with the hopes of catching Murray and ending this match before the tired giant couldn't stand anymore.

Yet the blow never met its target. Murray ducked and the trajectory of the attack spun his opponent around. The man was wobbling with dizziness but remained on his feet. Murray casually walked over to face him, put one hand on his head and pushed him to the ground. The fight was over. The bell rang and the little crowd booed, but above them the cheers of Corenswet echoed from his private viewing room.

Graves looked back at Greem, Crockett and Dormus. The old man was pointing at Murray and the other two were nodding at him and clapping. They were loyal to Bench, for sure. Not once during the entire fight had they looked back at Graves. Not once did they acknowledge his presence. Men who feared for their lives always would give some recognition to the one who held their life in his hands. Some form of delay or begging. Not them.

It was all up to Graves now. He was just waiting for the time to come, slip his guard, and take out Murray Bench and his crew, once and for all.

———

"No, not that way. You're close, but I need you to bring your left leg back further. This throw is going to require a low center of gravity. Focus your energy downward. Use your mind to push every part of you down to the ground. Imagine yourself glued to the ground and bonded to it. You're an unbreakable force. Now grab his foot and throw him!"

Cyrus Greem clutched the ankle of his former partner, swinging him and carrying the momentum of the kick through his body, behind him and to the ground. Matt flew around him and landed in a pile against the wall while Cyrus stayed fixed in his defensive position as if Matt had weighed as much as a feather. At least that's what Cyrus saw happening in his mind. He'd managed to catch Matt's kick, carry the momentum and throw Matt, but also threw himself and ended up in a pile next to his friend.

"Good. That's fantastic work," Murray congratulated.

"What are you talking about? I did as much damage to myself as I did to Matt," Cyrus replied as he stood up and adjusted his jumpsuit, which had become as twisted as its wearer was.

"Yes, you did, but I could see that you felt yourself becoming planted and unmovable," Murray answered. "Your mind followed where your body could not. Getting your limbs to do what you want them to do is hard, but training your mind is the most difficult task in *Daito-Ryu*."

Cyrus looked at Master Jan Liu to see if he showed any sign of input. Liu walked over to him and struck the defensive stance Cyrus and Matt were practicing.

"Find your balance. In your center, here," Liu instructed motioning to his hips. "Channel your focus towards this spot. Guide your attack around it."

Cyrus shook his head in frustration. "I'm just not cut out for this."

"Doubt is a powerful weapon, but for your enemy," Liu added. "Belief is the side you must align yourself with."

"This is a good break point. You both have a lot of information that needs to sink into your brains and I don't want to overload them," Murray instructed as he helped Matt get to his feet. "I know how smart you cops are," he said sarcastically and smiled.

Despite the joking Murray was proud of his students. He and Liu had started training the pair in *Daito-Ryu* just two weeks ago and they were like sponges. They were soaking it in and moving at a faster pace that either he or Liu could have guessed. They said that the LAPD had offered a mixed martial arts class about two years ago that they both had taken. The instructor had trained with a number of UFC fighters like Kimbo Slice, Shawn Tompkins and Bas Rutten. They loved watching UFC fights, so the chance to meet and work with someone who knew the stars was too irresistible to pass up. They had learned quite a bit and had built a good foundation to work from.

Matt and Cyrus grabbed a couple of towels and did their best to dry the sweat off their faces and arms and sat down in their usual chairs in the little training room/textiles department of the FF. Murray handed them a couple of waters and sat down beside them.

"So what do you guys feel like doing tonight?" he asked. "The NBA Finals are on. We could watch that. Mouse was also talking about getting a game of cribbage going. Maybe I could win back some of what I owe you sharks."

"I'm good with either," Cy replied. "It's still pretty early in the playoffs so we can skip that if we want."

"I was actually thinking about going to bed a little early tonight," Matt said. "This workout shit is kicking my ass."

"Oh, come on. I want you to stay up until at least 10pm. If you get too much sleep you'll be groggy. And if someone savvy notices you going to bed early each night, they might think something is up. They might come knocking on our door and find out about me teaching you guys martial arts."

"So what if they do, Murray?" Cyrus asked. "The warden signed off on us being here. He knows that you're training us. He's all for it. What difference would it make at this point?"

"All the difference in the world if we let our guard down and underestimate our enemies," Liu interjected, looking up from the tapestry work he'd started since the workout ended. "The less they know the better."

Murray smirked and nodded at his apprentices. He confirmed what the master was cautioning with his expression.

"Fine. No going to bed early," Matt said. "I think I'll spend the evening reading then. If that's cool with you guys."

"Cyrus?" Murray asked. "Playoffs?"

"Actually I was hoping we could talk about something. You mind?"

Murray shook his head, "Bleachers?"

Cyrus knew the location would suit what he wanted to discuss. The pair waved goodnight to Liu and Matt and walked out from the FF.

"What's on your mind?" Murray asked.

"You don't belong here, Murray," Cyrus told him. "You have too much to offer the world outside."

"I appreciate the compliment... Kinda weird thing to say randomly, but thanks?" Murray replied, confused.

"I mean it," Cyrus said. "You shouldn't have pled guilty that day."

"No, you're wrong. I need to do my time, just like you. I owe this community for what I did and thought was acceptable behavior. And until my peers say I'm ready to be a part of that again, then I'm good where I'm at."

"I can't agree with you on that. If that's how you really feel, then great. You've got your way of thinking and I know you well enough to understand how difficult it is to change your mind. You're a stubborn man, Murray Bench."

"I get that from my father."

By that point the pair had made it around the ball field and sat down at the bleachers next to them.

"I wish I could have met him," Cyrus confessed.

"Who? My dad? He was a kind and gentle man. He never wanted to hurt anyone and went out of his way to avoid doing so. You can imagine how that conflicted with his job. Still he made his career his own. He even taught a course for the Sacramento PD where he taught peaceful arrest procedures and de-escalation tactics."

"We could have used someone like him in my department. The mentality there is just so fucked up. You don't see it when you're there, though. You just accept that this is how things are done and you follow suit."

"What do you mean?" Murray asked.

"Well...it's like this. You know how in high school there's always this group of bigger guys that act like they are in charge of everything behind the scenes? The teachers, parents, and the principal don't make the rules-- they do. You remember those pricks?"

"Yes, yes I do," Murray said as he recalled how his younger and less muscular days went.

"Well they're right. They do make the rules. Because no one wants to stick their neck out to change the system. Say you're the new kid in school. You're going to get it worse from them than anyone if you get on their radar. So you don't make waves. You try to stay unnoticed. Just do what you're there to do, try to do as much good as you can in your role, but the whole time play by those rules, whether you agree with them or not."

"Okay. How's this relate?"

"It's like that on the force. You show up thinking that you're going to change the world. You're going to serve and protect. Then you find out that you can't do anything because there's a culture there. There's these unspoken rules that don't benefit society or the people you're trying to help. They are there because someone bigger and badder than you says they are there. So you just try to do what little good you can actually do without getting noticed."

"What rules do you mean?" Murray asked.

"Like, we don't try to ever disarm someone. We see a weapon, we're trained to shoot. Period. It's in our training. It's in the culture."

"Your training teaches you to shoot first?" Murray asked.

"Not intentionally. The courses don't teach it, but it's the result. We're taught to protect ourselves first and foremost. Then we're taught these tactics of arrest procedures that mostly consist of shouting orders. I mean lots of shouting. So before anything starts everyone is on edge. Then emotions run even hotter with all the yelling. Some guy starts in with verbal abuse. So now the perp is pissed and amped up. There's nothing taught about controlling the situation, either. So it's pretty easy for something simple to get ugly."

Murray listened intently, drawing connections to similar moments he'd seen in LA and Sacramento.

"You hear guys talk about it all the time. 'I see a gun, I'm shooting mine. I'm not getting shot for this job.' There's never a thought of 'Well, then why did you take this job?' It can't be the pay. And then there's no sense of how to treat people. Hey, if you're a nice guy then you'll be nice to people, right? Even as a cop. But it's the people that are pricks that are the problem. Especially the racist ones, like Johns. You put a gun and a badge on some racist asshole and you're gonna have a problem at some point."

Murray chuckled. "I was down in Santa Monica one day. Just to enjoy the weather and the beach, you know. There was some parade or something happening down the street. It was loud and there were people everywhere yelling and screaming and it just wasn't the quiet environment I was wanting. So I bailed. There were all these roads that were completely blocked off on the way that I would take, and there were cops everywhere. A lot of them were dressed in riot gear. It turned out the parade was a gay pride parade and they were expecting something bad to happen, I guess. Fine, whatever. So I'm walking down this street of apartments and there's just tons of people out. And I see this guy at one of the roadblocks and he's saying that he lives in one of the apartments behind it. He's just wanting to go home. But the cop at the roadblock says something like 'Turn around or I'm going to put you on your knees'. And I could see this guy, the one that was going to his apartment?"

"Mmm hmm," Cyrus answered.

"He was not having a good day. He looked just beat and tired. You could tell he just wanted to go home. And it wasn't like he was a threat. He's this fat guy in shorts and sandals. So he asks the cop again and he's like 'Isn't this roadblock for vehicle traffic? I'm on foot. Just let me go to my place. I can see it from here, asshole.' It was the 'asshole' that put this cop over the edge. The guy said it just in passing, not threatening in anyway. More complaining. Still the cop started towards this fat kid and reaching for his baton and I'm thinking, 'Oh shit, this is how riots get started.'"

"No kidding," Cyrus agreed.

"But, thankfully, this other officer--you could tell he was older-- steps in between the cop and this kid and he says in this calm and friendly voice, 'I'm sorry, buddy. Could you just go around? It's for your own safety.' And I could see everyone relax around me, including the kid who'd tensed up and clenched his fists. I think he was going to try to defend himself. And now he just says, 'Yeah. Sure, no problem, officer' and walks away. The stupid cop with the baton completely forgot about him and just started barking at other people. The entire incident had meant absolutely nothing to him. I bet that kid never forgot about it though."

"Yep. I saw stuff like that all the time. All you could do was try to mitigate the disasters that were happening around you. You couldn't do anything to stop the problem officers. You just had to try and wrangle them. I guess that's what got me here."

"Hey, I understand. Just one officer trying to make any difference is a step in the right direction. It could be that the good you did will have an effect on someone else and then they make an even bigger difference. Change happens slowly sometimes."

"Thanks Murray. I just wish I could have...and I should have, done something that changed your situation."

Murray didn't really know how to feel about that sentiment. He looked out at the setting sun over the prison walls, searching for the answer and finding one within himself.

"Look, there's a problem with bad police officers for sure. That doesn't change or have anything to do with me. I'm the one at fault for my actions. I'm not blaming anyone else for something I did. It's not just the police that need to take accountability for their actions. It's the people they were sworn to protect too, you know."

"Yeah, but I need to take that same accountability for inaction," Cyrus said. "It's not just what we do that matters but also what we don't do. I swear to you and to myself that I will never stand by and do nothing again, no matter the cost."

"Take it easy, buddy. You sound like a comic book superhero in their origin story a little. You need to sometimes pick your battles. You picked the wrong ones and not the right ones before you got here."

Cyrus paused. "I guess it's time to change all that."

———

While Murray and Cyrus were having their discussion, Crockett changed his mind on reading in his cell and instead found a poker game. About five hands in, he caught one of his opponents cheating, an inmate named Rogers. When he called the card thief on his game, tempers quickly got out of control and Crockett was threatened by the cheat.

"Give me one reason," Rogers said, "And I'll gladly take you out and make Graves a very happy man. Then when I get out of here, I'll rape and kill any woman you've ever cared about, however old they are."

Matt set his cards down and walked away, wisely. He found Murray and Cyrus at the bleachers and explained what had happened.

"He threatened to headhunt you?" Cyrus asked. "For Graves?"

"Yeah. He wasn't worried about the Ghost at all."

"We need to take this up a notch then. Tonight," Murray said. "I'll go get Jan."

That night, the Night's Ghost paid Rogers a visit. When he excused himself from the mess hall to use the restroom, Murray and his crew followed him. Rogers was known for relieving himself in private only. He refused to use the toilets next to the dining hall, so he always walked out and used the bathrooms in the library next door. While in the middle of his business, Murray snuck behind him as he stood at the urinal. A burlap sack was quickly placed over his head and Murray dragged him into one of the stalls.

"You'll find that threatening someone under the watch of the Night's Ghost will have very dire consequences," he said in a disguised voice. Cyrus joked that he sounded like Batman. "You won't want to forget that, so The Ghost will help you remember."

While Murray and Matt held the frightened prisoner to the toilet, Cyrus pulled his right arm forward and turned it upwards. Liu opened his bag of tools and dyes. The instruments were what he used to recolor dingy rugs and tapestries, but tonight they were going to act as an impromptu tattoo kit. He dipped his needle into dark red dye and proceeded to puncture the man's skin. The cheat cried out in horrible pain, as the size of the needle was not like anything one would find at a tattoo parlor. This needle was used for pushing through the thick backing that kept the tufts of wool attached to a rug. Liu drew the kanji character that translated to "The Ghost walks among you" on the man's arm. The kanji had become the adopted symbol of the Night's Ghost and the group had made sure it was seen by anyone living in Santa Mira.

When Liu was done with the tattoo, he disinfected the wounds and bandaged them. He nodded to Cyrus who let go of the arm.

"Now, you'll go straight to the infirmary," Murray went on in the Bat-voice. "They will see that you don't bleed to death. Nevertheless, you will bear this reminder for the rest of your days. See that it is heeded."

Murray tied a simple knot in the drawstring of the sack around the bleeding man's neck and then the four of them left him. Murray heard from Mouse the next day about Rogers coming into the infirmary and hysterically screaming that the Ghost had got him. The nurses patched his arm up just fine, but they found that the man had defecated in his prison jumper. He literally had shit himself while sitting on a toilet. It took Murray several minutes to stop laughing.

The looming threat of Irvine Graves burned in Murray's mind, though. He kept his fears to himself, but each day that passed he found himself asking, "Is it today? Is today the day that Graves begins a war against us?"

Murray's fears were warranted, and little did he realize, their attack on Rogers was the breaking point that Graves was waiting for. Rogers had a cousin that no one else knew about. His name was Luke Rogers, a guard at the prison. It was a common name inside, there were at least a dozen Rogers at Santa Mira. The relation had been wisely kept secret from the other inmates. It would have been a death sentence for Rogers, the prisoner, to be connected to one of the guards. There were no secrets that Irvine Graves didn't know, however. His eyes and ears were everywhere and it just so happened Luke Rogers was on his payroll. This incident had kick-started the beginning of the end for Murray Bench and only his greatest enemy knew it. It made Graves all too exhilarated to be this close to his ultimate revenge.

CHAPTER 33

Six pm, the following evening:

It was the end of another day of work in the Furniture Factory. First, their duties to their individual jobs and then another hour of Murray and Liu training their new-found allies. It was exhausting work, yet Matt and Cyrus were coming along just fine. With each day they understood the finer nuances of *Daito-Ryu* more and more. If their bodies would only progress at the same rates their minds did in the martial art, they would be near able to take on anyone but their trainers. Now Murray and the two students were tired and hungry. Time to get some dinner. Closing up the FF for the night, they left the building with Liu disappearing inside as he usually did.

Outside the door, seven men were waiting for them. Murray recognized four of them as inmates, but only knew one of them by name. He was the scumbag named Beckton, and Murray knew him all too well. He wasn't anything to worry about physically--he'd already beat him twice--but worry Murray did. Each of the inmates held baseball bats and things only got worse when it came to the other three men. Each wore guards' uniforms, each had a name tag. Burks, Rogers and Pinkman were the names displayed. These weren't inmates who had stolen uniforms somehow. These were the real deal, as evidenced by the collapsible metal batons each carried bouncing up and down in their hands. This was no ordinary group looking for trouble: this was a planned formation.

"What do you want?" Murray asked boldly. He thought that showing no fear might discourage the rabble from continuing whatever plan it was that had brought them into the alley outside the Furniture Factory.

"You guys are staying here pretty late each night, we've noticed," Beckton said as he moved to the front of the group to face Murray directly. He looked around. "Only guards I see around are the ones I brought with me. How come you don't have any guards following you around?"

"What we do has nothing to do with you," Murray said calmly. "If you've got a problem with the way things are then I suggest we take this matter to the administration department. If you want, I'd be happy to go with you first thing in the morning."

Beckton moved a couple of steps closer to Murray. The two were at arms-length. It was a distance Murray didn't feel comfortable about. His words hadn't defused this situation.

"You must think you're pretty special, getting to go and do what you want around here, while the rest of us have to follow all kinds of strict rules and stay within boundaries. We aren't really very happy about that."

Behind Beckton the other inmates shouted their support. Luke Rogers stepped out from the rest of the group. His face was twisted in anger.

"Enough games, Beckton. These fuckers have to pay for what they did to my cousin."

Murray tried harder to quell the situation. It was accelerating too quickly.

"Let's just settle down. I'm sure this is just a misunderstanding. I don't know who your cousin is, sir. Maybe you've confused us with someone else."

Beckton pounced on this. "Oh, there's no confusion. You fucked up. The inmate you tattooed last night." Seeing the recognition on Murray's face only encouraged him. Having six men with him didn't hinder his audacity either. "Yeah, you see. You know who I'm talking about."

There was no way that this was going to end without all three going to the infirmary. There were just too many of them. Reasoning with them wasn't working. Maybe he could bluff.

"This is not something you want to do, Beckton. I already kicked your ass, and now you want to try again with two LAPD on my side? You didn't bring enough men."

Beckton took another couple of steps forward. Behind him, his men followed suit and spread out in a half circle around them with the Furniture Factory at their backs. Beckton was now so close that Murray could smell his breath. It smelled nauseatingly of gum disease and stomach gases.

"That's a laugh. He doesn't know, boys!" Beckton chuckled. Behind him, the group joined in the merriment. "These two ain't with you Murray. They been working for Graves this whole time. Just like their other piggie pals."

What? He's lying, Murray thought. *Right?*

"Just like the one Graves cut open and spilled his guts out. Just like we're going to do to you tonight!"

Murray had no time to react to the accusation. Beckton stood aside and the first inmate ran straight at Murray, screaming as he arched his bat behind him to strike. Murray's training had prepared him for this, though. He knew to expect the unexpected and that an attack could come from anywhere at anytime. The bat swung around with its wielder still running at full force. Murray caught the blow between his side and arm, cradling the bat in the hard muscle of his trap. He shifted on his back foot and let the force continue its path around him, stumbling the attacker and sending him headfirst into the wall of the FF.

The next assault came towards his face from his right, but Murray again was ready. He dropped to the ground, landing on his back, and shoved his foot forward into the knee of the attacker. The knee snapped backwards, shredding ligaments and sinews. A howl of pain sprung from the wounded man as he fell to the ground in agony. Murray shifted to a crouching position just in time for the last of Beckton's goons to get his testicles crushed by Murray's fierce grip. He pulled down on the screaming man's groin, using it as a pulley to stand up.

He was moving like a force of nature. His movements were blindingly fast and he was running on full instinct and muscle memory. He hadn't planned his response to these attacks, there was no time. He just slipped into a different state of consciousness that allowed for his body and training to take over. Three of the attackers were dispatched before Murray's conscious mind knew what had transpired.

He spun to face Beckton and the remaining guards, but it was too late. Despite his efficient speed in taking the men carrying the baseball bats, the three guards had moved around and encircled him. He was surrounded. Alone. Betrayed.

Beckton sneered. Luke Rogers growled. The circle closed. Murray braced for the final attack.

Two bodies jumped onto the backs of the guards. Hammering elbows into their shoulders, Cyrus and Matt had joined the fray. Beckton's jaw dropped in shock.

"You motherfuckers! You'll pay for this with your lives!"

Murray's fears had been for naught. Cyrus and Matt had never been working for Graves--they had been playing him. The shoe was on the other foot now. The odds had been evened in this fight.

The guards had managed to wrest Cyrus and Matt from their backs and were now in hand-to-hand combat with them. Murray turned to face Beckton and Rogers. He was too late to manage them both. Rogers had joined his fellow guards in the attack on Cyrus and Matt. They were outnumbered. The pair of former cops were doing their best to defend themselves, using what knowledge of *Daito-Ryu* they could muster. Still, their bodies hadn't become one with the complicated martial arts. They were still moving with thought and they were just too slow. The guards were overpowering them.

Murray moved in to help, but the first inmate had recovered and now stood with Beckton blocking Murray from his endangered friends. Beckton bent down and retrieved a second baseball bat, a fresh weapon to tilt the advantage. The pair split apart and moved around Murray, forcing him to turn his back towards Greem and Crockett. He could only hope that they could hold out for a little longer, until he could dispatch the two he was facing, but he knew that the odds weren't good. Just one crack from a guard's baton to the base of the skull could kill them. He couldn't let that happen. Not again.

Before he could make his move though, something large cut through the air behind him. Another swift whoosh and a snap and then another came to his ears. He dared not turn around while Beckton and his boy were still within striking distance.

"Cyrus? Matt?" he called out, hoping to hear a response that let him know they were okay. There was no answer. He had to turn. If his friends were hurt or worse, then he was now surrounded. He'd have two inmates in front of him and three guards behind him and closing. His only chance was to break through the guards and run. He turned but there were not three guards coming for him. Just the stunned faces of his friends, standing over the unconscious guards on the ground. Another sound came from behind him, he spun. The first inmate was coming at him at full force, but a flying kick across the face sent him spinning to the ground.

Master Jan Liu had flown out from the shadows and caught him perfectly across the head.

Now there was only Beckton and his two bats. Murray and Liu both went into defensive stances. Their legs shifted and braced, sending their energy down and becoming fixed with the earth. Their arms repositioned, one ready to catch an attack, the other pinned back ready to strike. Beckton was outmatched and he knew it. Both bats fell to the ground and Graves's man fled into the shadows.

"We have to stop him," Murray shouted and began to run. "He's our one chance to take down Graves."

The quartet gave chase in the direction Beckton had run off. Sprinting as fast as they could with Liu and Murray at the front, the four moved with purpose. They were all in excellent physical shape for the chase; Beckton wouldn't be hard to catch up to.

"How's he going to help us take down Graves?" yelled Crockett ahead to Murray.

"He knows about Rodihan. We take him to the warden!" Murray answered back.

They ran along the wall between the vocational offices and the main prison yard until they reached the opening that led out into the yard. There was no sign of Beckton. The four stopped and looked around them. There was no movement in the open area and only one light that shined down to where they were standing. The rest was shrouded in darkness. The prison was shutting down for the night. It wouldn't be long before they were all missed and a search was formed to find them. Then it would be too late to do anything about Beckton.

"I don't see anything," Cyrus said.

"Me neither," Matt concurred.

"What's so important about catching him, Murray?" Cyrus asked. "We could just go to the warden now and all tell him that Beckton confessed. He could then send out someone to find him in the morning."

"We can't let him get away. Too much risk. Graves could hide him. Or he could have another attack coming our way. We have to find that little bastard and end this," Murray said and looked around. "Okay, we need to split up. Jan, you go back towards the FF. Maybe he doubled back on us. Cyrus you head up towards the vocational offices and look around there. Matt, you keep heading along the wall towards the clothing shop. I'm going to go into the yard. If you don't find him in three minutes, come back here and meet. We'll have to figure something else out. Now go."

The four moved into their specified directions, but before they could take three steps Beckton bolted out from behind the wall and ran into the prison yard. All four had to change direction and Beckton already had a sizable lead on them. The pursuit began anew, but this time they had too much ground to make up and a lot bigger area to search if they lost him again. They continued on in the direction they had last seen Beckton run, straight towards the little storage buildings that lined the athletic fields. They reached the first building and turned the corner towards the gymnasium.

Irvine Graves stepped out in front of them. In his arms was Beckton. Graves had one arm around his neck and the other against his head. Murray could tell that Beckton was frightened now. Behind him, Murray spotted the bouncing rays through the dark of flashlights headed in their direction. The guards had begun their search for the missing inmates.

"It seems you've lost something, Bench" Graves called out, his voice like razors. "What could you possibly want from this piece of human waste? Perhaps he's got a secret to tell?"

"Let him go, Graves," Murray ordered.

"Or perhaps he's just someone who sniffs around where he shouldn't and should be disposed of like the trash he is," Graves answered.

A look of disbelief shot across Beckton's face and Murray thought he heard him say something to Graves faintly. Graves smiled at Murray, a disgusting grin that sent a chill through him.

"I think it's the latter."

Graves took a deep breath in, kissed the side of Beckton's head. Murray lunged forward, but it was too much distance to stop anything. In a swift movement, Graves squeezed and pushed against Beckton's head. A sharp snap echoed through the courtyard.

"It seems I've done you a great favor, Murray Bench," Graves calmly said. He let go of the dead man, then turned and dropped to his knees. Two guards grabbed him and dragged him away. Murray and his friends stood in shock and horror; the light from the flashlights now pointing directly at Beckton with his neck twisted and broken, before they too were taken away by the guards.

CHAPTER 34

"You see how the fibers react to the cleaning mix? They are changing color. This once deep red is now a pink. If this had been the original, this 450 year old tapestry would have been destroyed and it would have been your fault. The mixture of the cleaning solution must be perfect."

Master Jan Liu sat next to Murray in the FF at one of their work stations. In Liu's hand was a swatch of carpet they had pulled from the scrap pile. It was time that Liu trained Murray on how to clean and preserve the antique European tapestries sent to the prison by the California Parks Department as part of the restoration process of Hearst Castle.

"Now this obviously isn't representative of the materials you will be working with, but the idea is the same," Liu explained further to Murray.

Murray nodded his head in agreement but remained silent.

"Okay, so you must understand your colors first and what chemicals react to what degree with each color. If you were to place 2 parts too much ammonia with only 1 part water, what reaction would it have to light blues?"

No answer came from the student.

"Murray?" Liu asked once again. Hearing no answer he slapped his pupil in the back of the head.

"Ow, what was that for?" Murray asked, rubbing the spot of impact.

"This is very important. You must be 100% attentive here. There's no room for errors. So pay attention."

"I'll try."

"No. You will do. If you are here to just try then we quit until you can focus. Tell me now. What will it be?"

Murray knew better than to lie to the former assassin who read people's behavior as part of his perfected skill in the murderous trade.

"It's last night. I can't get it out of my mind. You saw what happened. Why would Graves have killed Beckton?"

"Because in Graves's messed up world that was a sign of intimidation."

"Uh, what?" Murray asked.

"Graves runs his business like it's an independent country and he's the dictator," Liu explained. "He would prefer to rule everything but he knows that in order to get there he's got to work with others. He can't beat the Night's Ghost, not alone. He needs the other gangs to focus their fears. It's better to have them fear him than the Ghost. Killing Beckton was a gesture of terrorism."

"By killing his own guy? How does that make the other gangs want to fight the Ghost?"

"It's a show of power. The Ghost is invisible, a shadow. He acts in secret, pulling strings, casting doubts. Backroom, covert. Graves went overt. He showed that he's willing to turn this whole place upside down to reach his goals," Liu said and turned back to the work. "It doesn't matter. Graves has been put in solitary. He'll be there for longer than you or Matt or Cyrus will be in Santa Mira.

Mouse said he's buried. No visitors. No communication with anyone. He gets to sit inside a cell with no windows for the foreseeable future."

"But what if that's all part of his plan somehow? I can't trust that this is over just because Graves is locked up. His power is too far-reaching. He's too much of a planner to make a mistake like that because he just wanted to intimidate a rival gang. Plus I swear I heard Beckton say something before he died."

"What?" Liu asked.

"It sounded like 'But you sent me to-' and then he was dead. Graves snapped his neck before he could get words out."

"'You sent me to' what?" Liu asked.

"I don't know. That's what's been driving me nuts. If Graves sent Beckton to do something, then again, it was planned. It seemed he sent him to kill us. Maybe that's why he killed him? He failed at his mission?"

Liu put down his tools and looked at Murray directly. Murray had seen this face before. It was the face he wore when he was frustrated with Murray.

"I can see that any skills taught today will go unlearned. So let's get this figured out so you can go back to work. Here's what we know: you were attacked by seven men, three of whom are guards. A collection like that doesn't just form on its own because they don't like someone. That means that they answer to someone. Graves. He put them together. The inmate he killed was part of his gang, or at least was under his control. We know that the inmate failed twice to kill you. He also said that Cyrus and Matt were working for Graves, or Graves was under the impression they were. One theory is that Graves sent him to check on their loyalties. He reported his findings and Graves killed him."

"That doesn't explain why he did it."

"He's a psychopath, Murray. You said so yourself. He kills because he enjoys it. This time he got to kill as part of his plan."

"What's his plan?"

"That I cannot tell you. Time will tell. Now, please, can we move on and go back to work?"

"No."

"No?"

"No. I've got to meet with Cyrus and Mouse," Murray said as he zipped up his jumper. "The basketball playoffs are on tonight and I promised them I would watch it with them. We'll pick this back up tomorrow. Do you want to join us?"

Hearing no answer Murray waved to Liu, but his nose was already buried in his work. His mentor wouldn't be joining them tonight.

———

"But you sent me to-," then snap. Dead. Dropped to the ground like garbage. The scene kept playing over and over in Murray's mind as he walked from the Furniture Factory to the South Cell Blocks. Beckton wasn't a good guy by any means. He was a villain. He'd hurt people. On the other hand, his murder was surely undeserved. The punishment for his crimes had been to serve at Santa Mira, not to be executed for the goals of one man, especially Irvine Graves.

Murray knew that Beckton had been sent by Graves to accomplish some task. Maybe Liu was right. Maybe it was to sniff out Matt and Cy. Maybe it was to kill him as he'd suspected before. Maybe it was a combination of both. So what? Graves had failed. He was locked away, completely isolated from any task he'd hoped to achieve before he killed Beckton. He'd surrendered to the guards, he knew that they were coming and yet he killed Beckton anyway. Why? The question gnawed at him. Had he been outwitted, or was Graves truly a psychopath? Whatever the answer, he was lost on how he would solve this mystery.

Reaching his destination, he opened the door and entered into the South Cell Block. Inside, he took a right turn at the waiting staircase that led up to the individual cells and entered through an open door that was painted blue, in contrast to the drab olive walls on either side. Beyond the door was a large common room, where a group of prisoners were sitting in metal folding chairs and glued to the TV hanging above them. The basketball game had already started. In the third row back from the front, Murray found Cyrus and Mouse waiting for him.

"Saved you a seat," Mouse said and nodded to the empty chair at his right.

"Where's Matt?" Murray asked as he sat down.

"You didn't hear?" Cyrus asked. "He's meeting with a parole board. There's a chance he's going to get out of here."

"What? That's fantastic!" Murray exclaimed. A look from the row in front silently told him to quiet down.

"Yeah, his family has hired an advocacy attorney who says that he might be able to get him on work release, due to his military background."

"Yeah you had mentioned that before," Murray said. "He's never brought it up to me, though."

"He doesn't like to talk much about it," Cyrus said. "The PTSD stuff, you know. He told me that no one knew what we were in for in Afghanistan but that was especially true for the first 'boots on the ground', as it were. He just wanted to fight the people who caused 9/11 but instead he found himself fighting everyone but them. Women, old ladies, kids...So when he was discharged he walked away and never looked back. It kind of messed him up. The problems didn't show up until after he'd been on the force for a little while, but he kept his mouth shut and did his job. He did his service for the country and that's being looked at now. Plus he's been pretty well behaved while he's been here."

"So what's that mean for you?" Mouse asked.

"Well, nothing really," Cyrus said, before joining the rest of the audience in celebration. Los Angeles had just hit a three pointer and then stole the ball on the ensuing defensive play. When a foul occurred, Cyrus continued.

"Aside from missing my friend, there's not much consequence to me. This attorney is pretty expensive from what I understand. Matt's family has money so they can spring it. My family is gone and I had zero dollars saved up, so for now you're stuck with me.

Besides it's not a done deal yet. Matt told me the process could take months."

"Better than years," Mouse chimed in.

How about that? Murray thought. *Matt might get out early, probably before Graves could get out.*

It was a possibly huge victory for him and his challenge to keep his team protected while serving their sentence, even if it meant losing a member of their ranks. Matt deserved the chance.

"Oh this fucking guy," Cyrus declared with sarcasm. The comment jarred Murray from his thoughts and he looked at the TV screen that Cyrus had gestured to. A commercial was playing. Patriotic music played over sweeping shots of Los Angeles and San Francisco. Between the city shots were pictures of people and families smiling. Murray couldn't help but notice how they all were white and appeared financially secure.

"He's so full of shit," Cyrus went on. "We had to deal with him a few times when we were on the force. He acts like he's this philanthropist and is working hard for the community, but he's as bad and greedy as anyone."

"Who are you talking about?" Murray asked, seeing only the same stock images from before.

"Welshing. Thomas Welshing. This is his commercial."

The images had ended and a salt-and-peppered man came on screen in front of a large building with the name "Welshing" written across the front. Murray had seen the building before but never the man. When he spoke he was eloquent, but Murray could hear a Bay Area accent come through.

"I'm Thomas Welshing, CEO of Welshing Construction and Real Estate, where we make California better for you and your business, one building at a time."

The camera zoomed outward and upward to a map of California. A graphic ran along the bottom of the screen and said "Welshing Construction and Real Estate - Building a Better California". On the left was the pronounced W over a black C that represented the logo of Welshing Construction. An odd sense hit Murray when he saw the logo. He'd seen it before somewhere, but couldn't place it. Somewhere and sometime long before he-

Cyrus nudged him. "He's exactly the type of guy who is killing the community. He's played a major part in what's happening in your old neighborhood. His goal is to make the rich stay rich and, well, everyone else...shoot them if they resist. No one knows it but he's a major reason why people are rioting over police violence. When neighborhoods get destroyed, guess who rebuilds them? With taxpayer money I might add. Scumbag."

The game had come back on and the moment was over but Murray was haunted by an unrecoverable memory from his past. Where had he seen that logo before?

He stewed over it, distracted from the ball game. He tried to focus and move on from it, but the image stuck like glue to his brain. It was the final quarter before the thought left his mind.

The game was close. The room was split between the home team and away team. There were some bad calls made by the referees and the room was starting to get a little heated. Insults were starting to flow out more and more. Slowly Murray, Mouse and Cyrus moved farther back away from the more angered front until they were against the back wall. Tempers often flared during sporting events. It was part of the way of life here. You just had to ignore it, stay clear, and keep enjoying the game until it calmed.

Tonight was different. It soon became clear that the anger wasn't about the basketball game, but about the death of Sam Beckton. Halfway through the fourth quarter, two inmates began pushing and shoving. Murray caught Beckton's name being said by both men. Then he heard one accuse the other of being part of the Night's Ghost. It was his crew's fault for Beckton's death. The pushing and shoving was quickly broken up by the guards in the room before things turned ugly, yet there was now a foul air in the room. Murray could feel the bad vibe in the awkward silence that fell after the scufflers were separated.

The silence lasted only minutes.

Again, the Ghost was brought up and arguments broke out. The guards asked for the inmates to settle down. Their pleas were ignored. Someone popped off about the warden. He was in on it, he had to be part of the Night's Ghost. Otherwise he wouldn't allow them to exist and get away with what they do. That turned the room into an all-out fistfight. The guards were attacked and fought back with their nightsticks. The brawl spread out through the room before Murray and his friends could escape it. Murray and Cyrus blocked Mouse away from the danger and within seconds they were swimming in bodies.

Someone grabbed Murray. It was Tony Clark, one of Graves' men. How had Murray not seen him earlier? No time to analyze that now, Murray settled into the *Daito-Ryu* defensive stance he favored. *Here we go again.*

Yet, Tony Clark just pulled him as close as he could and gave out a warning.

"You watch your back, Bench. We've got a war coming. All Hell is headed your way and it's the end of you and your little rabble's lives."

He spat in Murray's face. Murray didn't budge, he didn't need to. A guard pulled Clark off him and slammed him to the ground. Clark stared up at Murray as he was zipped-tied by the guard.

"It's coming, you son of a whore."

"Shut it!" the guard said and yanked him to his feet. The fight had been contained. The guards had regained control.

"Bench, warden's office now!" the guard yelled at him.

Murray looked at his friends and shrugged. "Busy night."

———

"Murray, what do you say we get you out of here," Corenswet said from across the desk to Murray. He sat with his hands folded together. He looked at Murray with his usual insincere expression. Murray didn't respond. He wasn't expecting what Corenswet was proposing.

"Your office?" he said in confusion.

"No, not my office. You've proved yourself time and again to me. You've been a model prisoner. I put you up against some of the best fighters Santa Mira has ever had reside within her. You've made me considerably wealthier. I'm indebted to you." Corenswet stopped this time, waiting for Murray's response.

"I'm just glad to have had the opportunity to keep boxing, sir." Murray replied, knowing he was saying exactly what Corenswet wanted to hear.

"Bullshit, Murray. You're a champion and I'm saying thank you."

"Well you're welcome, Warden Corenswet."

Corenswet smiled predictably. Then he said something that Murray didn't expect. "I think it's quite clear that you're no threat to society and are ready to reenter the rest of civilization outside these walls. What do you think? Would you like that?"

Murray's jaw dropped in surprise; he was expecting to serve his full sentence or for as long as Corenswet was making money off him.

"I don't know what to say. Of course, I'd be happy to. But what about the parole board? I'm not scheduled to meet with them for another three months."

"I've spoken with the board and all is taken care of. I told them what you did during the earthquake, the horror you endured at Oroville and how you've behaved in your time here. Trust me, Murray, when I want something done, I have considerable pull to make it happen."

"Well that's fantastic news. When does this all take place? What happens next? I have to go tell Master Liu and Mouse," Murray stood as he spoke.

"Not quite so fast, Mr. Bench," Corenswet said as he waved his hand, gesturing Murray to sit back down. Mitchell, who had been standing beside Murray, put his hand on his shoulder firmly but not to give injury, giving the warden the illusion that Mitchell would force Murray down in case the inmate didn't comply.

Corenswet continued as Murray slinked back into his chair. "I have one more thing I need you to do for me, Murray. The governor is coming to visit the prison next week to inspect the damages done after quake and to potentially dedicate more funds towards additional men, better defenses, guard riot gear and training. His visit will mean a great deal to this prison's future. Still that isn't why I need you. As you well know, the governor is a huge fan of yours and wants me to arrange a final fight for you."

"Well, that is understandable. I've waited this long to leave. I think I can wait another week," Murray replied in earnest.

Corenswet looked at him and smiled in a condescending way, like a teacher looking at a naïve child. "That's why you've been so great here, Murray. Always understanding and willing to sacrifice yourself for others. But I'm afraid this isn't going to be your usual fight. You'll be facing off against Ed Rains. I believe he likes to call himself Pain Rains--a narcissistic alias if you ask me, but it seems to have worked for him."

"Yeah, I know Rains. The man is a buffoon. A dangerous one, but a buffoon. I can take him."

"Well that's the point at issue, Murray. I need you to lose this fight."

"You want me to take a dive? Why? I can beat Rains. I've never lost a fight here and you've bet on me every time and won. Why would you want me to lose?" Murray was despondent.

"Because everyone knows you can beat Rains. There's no money in betting on the horse that's a lock. I'm betting against you this time, Murray, and I need you to go down," Corenswet's tone had become serious.

"Well the answer is no, then. I won't do it."

"Murray, don't be so proud that you won't let anyone see you lose."

"It's not about pride, sir. It's dishonest. It's cheating. It goes against everything that I stand for and believe in, exactly why you think highly of me, as do others. I can't betray that just because it gets me out of here. I'll wait for the three months to talk to the parole board."

"You won't be speaking to the parole board, Murray. I'll see to that," Corenswet had never been so malignant.

"The answer is still no, sir. I'm sorry."

"Then you'll also want to apologize to your little friend. What's his name? Dormus? I believe you call him Mouse."

"You leave him out of this," Murray stood up now. Corenswet had gone too far. Mitchell again put his hand on Murray, but this time forced him back down. Murray looked at Mitchell, who gave him the slightest head shake, so slight that only he noticed. It was Mitchell's way of pleading, "Do what he says." Murray didn't know what to make of it.

Corenswet waved Mitchell off and he moved away from Murray. Corenswet went on. "Mr. Dormus has a life sentence here, Mr. Bench. You and I both know he will never step outside of Santa Mira again. He'll die here. I'll get right to it. If you don't do this, Murray, Mr. Dormus will spend the rest of his time in solitary. He'll never come out. He'll die alone and much sooner, all thanks to your inflated sense of honor. And since you'll still be here as well, I'll make sure you watch as he slowly withers away and steadily loses his mind. Or I could have the Mannequin sent to death row for the murder of Louis Rodihan as head of the violent and horrific gang, The Night's Ghost."

Murray's tense frame slumped as Corenswet spoke. "You couldn't...." he started.

"Oh, I could and I will, unless you do this simple task. You do that and I'll see that Mr. Dormus is treated as well as you have been here. He'll have protection. I'll have someone else take over in the vocational office if that's what he wants. He'll be able to enjoy the rest of his time here more than anyone could hope for. And you'll be free to call or visit him whenever you'd like. All you have to do is let Rains win. Everyone loses sometime, Murray. It's a fact of life. Now is your time."

Murray had been beaten. He'd already lost. "You win," he choked on the words. "I'll do it."

———

At the end of a white hall lay a single cell. A metal door with a small barred window was the only means of seeing the huddled figure within its confines. Nate Johns strode through the hallway, having greeted the guard at the front. He was expected. Irvine Graves had sent for him.

"Mr. Graves?" Johns called out through the window. "It's Nate Johns. I have news."

The man inside came forth from a shadowed corner silently. His hair was matted and he smelled awful but Johns held his posture to not offend his employer.

"What news do you have, Nathan?"

"It's from Luke Rogers. He said he had news from the warden's office."

"Am I being released?" Graves puzzled. "This soon?"

"No sir. Not you. Bench. The warden is giving him early release."

The news was not what Graves had wanted to hear, of course. He didn't panic, though. His prey would think he was slipping away. Graves was ready. It was time to strike.

"How long?" he asked in a low voice.

"Two days. Friday at around noon. He wants Bench to fight one more fight before he goes."

"I see," Graves fell silent.

"Your orders?" Johns asked after a minute.

"It's time for the show to end. Get me a notepad. I've got something to confess." Graves said and sat down.

"Yes sir."

CHAPTER 35

The next morning, all of Santa Mira had seen the statement from Irvine Graves. It was taped to each cell, placed in each mailbox, and delivered to staff offices by a group of workers under Graves' employ in the dead of night.

To the denizens of Santa Mira prison, staff, guards and Warden Corenswet,

I, Irvine Graves, am making the following statement regarding the murder of Sam Beckton. I am wrongfully accused of this heinous act. I have been placed in solitary confinement for a crime I did not and would not commit. Sam Beckton sent me a message that he had vital information regarding the identity of the Night's Ghost, the most wicked and murderous group of evil any prison has ever seen. He and I were to meet at a secret location so that he could share this info with me and I could get the message to the proper authorities and finally end the chaos within this institution. When I arrived at the location, Sam Beckton was not alone. He was surrounded by a rabble who, it seemed, had chased him to that spot. He was desperate for my help, but I was too late. I watched as one grabbed him and snapped his neck, then tossed his body in the dirt like some piece of trash. This was a human life! When I picked him up to check his condition, guards came upon me and placed me in shackles. I tried to explain to them what happened but the conspiracy surrounding this event runs deep through this prison.

Just before my arrest, the villains that perpetrated this left and were not seen by the guards. However, I saw them clear as day. The men who had chased him were four guards, led by Steven Mitchell, the warden's personal guard. It was Mitchell who had dealt the final blow and killed poor Sam. I can only assume that they found out what he was trying to tell me and killed him for it. They must be members of the Night's Ghost, if not their leadership.

Sam was my friend. He was kind and loyal. He did not deserve this. I only hope that this letter can find those who will do what is necessary to see that this great misdeed will be resolved and that the perpetrators will find justice.

Irvine Graves

Murray's crew met again in the FF training room. In light of the bombshell from Graves, Murray had called an emergency meeting. Things were beginning to accelerate and Graves had just revealed a large portion of his plan. He was trying to turn the inmates against the prison guards. Tensions were tough already with the Night's Ghost and now by revealing the entire gang to be a conspiracy that could go all the way up to the warden, things were being set in motion that were beyond Murray's control. Now he was leaving Santa Mira and he worried that he would be deserting his friends, possibly exactly what Graves wanted.

"So what does this mean?" Mouse asked first.

"It's just more of Graves's mind games," Murray shrugged the question off.

"You saw what it's like out there though," Mouse went on. "Everyone is going nuts. They think it's real. They think the guards are out to get them."

Matt laughed. "In a sense, they ARE out to get them."

"Just not the way this makes it seem," Cyrus confirmed.

"Well, we know that Graves is lying," Murray said. "He knows that the Night's Ghost was made by us."

"Could it be some move to get out of solitary? Or to make an escape?" Liu theorized.

"I don't think so," Murray answered. "He wouldn't jump ship without dealing with me first. He's trying to use our own weapon against us. I think he's still got more planned."

"Well, unless he gets out in the next few days, he can't touch all of us, at least," Matt said, beaming a smile.

"What do you mean?" Murray asked.

"My release has been approved. I'm getting out of here as soon as the paperwork is signed."

Congratulations were given throughout the group. Mouse shook Matt's hand and gave him a pat on the shoulder.

"That's fantastic news! How long did they say it will take?" the old man asked.

"Couple days, maybe longer if they don't get it done by the weekend."

"So Monday at the latest," Murray stated. "That's five days we have to keep just one of us safe. After that..."

"Murray, Graves is still in solitary," Mouse replied. "The warden knew his report was bullshit. If Graves is in solitary, he can't touch us. The prison may think he's telling the truth, but they also think that anyone could be a member too."

"Mouse is right," Matt added. "He can't try to kill any of us himself. Nor can he have any of his cronies do it."

"I agree," Cyrus said. "True, he's not going to be there forever. Fine. Matt's going to be out of here shortly. If he's out, then maybe I can find an easier legal path out of here too, right? And you're leaving Sunday, Murray. We'll be fine."

Before the discussion could continue, the overhead speaker crackled to life. The prison speaker system only sounded off when there was an alarm or if there was a special announcement to be made. Everyone gathered in the little FF room hoped for the latter.

"Attention all inmates," the voice of Corenswet boomed through the prison. "The letter that you received earlier today is a complete and total fabrication. My men were not involved in the death of Sam Beckton. The suspect for the murder has been detained and is awaiting trial. Furthermore, there is no gang in Santa Mira called 'The Night's Ghost'. This myth is another pure and total fabrication spread by yourselves in superstition. This matter ends right now. Any further rumors spread about this matter will be dealt with harshly. Lastly, any actions taken against any of the staff or guards will be punished to the fullest extent of the law. You WILL let this go and understand the truth, not the lies being spread. You will resume your normal activities and duties. All scheduled events will proceed as before. I expect this little issue to now be resolved. Thank you."

With that, the speaker went silent.

"Well, THAT should clear things up," Liu said sarcastically and rolled his eyes.

Murray looked up at the clock and saw that it was time to adjourn.

"Look, I've got to go get ready for the fight with Rains. 'Fight...' That's a laugh."

Mouse met him at the door.

"Are you sure you want to do this, Murray? Take the dive I mean."

"I kind of have to. The sooner I can get away from Graves the sooner the rest of you are safe." Murray didn't think it a good idea to mention the threat to Mouse and Liu by the warden. "Look, I'm sure things will be fine. Just keep an eye out for trouble and if you see something weird then get clear of it."

Before he could open the door, Liu was standing next to Mouse.

"Murray, there's something we need to talk about," Liu said.

"We'll have lots of time after the fight, but I really have to go. I don't want to blow this chance."

"It's important," Liu urged.

"After the fight." Murray side-stepped his friends and left the FF.

———

Murray didn't renege on his promise to the warden. He took the dive. He let Rains hit him and fell in an act. A ten count later, and he had lost his first fight.

In the locker room, he was still staring at his golden right when the door opened and in walked a guard, followed by Ed "Pain" Rains. Murray looked up at him silently. Rains strode in confidently and when he saw Murray he sneered at him and snickered. He opened his locker and began unwrapping the athletic tape from his hands.

"Just shows you who the best really is. Fight should've happened a long time ago, Bench. You wouldn'ta been such hot shit this whole time. But now it's time for all to respect Pain," Rains said.

Murray didn't reply but thought to himself, *Nothing changes for you, Rains. You'll still be the same idiot tomorrow. Enjoy how this feels; it'll be short lived.* He finished patching the cut on his head with gauze, changed his clothes and headed for the door. "Congratulations on the victory," he said to Rains as he passed.

"Keep it. You're my bitch now. That's my victory. I'll see you soon," Rains bellowed. Murray stopped briefly but then continued out the door. "You won't ever see me again, Ed," Murray muttered to himself and left the locker room.

In the gym, Corenswet's men had cleared out the last of the prisoners and guards who had lost money by betting on Murray. The warden had taken extra precautions to ensure that Murray was going to leave the prison safely. The gym was completely silent now, and he exited it without looking back.

Across the yard he walked. Just one more meeting with his friends. He'd be telling them goodbye soon. Sad, yet there was hope in his leaving. Maybe he'd have the chance to see them again, outside of Santa Mira.

On his left, the sounds of a baseball game came to him. Today was the biannual guards versus inmates game and the cheers reassured him. *See, all good. Business as usual. The warden's message worked just fine and Graves can't do shit. Let him rot in that cell, warden. Let him rot.*

If only Murray had been near the field for just a few more minutes, he would have been alerted to the fact that everything was not "just fine".

———

For two innings, the game went well. The teams were playing competitively, but in a fair and peaceful way. The tone of the game changed during the top of the third, when a guard was struck in the leg by an errant pitch. The guard, while not seriously injured, was angry and judged the pitch to have been thrown at him with malice. He threw the bat to the ground and began walking towards the pitcher's mound, shedding his gloves and helmet along the way. The umpires quickly ran in front of him and stopped him from doing something he would regret only a few paces in. The guard calmed down after sitting in the dugout for about ten minutes and the game went on.

For the next three innings, the game grew steadily more vocal on both sides. Calls began to be questioned, accusations of cheating were cast by each team. This was nothing new, though. Any sporting activity at Santa Mira went this way, whether the guards were involved or not. People would yell and cuss at each other, but nothing would come of it. If someone's temper did flare out of control, it was usually an isolated incident between just a couple of people. They would be separated and the event would continue. It was prison policy to not punish the many because of the actions of the few. Only the few were punished. It was one of the policies and attitudes Corenswet had changed when he took over.

And so, despite the name calling and the temperament, the game went on. However it ended abruptly in the sixth inning, when a well-liked young black inmate named Gibson was called out after sliding in to home plate. The inmate stood up and yelled at the umpire, a prison guard, and accused him of cheating in favor of his colleagues. The argument should have been broken up, but instead a relatively new prison guard named Gerbaux grabbed a bat and joined into the argument.

Nate Johns and his team had been watching the game, waiting for the moment that Graves had said would come. This, they determined, was that moment. Johns glanced over to Ryan Davison and Frank Pergent sitting just a few rows behind him. He nodded quickly and they returned the gesture in recognition. It was time.

Johns stood up and yelled out that Gerbaux was a Night's Ghost. The other pair joined in, building the frenzy. Johns kept going, screaming that Gerbaux was going to hit the inmate with the bat, that it was all part of the Night's Ghost agenda. By the time the rest of the team and the inmates watching had joined into the accusation, the guards were losing control of the situation. Frightened, the ones by Gerbaux backed away and the rest told the inmates to quiet down.

It was far too late and the final straw was about to be tossed.

Johns looked down to Kelsal and nodded a signal to him. Kelsal stood up and yelled as loud as he could.

"Gerbaux was one of the guards that killed Beckton. I saw him do it."

The rest of the inmates never questioned the validity of what he was saying. They all stood and began to make their way towards the field. Into the faces of the guards, they screamed. Pushing and shoving began. And then it happened.

Gerbaux, nervous and afraid, panicked and hit poor, innocent Gibson in the back of the head at the base of the skull. He dropped to the ground immediately. The turmoil stopped as everyone stared at what had happened. The unconscious and bleeding boy was carried off the field on a stretcher and rushed to the infirmary. On the baseball field an eerie silence replaced the screaming and yelling. Gerbaux was escorted off the field. The rest sat and waited for news about Gibson. Both the guard's team and the inmates sat on their opposing sides, all part of the plan for Johns and his men. Whether or not the boy lived, they would see this riot start. They held the gasoline, now they waited to find out if the match was going to be lit for them.

A few spectators left the field to tell other inmates about what happened. At this time, most of the inmates who were not watching the baseball game were grouped together in the common areas of the cell blocks. The news spread quickly. In just a few minutes, 90% of the inmates had heard of the events that took place on the field and waited tensely to hear the condition of the boy. It wasn't more than fifteen minutes before news came out of the infirmary and swept through the prison. The young inmate had suffered a shattered spine and died within minutes of reaching the doctors.

The prison exploded. Inmates overpowered the guards in the cell blocks. The majority of the guards were clustered at the baseball field, so the ones inside were no match for the volume of inmates grouped together. The real battle took place on the field. The inmates were already armed with bats, and the guards were not in protective riot gear. It was an even match. Both benches and sections of bleachers were cleared and met on the baseball diamond. Bats and fists struck against blood and bone with equal casualties on each side. What had just minutes ago been a dusty field for America's pastime was now a blood-soaked quagmire of hatred and violence.

The alarms rang out and snipers from watchtowers did their best to protect their colleagues, but it was too difficult to take a shot without risking the lives of the guards in the melee. On the field both sides were losing men at a steady pace, but that wasn't good for the staff of Santa Mira; the prisoners had many more able bodies than the guards ever did. Inside the South Cell Block, the remaining guards had been defeated, left bleeding and broken on the floors of the building. It was here that Tony Clark became the leader of the riot. He knew exactly what to do. His boss had coached him well. Once the last of the guards had been dispatched and the block was theirs, he ran to the second story and yelled down to the inmates below.

"We must free our brothers in the other blocks before the riot team is assembled. We need weapons!" he yelled and was rewarded with cheers. "We're going to take over the industrial facilities. Grab hammers, screwdrivers, wrenches...anything you can find!"

More cheers were yelled up at him and his army marched out the front doors of the block and began making their trek to the vocational buildings at the north wall. Clark wasn't among them, though. He met Johns, Kelsal, Pergent, and Davison next to the baseball field and made a path towards the west, a path that lead to solitary confinement.

CHAPTER 36

Murray was just walking into the workshop at the FF when the riot started and was fairly oblivious to the events that were transpiring outside. He and Liu were finally about to have that promised discussion.

"What's on your mind, Jan?" he asked.

The master of *Daito-Ryu* put a hand on his shoulder. "Your friendship has meant a great deal to me, Murray Bench. And to John. We're indebted to you."

"Yeah," Murray answered unfamiliar with how to express his feelings the same way. "Me too. You guys have been great. We'll see each other again. Life has a way of working out sometimes."

"Funny you should say that," Liu grinned. "Murray, John and I—"

The door flew open and Mouse ran in.

"Riot!" he yelled.

"What?" Murray and Liu said at the same time.

"The whole place has erupted. Some guard killed a kid. They think the guard was the Night's Ghost. It's mayhem out there. There's a group headed straight this way."

Then the sounds of the violence breached the walls of the FF. Outside they could hear shouting, screaming, and sounds of bodies hitting against the walls.

"If they can get in, then they can get weapons," Mouse said in a huff. "The guards won't fight fairly then. Instead of batons and shields, they'll switch to pistols and rifles. This place will turn into a bloodbath."

"Jan, go get Matt and Cyrus," Murray ordered. Liu nodded and headed out of the room and down the hall to the wood shop where Matt and Cyrus were working.

"We have to try to keep them out," Mouse said to Murray. "Can we block them from getting in somehow?"

"There are too many entrances for the five of us to hold," Murray replied. "They are going to come in. We can't stop that."

"Well, we'll have to defend this place," Mouse suggested.

"There's way too many of them, John," Murray cautioned. "Even for Master Liu and I. We have to get everyone to some place safe."

Almost on cue, Mitchell rushed through the door into the little section of the FF where Mouse and Murray were waiting. His uniform was dirtied and torn. He had a large cut running across his neck and a bruise forming on his already ruined cheek. In his hand, he held a baton that had been used recently, with flecks of blood on the end of it. He strode right up to Murray and grabbed his arm.

"Corenswet wants to protect his promise. You are to come with me to his office," Mitchell spoke. "We've locked down the elevators; no one can reach the top floor without the proper access code. You will be safe there."

"I'm not going anywhere without my friends," Murray rebutted.

"Warden only said to bring you," Mitchell stated as he pulled Murray.

Murray slipped the giant's grip, while repositioning Mitchell's arm in a way that pressured his elbow to a point of breaking. "I only go if Mouse comes too."

"Fine, but don't ever try this ninja shit on me again," Mitchell said in pain and Murray released his grip.

"We have to wait for the others," Mouse objected.

"They're with Liu. He can take care of them. I've got to get you out of here."

Mouse looked at Murray defiantly. "I'm old but I'm not useless."

"This is not a time for heroes, John," Murray said. "I need to get you someplace safe and the warden's office is the best shot we've got. Trust me on this." He strode over and put his hand on the old man's shoulder after seeing his friend's look of defiance. "I need you to trust me on this."

Mouse sighed, giving up his last self-delusion of youth, and nodded. "Thank you," Murray said and turned toward Mitchell.

"Lead on."

Murray and Mouse followed Mitchell to a small, hidden side door at the back of the FF that was mostly unused and thus most likely to be clear of any rioters. When they reached the outside, they ran along the wall of the building to the south. Turning the corner, they could see a mob of about forty inmates reaching the front doors of the building. Yet the group was stopped, they couldn't open them. Something had jammed them shut.

Liu, Murray thought as the group was forced to move away to the other side of the building. The trio took advantage of the empty path in front of them and ran through the opening in the wall where just three nights before, Murray had chased Beckton to his death. In the main prison yard, the battle at the baseball field had ended. The guards had lost. Inmates were caring for their friends who had been injured while others continued to kick and beat the guards who had been too crippled to crawl away.

"My God," Mouse said as he stopped to look. Murray turned back and grabbed him, jolting him back on the path to the Administrative building. They passed storage buildings with walls splattered by blood and unconscious (or worse) men slumped against the sides. Ahead, their destination came into view and the path was clear for them to reach it and the hope of safety.

Inside, the ground floor of the building was completely empty. The security desk was unmanned, and above it security monitors showed the violence continuing outside. The remainder of the cell blocks had been taken over and more inmates were pouring out into the yard. There was no screen that showed the vocational buildings, no sign of Murray's absent friends. Mitchell pushed his charges forward and they ducked inside the elevator. Mitchell hit the button for the top floor and then rapidly entered in a series of numbers (which Murray couldn't determine) that allowed the elevator to move up to the top. The old car jerked upward and the motor loudly screeched out in labor. Inside the car was a different picture. No one spoke as the car rose to the top floor; the only sound from within were the taps of Mouse's nervous fingers along the handrail. The doors opened and Murray could see no signs of violence down the empty wooden hallway. They ran to Corenswet's office and entered. Corenswet was waiting inside.

"Excellent work again, Mitchell," Corenswet congratulated. "Mr. Bench, I see you've brought your little friend. As long as you are here, it matters not."

Murray ignored him, still angry by Corenswet's earlier threat on his friends and looked down on the mayhem below. Through the big windows behind Corenswet's desk Murray could see what was unfolding outside. The guards and inmates were all engaged in what looked like a scene out of a Lord of the Rings movie. There were groups clashing on the baseball field again and around the cell blocks, with more inmates pouring in from the beyond the wall that separated the yard from the vocational buildings and the FF. Everyone was fighting hand to hand combat and the remaining guards were clearly losing.

"They will be coming here, warden," Murray warned. "If they can take you, then they will be able to use you as a hostage."

"I've called in the situation. We'll have a full battalion of officers in full riot gear within minutes," Corenswet replied. "We just need to hold tight."

———

"You both need to come with me, now!" Liu shouted in the doorway to the Wood Shop.

Matt and Cyrus were just removing their gloves and safety goggles when the Master of *Daito-Ryu* appeared. The pair had been using the loud wood planer when the riot began and had heard nothing until they had shut the machine off. Through the sheet-metal walls they heard shouting and banging of fists along them. Alone in the shop, they had decided to go find Murray when Liu cut them off.

"What the hell is going on?" Cyrus asked.

"A riot. We're leaving," Liu responded.

The trio rushed down the hallway and into the great room that made up the storage area of the Furniture Factory. On either side were racks of milled wood waiting to be shaped into chairs and tables, and roll after roll of carpet ready to be shipped out. At the end of the room stood the sliding barn-style doors that were big enough for delivery trucks to enter through. The doors were shut for now, but Liu knew that it would be the first place any invader would try to enter by. The fact that it was still shut and locked was a very good sign for their successful escape.

They ran across the open room and entered into the hallway that led back to the tapestry room where Liu had left Mouse and Murray. They found their usual hangout empty. There were no signs of their friends, nor any clues as to where they had gone.

"Change of plan. We get to the library," Liu ordered. He turned and ran before Cyrus or Matt could respond. They chased him back into the great room and found him heading for the sliding barn door. Cyrus caught him first and stopped him.

"The library? Why there?"

"Only two small entrances, lots of hiding places, no weapons there."

"Why not Mouse's office? There's only the one front entrance. It's closer." Matt suggested.

"No. Always have an escape route. There are two entrances in the library. We go there," Liu stated adamantly.

The doors shook and jerked from the outside, cutting off any argument. Without a word, Liu darted over to a nearby table and grabbed a blade screwdriver from it. He swiftly moved back to the doors and wedged the blade into the bar-lock that held the pair in place. The doors separated slightly as the inmates outside pushed but jammed against the screwdriver, blocking their entrance.

"That won't hold for long," Cyrus said. "If they get in here..."

He looked around the room and saw hundreds of potential weapons. Although it wasn't the tools that gave him pause. It was the four forklifts positioned around them that made Cyrus worry. If the inmates could get through this door and then drive the forklifts outside, they could use them to ram through any door they wanted, with exception of the prison entrance. The solid front gate would hold against all four of the trucks at once, but not against the freight trucks parked in the garage. The only thing keeping the trucks secured was a garage door that would be no match for the bladed lifts of the motored carriers.

"We've got to block...those...off..." Cyrus trailed off as he heard the engine from one of the lifts start. He turned in time to see Matt bring one of them around, loaded with two rolls of carpet each weighing 400lbs. He drove the lift straight over to the wall and emptied the load, laying the carpet rolls alongside and jamming them against the castors of the sliding doors. He repeated the process for the other side. Matt parked the lift at the end of the rolls and engaged the parking brake.

"There. That oughta hold them for a little while at least," he said as he hopped out of the driver's seat.

"There's still three entrances," Liu stated. "We need to go."

Liu ran to the stairs that led up to the second floor. Cyrus followed, leaving Matt behind.

"Well, don't everyone thank me at once," he muttered and then pursued his friends.

Reaching the top, he found Cyrus and Liu at the end of a hallway that led to a window overlooking the vocational buildings. Outside the window was a stretch of roof that ran down to a gap of ten feet before the roof of the next building started. Liu smashed the window open with his elbow and cleared the remaining glass from the frame with work gloves.

"Go," he said to Matt and Cyrus.

First Matt, then Cyrus climbed out onto the roof. Cyrus turned back to Liu and extended his hand to help. Liu ignored his offer and looked back into the FF. He could hear voices coming from the first floor; the inmates had entered through a side door.

"You have to go now," Liu said turning back to his friends. "If they find you, they will kill you. Go to the library. I will keep them off you."

"Liu," Cyrus began, but the Master had already left the window and descended back down the hallway to the staircase. There was no turning back now. "Dammit," Cyrus cursed.

Below them they could still hear the sounds of men fighting and banging on the walls of the FF. Screams sprung up as the voices of the fight signaled the death of an enemy. Whether it was guards or inmates was impossible to tell. Cyrus and Matt could only hear the horror, the rooftop blocking their vision to it.

The pair fled along the roof top to the edge and never slowed to make the jump needed to clear the gap. Over the rioting men, they leaped, but it was Cyrus who lost his footing on the landing and began to slide down towards the ground below.

"Matt!" he called out. His partner turned to see him sliding off the edge of the roof, three stories above the ground into the violence and murder below.

CHAPTER 37

Matt dove to catch his former partner just as he slipped over. Too slow. His momentum carried him right to the edge of the roof. Matt was quick and caught an exposed exhaust pipe protruding upwards. He stopped and looked over for Cyrus. There, hooked into Cyrus' jumpsuit, part of the metal roof had caught him. He was hanging by the back of this suit over the ground like a flag blowing in the wind.

"Get me up! Get me up!" he yelled. Below him, rioters had begun to take a notice. He made an easy target. They had already started throwing rocks, trying to knock him down. It was like a game. Matt might have found the situation comical, if both of their lives weren't on the line. He latched his grip around the collar of Cyrus's jumpsuit and pulled him up onto the roof.

"Thanks. I felt like a piñata."

"You do that again, and I might take a swing at you."

Both rose to their feet and continued on their flight. The other side of the building sloped down, and from there it was an easy climb to the ground below. They sprinted past the end of the ruined offices in the middle of the vocational buildings. So far so good; there were no inmates in their sight. The rioters had headed straight for the Furniture Factory, leaving the rest of the area empty. Now Matt and Cyrus just needed to get outside the wall and from there make a straight shot to the library. The only thing between them and their destination were the mattress factory, the laundry facility and solitary confinement.

They had seen no sign of Liu since they left him at the second story window. They could only hope that he found a way out before the rioters found him. On either side of them they could hear shouting and fighting. It was a cacophony of pain and anger and it chilled them to the core. They knew that people were dying, people they knew, people sworn to protect them. Now they were alone and making a gamble on reaching safety that could instead be their death sentence.

They raced along the long wall of the Mattress Factory. The dirt below them was trampled from the crowd of inmates who had just run this route in the opposite direction in their search for weapons. Debris littered the path in spots. Metal shelves had been turned over. Old mattress materials had been strewn about. The obstacles slowed them down, finally resulting in Matt's foot getting caught in a wire coil. He hit the ground hard and landed on his shoulder in a bad way. He cried out in pain, causing Cyrus to stop in his tracks and check on his friend. Helping Matt back to his feet, it was clear that the fall had caused a dislocated shoulder. He'd be all right, but his left arm was now useless.

"Well, you're never gonna play in the big leagues now," Cyrus jested.

"Don't even talk about baseball right now," Matt replied. "If everyone had been playing shuffleboard we might not be in this mess."

The pair laughed for a minute and then caught their breath. That was when they realized the fighting had stopped. They couldn't hear the clash and shouting anymore, just people crying out in pain from their injuries and a strange whooshing sound from in front of them.

"That sounds like..." Cyrus started.

"Water. It's the water hose!" Matt exclaimed. "Someone got on top of the library and is spraying the rioters down. We might get out of this yet."

"Should we keep going?" Cyrus asked. "If they're in range of the library turret then our path may be blocked."

Matt didn't have time to answer. Another voice came from down the path. It was a familiar voice that neither of them had wanted to hear. It was Nate Johns.

"Your path is already blocked, bitches," Johns taunted. Behind him, Pergent, and Clark sneered from behind their leader, their faces expressing the eagerness for the confrontation that was now inevitable.

"It's time to pay the piper for getting me locked away in this shithole with you," Johns threatened. "You betrayed me and Louis. You lied about destroying the evidence. And now you're gonna die for what you did."

———

"It's a war zone out there," Mouse stated plainly.

Concern ran across Murray's face as he looked at his friend. The old man looked back at him with the same expression. Things were getting worse, and it worried Murray that his other friends were out there in the middle of it. Maybe he should have stayed in the FF and waited for them. Maybe the five of them could have held off the intruders coming to look for weapons until help arrived. Maybe he didn't need to be so protective of Mouse. The old guy had survived this long at Santa Mira, maybe he could take care of himself. It was a lot of maybes that he was coming up with but for now at least, he and John were safe. He turned back to the window that he and Mouse stood next to in Corenswet's office.

The remaining guards outside who could still fight were retreating back to regroup. More inmates were rushing from the vocational buildings and into the yard. He could see that they had successfully entered the FF as he spotted them carrying tools from the wood shop as weapons. The group of guards braced for the fight to begin. The inmates were far too many though; the guards would surely be overrun, but the first good sign came since the riot began. The inmates had made a serious miscalculation in their route. They'd moved right into the line of the high-pressure water turret that sat atop the tower by the library. Two members of the prison staff (Murray thought they looked like they were cooks) had climbed the tower and were now spraying jets of water at the invaders. The ones in range tumbled to the ground in agony as their skin was hit with hundreds of gallons of water each second. The inmates retreated back out of range of the hoses. It seemed that for now their advance was through.

"Bench."

Murray heard his name called from behind him. He knew the voice without looking. No one could mistake the deep rasp of Mitchell. Murray walked over to the guard, who beckoned him from the far corner of the room that was partially blocked off by bookcases.

"Mitchell?" he asked.

"I need to speak with you," the guard replied.

"Now? This isn't really the best time."

"It may be the only time. Listen," The guard brought the volume of his voice down to almost a whisper. "I'm the one that gave you Graves. I got you that note."

Murray was surprised. Mitchell had always appeared to be Corenswet's brainless muscle, showing no sign of independent motivation. Yet here he was, confessing that he'd reached out to Murray against the warden's wishes. It filled Murray with wonder and fright. Wonder at what would cause Mitchell to step out of line, and fright at the consequences. Mitchell saw the look on Murray's face and didn't wait for the questions.

"Graves is blackmailing my family. He has been for years, before he even came to Santa Mira. My father was an executive for a labor union of dockworkers. Some of his guys worked for Graves at the docks. He knew that Graves was dirty, but he just thought he was smuggling in pot from Mexico. He didn't know the man was a psychopath. One day he found out. One of his boys opened the wrong shipping container. Inside were people: all women, all young. All had been kidnapped."

Mitchell paused here for a moment. It was obvious speaking of this brought about emotional pain.

"Graves was shipping them to Thailand," he continued after partially recovering. "Human trafficking thing. My father refused to let his men work for him. He called the cops but they found nothing. My father stuck to his guns and told Graves to go fuck himself. My father...he was a good man. He loved his family very much. But Graves found out about my sister. She was a student at Berkeley."

The giant with the scarred face who'd always looked so fierce now looked like a frightened child.

"He got her. He took Stacia. He said, 'You'll do what I tell you' or he'd…" Mitchell trailed off. Murray didn't need to hear the rest of the sentence to know what Graves was willing to do. "So we played ball with the devil. We did what he asked, when he asked. Each time, Graves promised us he'd return my sister. He'd say, 'Just this last thing and then she can come home.' But she never did. We knew she was alive because he'd send us pictures of her. Despite everything she looked like she was well cared for. For years this went on, until my dad died. He was only 53. His heart just couldn't take the stress. So what does Graves do? He turns to me. He put himself in Santa Mira because he knew he had someone who would do his bidding. It's me that gets him what he needs. It's me that allows that motherfucker to operate behind these walls. I'm the one that got him the drugs to kill that cop. I'm the one that spread his 'confession'. I just want it to stop."

"And that's where I come in?" Murray asked.

"You aren't going to be here for long. I know you. I know you can get things done. You're the only person that can help me and my poor mom. You gotta find Stacia, Murray. Please."

"I'll do whatever I can, Mitchell."

"Murray! You better get over here," Mouse called to him from the window. "Things have gone to shit again."

———

"Matt, we gotta turn back" Cyrus declared. "You can't fight now and there's too many for me."

Matt nodded and followed Cyrus in his retreat. Behind them Johns shouted, "Get them!" and the pursuit was on. Retracing their steps from just moments before, Matt and Cyrus sprinted as hard as they could along the side of the Mattress Factory. Their pursuers were forced to slow as they traversed the debris that had caught Matt so badly. It was just the break that they needed. Matt and Cyrus were in much better shape than the pursuing convicts. With each step, they were widening the gap between them and their would-be murderers. They rounded the corner of the mattress building and what lay in their path crushed all the confidence they had built up. Ahead of them a group of twenty or so rioters had broken off from the main group and were searching for an alternate path to the library. They were going to try to take the operator of the water cannon out so the main body could advance the attack.

Cyrus pulled Matt back against the wall and slid behind a delivery truck sitting at the ready to receive materials that wouldn't be coming today. The rioters didn't see them and continued past. They would run into Johns's men at any moment. Maybe they would get lucky and a fight would ensue. The pair waited in silence for any sound coming from either group. They didn't have to wait long, but their hopes weren't fulfilled. They couldn't hear the words being said, but they clearly heard Johns talking to the rioters. His voice was calm and showed no sign of an impending confrontation. The groups broke off and resumed their missions, with Johns, Pergent and Clark heading straight for Matt and Cyrus.

Their retreat was blocked now. They couldn't go back without running into Johns. Only further into the parking lot could they move. Ducking behind the rows of delivery trucks, the pair moved in silence. Behind them they could hear their pursuers split up, to either follow them or to search from the front of the trucks. Matt and Cyrus had only one option now: they had to enter the Mattress Factory and try to find another exit that would take them past Johns and put them back on the route to the sanctuary of the library.

They ran through the Mattress Factory loading entrance. The lights were on in the building and the equipment still hummed with life, but no sign of any workers remained. Just like the rest of the vocational buildings, this one had been deserted. They looked for any sign of an exit, but the large machines used to coil springs and stitch the foam layers of mattresses blocked any view they might have of the other end. They could see that the interior of this building was the same as the Furniture Factory though. A large open room in the middle, hallways on either side with individual work rooms on the ends, a second story for storage above them. The only difference was that catwalks spanned the middle area and connected each side of the building overhead.

"Come on, I think I know a way out," Cyrus said, hoping that the locations of exits would be the same as the FF. They moved further in.

"There they are!" a voice shouted, and the foot chase was back on.

Matt and Cyrus moved through the machinery as fast as they could on a path to the opposite end of the building. If the layout was indeed the same there would be a back door off to the left at the end. If they could reach that, they would be back on the path to the library and in better position than when they first ran into Johns and his goons outside.

They jumped over desks, circled around stacks of finished spring frames, ducked under tables and slid past spring coilers. Cyrus took a chance to look back for pursuers but could see none. He could hear them though. They called out to each other for signs of their fleeing prey from both sides. How did they get around them so fast?

Finally, they reached a gap in the equipment and machines and entered into a more open area that contained four large vats. Inside each vat, large mixers stirred a dull orange thick liquid, the compound for the mattress foam. On either side of the room a conveyor belt moved the hardened foam from a processor into the vats down to a machine that cut the foam in perfect sizes. On a normal day, inmates would be stacking these foam cutouts, but in the emptiness of the factory, the foam sheets just piled up at the end, littering the floor ahead of them and blocking their path. Cyrus and Matt looked around for another route when Clark came out from the hallway on their left. Matt and Cyrus turned away towards the other hall and saw Pergent emerge from the opposite hallway. Between them lay Matt and Cyrus's only route, the staircase that led to the second story. Without thought the pair darted for it with pursuers closing from all sides.

Atop the staircase they moved out to the catwalk above the foam vats. They needed to get to the other side of the building; there was no exit on the side they were on. The metal catwalk shook at its mounts as they hurried across, causing a loud clang with each footfall. Below them they could see Clark and Pergent split up and head for the staircases on either side. Now they were trapped. In front of them, Clark reached the catwalk, blocking their path. Turning back meant facing Pergent.

"We have to take a stand, Matt," Cyrus said. "We fight back to back and take them out. Then we move."

"I'm with you. Let's fuck these scumbags up."

Matt and Cyrus both went into defensive stances. While outnumbered, they now had an advantage. They were trained by Murray in *Daito-Ryu* and were in better condition than their opponents. The chase had taken a toll on their pursuers. Both were visibly breathing hard. What exercise the convicts had done before today was clearly not enough, neither had the stamina for this type of fight. The pair of former LAPD centered their mass and focused their energy on becoming one with their footing. Their heart rates slowed and calm washed over them. They were ready.

The convicts closed the gap on either side as they hastily came forward on the bridge. Their heavy steps shook the catwalk that was now reaching its weight capacity. Clark came first, followed closely by Pergent. Matt and Cyrus took one last deep breath before the fight began.

The first clash was brief. The convicts were no match for Matt and Cyrus. Both went down in a flurry of blows after attacking directly. Their lumbering punches were easily dodged as they both tried to go for a killing blow on their first strike. Matt and Cyrus quickly countered, deflecting the momentum and bringing their return down hard on their opponents. Pergent crumbled to the ground under Matt's downward elbow strike to the neck. Clark flew backwards onto the catwalk from Cyrus' kick to the chest.

"Man, get off me," Pergent shouted, pushing his way to his feet. Clark had risen and now the second round of the attack was coming. The first volley had forced Matt and Cyrus backwards and now they stood at each other's backs in the middle of the catwalk. Again, they centered themselves and focused on Murray's training.

The second wave never came. As the heavy convicts approached on the bridge, the bolts holding the structure together finally gave out. The gangway teetered back and forth for a moment and then split on the side, causing all its occupants to fall. It was unexpected and Matt and Cyrus, despite their athleticism, were not prepared.

All four tumbled to the floor below with the convicts bouncing off the stacks of mattress foam on their way down. The impacts were hard and Clark suffered a dislocated shoulder, while Pergent hit his head against an iron bar, causing him to see stars.

Cyrus was lucky. He caught the railing with his hand and slowly slid down, giving him time to adjust and land safely upright. He only dropped about 10 feet. Matt had not been so fortuitous. The railing and catwalk had split directly underneath him and he'd dropped straight down towards the vats below. He did his best to twist his body midair to avoid a landing inside the vat, which would surely have swallowed him whole in the boiling foam mixture. He bounced off the edge of the tank and onto the ground, but the initial impact was squarely against his back. When he hit the ground he didn't move. Cyrus ran over to him. He was breathing but not conscious.

"Matt!" he yelled, but there was no response.

"Looks like it's just you now," Clark threatened from behind him.

Cyrus stood back up to see Clark and Pergent coming towards him. Two on one; there was no way. He could run-- the way was clear to the exits. The bruised and battered villains would never catch him now. Yet that would leave Matt defenseless. It wasn't a choice at all. He had to stand his ground and protect his friend.

The sound of falling metal came across to them from one of the machines in the back of the room. The convicts turned to it. Someone else was inside. Clark let out a cry, then was silenced. Pergent turned in time to feel his legs go out from under him as his right knee bent sideways, tearing through ligaments and tissue. It was the last thing Pergent would feel before a pipe came across the back of his head, knocking him out to the ground.

From behind rows of machines and through the shadows of the room, Master Jan Liu stepped into the light. Cyrus smiled when he saw him. The Mannequin had arrived just in time.

"Matt's hurt. We need to get him some medical help," Cyrus pleaded, wasting no time to celebrate.

"Don't move him. I'll go get someone," Jan stated. "You stay with him but don't touch him."

"Got it. Hurry."

Jan turned towards the exit leaving Cyrus to care for his former partner. He crouched down by Matt and looked out the door in anxious hope of Liu's quick return with help.

Then Nate Johns stepped out from the shadows, into Cyrus's view. Nate Johns smiled in menace at Cyrus.

"Hello, officer. What seems to be the problem?"

CHAPTER 38

"Looks like you backed the wrong horse again," Johns threatened. "I'm almost glad those other bozos left you alive. It'll be my pleasure to be the one that ends your life. Same with that piece of shit next to you."

Cyrus Greem had known in the back of his mind that this day would come, the day that he would have to face Nate Johns for his crimes. He'd hoped that day would have been when he testified against him, yet that obviously hadn't been enough. Here he was, standing in front of him, ready to kill Greem and his injured friend. No more. Cyrus decided that this was going to end with only one of them walking out of there.

"I'm not even interested in your drivel, Nate," Cyrus returned. "You're a waste of life. You've always been a drain on the world and someone else's lackey. Now you're Graves's bitch-boy. The cycle of you just repeats."

Johns had reached the small clearing of the Mattress Factory where Cyrus protected the still body of Matt Crockett. Greem took a quick moment to look down at his friend. Matt was breathing, barely. Cyrus knew that he had to end this incoming fight soon. Cyrus's concern for Matt didn't escape Johns's attention.

"Always protecting him aren't you?" he hissed, circling Cyrus. "Choosing that mental patient over your fellow officers who were actually making a difference against the scumbag pieces of shit that are destroying this country."

"That's a fucking laugh," Cyrus jibed. "I spent more time cleaning up after you than I did helping the people I was sworn to protect. That's on me. I'm paying for that now. But I'm done. It's time I got out from the sin of sheltering you from justice. This ends now."

"As you wish," Johns chided.

Cyrus again focused on the training he received from Murray. He steadied himself in advance of the attack. It came quickly. Johns was nothing like Pergent and Clark. He'd had the same training as Cyrus when they were in the LAPD and he was adept in hand-to-hand combat. His blows came swiftly, one after another. Cyrus could only block them with his forearms. The defense was working well, but Cyrus knew it couldn't last. Something had to break eventually. He had to ensure it wasn't him.

Johns was a machine. He wasn't tiring. He just kept coming like he was possessed. He struck with every limb of his body, kicks and punches. It was all Cy could do to keep up. An opening came. Johns had repeated the same strike pattern three times in a row. Cyrus spotted the flaw, and on the fourth rotation caught Johns' right arm and applied a redirection technique Liu had taught him.

Johns was too strong. Cyrus couldn't finish the move and the pair fought for position against the other. If Johns gained the advantage here, Cyrus would not be in a position to defend. He struggled against the power of Johns as best he could but he was losing. He had to try something else. He grabbed Johns with both arms and pulled his legs up into his opponent's chest, a double kick square into his middle. The pair blasted apart, Cyrus going to the ground hard on his back, Johns skittering backwards into a tool rack. Tools fell to the ground upon impact and slid across the concrete floor.

Between them, a heavy pipe-wrench dropped. The fighters both spotted it and dove. Equally timed, they grabbed onto the wrench. They wrestled for control, both desperate to use the tool to strike their nemesis down. They fought each other upwards, rising to their feet. Once again, Johns's strength was his advantage. He was prying Cyrus's hands off. Another moment and he would have the weapon. Cyrus let go. The sudden change in momentum threw Johns backwards.

"Time to die, asshole!" Johns yelled and ran straight at Cyrus, wrench raised for the killing blow.

It was exactly what Cyrus hoped he'd do.

Greem cleared the distance with a giant leap, extending his leg in front of him. The *Daito-Ryu* student landed his kick in Johns's stomach, doubling him over and sending him backwards. He landed hard against the spring coiler behind him. His arm flew backwards on impact, causing the handle of his weapon to hit the machine's 'Bind' button. Before he could react, the coils looped around him and began to tighten.

"Stop it! You gotta stop it! AGHHH-" his last words cut short by a squelching report that echoed through the room as the coils tightened and didn't stop until they were only two inches in diameter. Nate Johns was no more.

———

Murray looked out the huge window down at the courtyard below. The water cannon had stopped firing. A group of inmates had flanked the turret and sent two men to the roof of the library. The cooks at the top of the tower were overpowered and the hose was shut off. The riot was back on.

Through the archway of the wall that separated the main grounds from the vocational buildings, rioters poured through. Makeshift weapons were abundant, their raid of the FF had been successful. There were far too many of them and the guards had no way to keep them from reaching the front doors of the Administrative building. Within seconds, they were crowding inside. Not long afterward, Murray could hear them coming up the stairwell and then banging on the door to the top floor.

"The door is quite secure." Corenswet said calmly. "Without any type of explosives, they will not be able to break it down. Right?" His last question directed at Mitchell, didn't give anyone in the room any reassurance. Mitchell just gave a look of doubt back.

The four people inside the office all looked towards the wooden doors of Corenswet's office, expecting to hear rioters entering the hallway at any time. None realized that one of the inmates had climbed to the level under them, broken out a window and started to climb around the front of the building and up to the large windows that Murray had just looked out of. A loud crash of glass filled the office as the inmate pounded inside with a hammer and then raised the hammer to strike Corenswet. It was Ryan Davison, Graves's thug. Murray moved on instinct, and in a flash had grabbed a letter opener on the desk, leaped over the top, and kicked the chair into Corenswet, knocking him out of harm's way. The new space gave Murray a window to plunge the letter opener deep into Davison's neck. The man struggled for a split second in complete shock and then fell backwards out the window, grasping at the blade in his throat.

Murray looked down at Corenswet who was lying on the ground where the chair had pushed him. The warden looked up at Murray as Mitchell helped him to his feet. He stared at Murray, speechless.

Then the phone rang.

The occupants of the room looked at each other, wondering what to do. Who would be calling now?

"Get me the phone!" Corenswet rhetorically commanding, then grabbed at it. "It's probably the reinforcements. Hello?"

The hope on Corenswet's face dropped. It wasn't his backup.

"It's for you," he said and then handed the phone to Murray.

Confusion and fear crossed Murray's face as he took the phone and said, "This is Bench."

"Hello, Murray." It was Graves.

"What do you want? Calling to gloat about your riot?"

"Actually you don't have time for that. I'm here with my friends Kelsal, Pergent and Clark. We've got your little pals, Greem, Crockett and Liu. It's a knife party and they're losing. Wanna play?"

"Let me talk to them!" he yelled.

"Too busy. So little time. If you'd like to say goodbye, we'll be waiting for you in the gym. Clock is ticking."

"Don't you dare do anything to them!" Too late, the line was dead.

"FUCK, FUCK, FUCK!" Murray ranted, slamming the phone into the desk repeatedly. The handset broke in half from the impact. "He's got Liu, Greem and Crockett. I have to go."

"We all have to go," Mitchell added. "That door doesn't sound like it's going to hold much longer."

"We all leave," Murray ordered. "And then you three get safe. You go to the infirmary and bolt everything shut."

"What about you?" Mouse asked.

"Where do you think I'm going?"

Louder the sounds of the reinforced door splitting apart came to them from the end of the hall. There was no more time. They had to make a rush for the elevator before the door gave out and armed inmates stormed the office. They would be trapped and far too outnumbered.

"GO!" Murray shouted.

Through the office door the four of them ran. Ahead they could see the faces of inmates who had broken the top of the door from its hinges. Another moment and they would have the other hinge busted and free. This was going to be close.

Mitchell reached the elevator door first and hit the button. The doors slowly started to open. He latched onto the doors and pushed against the slow motors. A loud whizz sound came as the motors sped up against the force. Into the elevator they piled and hit the close door button.

POP! The final hinge came off and inmates crammed into the hallway. They ran straight at the elevator and Murray braced for the attack. *Come on, goddammit,* he begged the doors to close. A filthy and bloodied lunatic was rushing them. He jabbed his hand through, thrusting a blade at the occupants. They dodged his blows as the doors of the elevator closed around his arm. He fought against them, pulling back. The doors safety feature engaged and attempted to reopen. Murray and Mitchell were fast though. They pushed against the doors, forcing them to close against the arm until it pulled back. The doors slammed shut. They were safe.

For now.

Mitchell input the code to return to the bottom floor, not bothering to conceal it this time. They were probably going to die, why worry about secrets? The elevator lurched downward on its old frame.

Must go faster!

Wham! Something landed on the roof of the elevator. Then another!

"They're trying to come in through the roof!" Mouse yelled. Murray quickly reached past Mitchell and hit the button for the second floor. Just in time. The elevator stopped abruptly and opened its doors.

The second floor was deserted. No inmates had even bothered to enter it, they had just ran straight up to the top floor, to Corenswet.

"What are we doing?" the warden asked. "We need to get to the bottom floor!"

"Come on," Murray ordered and pushed the warden out. "We take the back stairs."

Down the hallway they ran to a single door with a blinking EXIT sign above it. Daylight poured through as they flew out and down the metal staircase that led to the ground.

"This way!" Mitchell shouted and turned the corner that led to the infirmary. Murray and the rest ran after him. They almost collided into his back. Mitchell had stopped in his tracks. Ahead of him, at least twenty inmates stood in their path. All armed and all surprised to see their prey had come to them.

"I'll handle this," Murray said faking confidence. "You guys find another way around."

Mitchell put his hands on his head and popped his neck and then his knuckles. "There is no other way around. We go through them."

"Oh fuck," Mouse whispered.

Mitchell rushed forward. The inmates reeled in shock at the mountain coming for them. The unyielding guard dove into them. He was like a tank, tossing them left and right. They piled forth upon him like a zombie horde, yet he shrugged them off. Grabbing, ripping, and tearing Mitchell flung his attackers aside. All Murray had to do was pick off any stragglers that Mitchell had missed. A path was clearing. One by one, two, no, three by three they went down.

"Go! Run!" Murray yelled when the way was clear enough for them to break free. Corenswet and Mouse ran forward through the piles of injured men around them. Ahead, the infirmary lay. Just a few more yards.

Behind them, Mitchell and Murray fought. Another wave was regrouping and coming forth. Mouse had time to look back as then ran inside. Mitchell and Murray were surrounded and swallowed up.

"Close the door!" Corenswet yelled. Mouse stuttered and the warden pushed him aside and slammed it shut.

Outside the infirmary the inmates struck. In the middle fought Murray and Mitchell. Their defense was beginning to buckle. *At least, Mouse is safe,* Murray thought in defeat.

Sirens! Murray could hear sirens approaching. Backup was on its way. The hope gave the pair new life. They thrust themselves back into the attack. Striking down opponents from all sides. Bones cracked, joints split, faces shattered, until a large enough opening was created for Murray to move on.

"Help your friends!" Mitchell ordered. "Go!"

Murray didn't question the command. The others needed him more than Mitchell did. He twisted free of the arm that had grabbed onto him in the fray and ran away.

To face Graves in the gymnasium.

———

Murray entered the gym to find it pitch black inside. It was silent. Struggling for his eyes to adjust he looked for any signs of his endangered friends and more so for the location of his enemies. He could see nothing.

His eyes were starting to become clear when the lights came on. One row after the next, the clunk of the overhead lamps fired up. Murray blinked against the sudden change in radiance, his eyes narrowing once again.

Overhead the speaker system of the gym boomed. The voice behind the microphone belonged to Murray's scourge.

"Now approaching the ring... Weighing in at a crying baby's weight and standing as tall as someone who's been beaten at every turn... It's the fool's champion, Murray Bench!"

"Cut the shit out, Graves," Murray shouted. "Get down here and tell me where my friends are."

"Fine, take the fun out of this, why don't you?" Graves set the microphone down and descended the stairs from the viewing room above the gym. "It's good to finally be alone with you, Murray. I don't think that we've ever been able to really let our hair down together. Talk about the past, like old friends do."

Murray's patience for this game was running out. "Where are they? Where's Liu, Cyrus and Matt?"

"Oh, I have no idea. It's just you and me, buddy boy," Graves said reaching the bottom of the staircase and walking calmly to Murray. "I just told you I had them so you would come. It's always been about just you, my boy. I couldn't give two shits about your little rabble. Just you."

"I'm leaving Santa Mira, Irvine. I'm leaving you here to rot. You'll never see me again."

"I'm afraid that isn't quite correct. You may have some little deal with the warden but I can tell you that he won't be able to keep his promise. You forget that I own Judge Simpson."

"I'll burn that bridge when I get there."

"Well, I wish you luck," Graves said flatly, reaching Murray. He was still relaxed. There was no sign of aggression coming from

Murray's enemy. "If by some chance you do get out of this, just know I will always be hunting you down. I will never lose sight of you until you are dead."

"Then I say we end this here and now," Murray provoked.

"That's what I came here to do," Graves confirmed.

The final fight was on.

Graves came to Murray first. His fist flew forth, past Murray's dodging frame. Downward Murray thrust his elbow, attempting to catch it in the extended forearm of Graves. Graves spotted the attack and spun, landing his other arm square into Murray's back. The blow knocked Murray forward, stumbling to regain his balance.

"You know, you've never asked me where I learned to fight," Graves stated casually. His tone was like that of someone discussing the weather. "I would think you'd like to know."

"Has nothing to do with me!" Murray returned and threw a breaking kick at Graves head. Graves ducked it and struck at Murray's crotch with an upward blow. Murray caught the fist and jammed it back into his attacker.

"Ooff, good one," Graves praised. "Actually it does have something to do with you. Four years ago, I was brokering a deal with a trafficking ring out of Pyongyang. You know, North Korea, dictator who loves cheese and has a bad haircut."

The fighters broke apart and shook off their first attacks. Graves bounced up and down, limbering up his legs. Murray just circled him, keeping his center low and squared to the ground.

"I met up with a special forces division there. Mean guys. Spent their whole lives being trained to kill. Since birth. Can't remember what they were called. Something mystical. Anyways."

Murray cut him off with a jab, followed by another, then a flurry of kicks. Graves returned them one for one. Murray reacted well, catching one kick and then sweeping Graves's planted leg out from him. He tumbled downwards but took Murray to the ground with him. The pair fought for position, trying to twist the other into an unbreakable hold. Neither could finish the other. Graves was the first to relent, jumping back to his feet and repeating the gentle bounce and circle from before. Murray pushed himself up and planted his feet once again.

"As I was saying, this military group. I was set up with them by a friend of mine. A colleague I guess. He's got a pretty special interest in you. Maybe I could take you to him. You surrender right now and I'll make sure you meet him before you die. How does that sound?"

"More of your games, Graves," Murray challenged. "I'm not playing them. This ends here."

"Well, all right," Graves said. "I hope he's not too disappointed when I kill you."

The fight resumed again, this time much more furious. Blows were coming fast from both sides and soon defenses were not even being put forward. It was all attacks. Fists slammed into bone. Skin splintered from impact. Blood sprayed out onto the ground. The fight was brutal, though both carried on. They ignored their injuries and threw more attacks at each other. Murray would catch Graves in the ribs, hammering his right into them, blistering the bones. Then Graves would gain ground, jamming Murray in the throat and cutting off his air. Murray gasped, coughing, struggling to maintain until his trachea opened again. Graves blasted him in the nose with his forehead. Blood rose in Murray's mouth, his eyes welled up in response to the trauma.

He couldn't see clearly. Graves was just a blob in front of him. He tried to retreat. There was nowhere to go. His back was literally against the wall. In front of him, the vague blob moved forward, confident in victory. Graves threw his hands around Murray's neck and began to squeeze. Already impaired from the previous impact, Murray's throat closed again. Graves had him. He pressed as hard as he could against the muscles in Murray's neck, cutting off the boxer's air. The edges of Murray's vision were beginning to darken around the tears in his eyes. He was running out of time.

No longer needing the image of his father's killer, Murray brought his right fist into Graves's face. The villain's face mashed against the impact but his grip didn't loosen. Again, Murray hit him with the right. Another. Wham. Graves's jaw dislocated. Another!

Wham! Graves's left cheek broke open against the blow. His mouth dangled open. Still he didn't let go. Murray was slipping away. Once more. One last with all you've got. The Golden Right launched again, blasting Graves in his glass eye. Knocked loose, the eye launched backwards through Graves's skull and into his brain.

The body slumped to the ground at Murray's feet. Irvine Graves was dead.

The door of the gym swung open and armed men rushed in. Murray was done. He slid down the wall behind him and sat next to Graves' body. He could breathe finally but still couldn't see. Exhausted, he fell unconscious as the men came to him.

He was out before he could tell that they were uniformed, a security force sent by the warden to find Murray. Corenswet's backup had finally arrived.

———

It took another hour, but the riot was contained. The officers moved in with non-lethal weapons and water hoses from cannons atop trucks. They first focused on the bulk of rioters that had formed at the Administration Building. Then they moved on to the remaining small bands that were still held up in various locations of the prison. In the East Cell Block, a band of twenty armed inmates had locked themselves inside with six hostages, some guards, and some inmates who had refused to take part in the violence. They demanded that they be released and that a boat would be brought to them so they could leave into international waters. Their demands were not met. After a twenty minute standoff, it took just one canister of tear gas sent into their refuge to take them down. All six hostages were rescued.

In total, the riot had cost the lives of seven guards. Seventeen more were injured in the madness. Fifteen inmates were dead, including Irvine Graves, Nate Johns and Ryan Davison. Over a hundred inmates had been injured. Corenswet sent thirty-two inmates into solitary confinement for over a month and twelve more were eventually tried and put onto death row for the killing of the guards, including Steven Kelsal. Santa Mira had faced its biggest challenge in the long history of the prison and survived. Life would go on for those left within the walls.

Still for Murray Bench, life would never be the same. He'd taken men's lives for the first time. It wouldn't be the last.

EPILOGUE

It had been just six days since the riot. Murray spent the first four of them in the infirmary, healing from his fight with Graves. His voice was hoarse and his throat hurt still. He had bruises all over his body and three fractured ribs on his left side. His nose had been broken and he had cracked four of his knuckles against Graves' face. He felt like hell, but it had been worth it.

The violence at the prison had made national news headlines. Voices shouted and argued across the political landscape and social media, demanding prison reform or fully privatizing America's prison system, depending on what side of the issue one was on.

But inside the walls of Santa Mira there were no arguments. Things were quiet. Cleanup crews had come and gone. The damaged structures were being repaired. The dead had been buried and the injured tended to, but the pains of the violence could still be felt throughout the prison. Matt Crockett had made it to the infirmary. He was alive, but sadly not whole. The impact of his landing had split his spinal cord at the base of his spine. He would never walk again. On Monday his release papers were signed. The next day he was transported to a rehabilitation hospital in San Jose, a free man but shackled for the rest of his life from his time at Santa Mira.

Before he left he had a surprise for Cyrus. Because the pair had been tried together, the court decided that they must be released together as well. No separate appeal would be needed. Cyrus Greem was leaving Santa Mira as well. Before he left with Matt he said goodbye to Murray.

"I can't thank you enough for what you did," he told his friend. "We never would have made it if it hadn't been for you, Murray. I owe you everything."

"I could give you some speech about how I just did what I had to do, but who wants to hear that? Cyrus, you're my friend and I'm going to miss you, but I'm thrilled to see you leave."

"When you get out, look me up. I'm going to stay in San Jose with Matt and his family for as long as it takes for him to adjust. Maybe forever."

"Actually, I think I'll be seeing you soon. I've got something I need to do and I think I'll need your help."

Cyrus smiled. "Murray, you ask for it and my help will always be there."

They shook hands and then hugged and smiled one last time. The last of The Brose Four walked out of the prison yard and through the doors of Santa Mira.

It was all over: the fights, his training, his time with Liu and Mouse, The Brose Four, their redemption--as well as his own, finding his justice for Anatoly, his entire life and home for the last three years. All that was left was to pick up his things in his cell, say goodbye to his two friends and then he was on his way to the discharge office. He limped across the prison yard for the final time clutching his side and entered his cell block. He passed through the halls in silence. It was deafening to him. He'd survived prison, yet he still felt like he'd lost part of himself to do so.

He made it to his cell and collected the only thing he wanted from it: "The Techniques of *Daito-ryu Aikijujutsu*", the book Mouse had given him so long ago. Leaving the cell block, he looked for Liu and Mouse. He tried the prison yard and asked around if anyone had seen them. No one had. He tried the FF and the library where Mouse worked. There was no sign. He realized he hadn't seen them at the breakfast that morning. He hadn't seen either of them since the previous night, when they celebrated Murray's last full day in Santa Mira. They had both been elusive, almost distant. He just thought they were sad to say goodbye. *Dammit, where could they be?* Frustrated he went to the administration building and went up the elevator to Corenswet's office.

Mitchell stood outside and stopped Murray as he approached. "The warden isn't in his office today," the guard spoke as he blocked Murray's path.

"Where is the warden? I need to talk to him." Murray said as he tried to look past the guard through the windows of the office door.

"The warden is not in his office today," the guard repeated.

"Yeah, I got that. I can't find Mouse or Liu. Have you seen them?"

"I haven't. It's time for you to go, Murray. You have a job to do," Mitchell said with hope. "I need you to find Stacia."

"I will, Steven. We'll see each other soon," Murray replied as he turned away.

Left with little choice, but deeply concerned for his friends, Murray went back downstairs and found his way to the discharge office. He entered and the attending officer inside asked "Are you Murray Bench, Inmate #78369836?"

"I am, or was, not sure which," Murray replied with his mind still on the whereabouts of his friends. Something had to be wrong. They wouldn't let him leave without saying goodbye. And did Corenswet have anything to do with it? Did he double cross Murray? What was going on?

"Yes or no, please," the guard said.

"I'm sorry, what?" Murray replied.

"Just answer the question yes or no. Are you Murray Bench, Inmate #78369836?" the guard asked again.

"Yes"

"Do you have dress outs?"

"I don't know what that is."

"Has someone sent you clothes to wear upon release?"

"I don't believe so, no"

"Come with me," the guard said as he led Murray to a small closet. Inside was clothing that had obviously come from a thrift store. Murray found a tacky Hawaiian shirt and a pair of jeans in his size and dressed. "Well, it isn't classy but it's better than an orange jumper," he thought.

"A ride is waiting outside for you in a blue sedan," the guard said. "Your caseworker is going to take you to where you need to go. Good luck to you. We look forward to seeing you again." Murray couldn't guess how many times the guard had said that and still thought it was funny.

They opened the door and Murray walked outside as a free man. A man in a suit stood next to a blue four-door car with government plates in the small parking lot. As he saw Murray, he opened the passenger door and said, "Mr. Bench. I am with the California Department of Corrections. Let me be the first to congratulate you on your release." He held out his hand and Murray shook it.

"It looks like you've had a rough day," the man said, nodding towards Murray's bandages.

"About the same as all the rest," Murray responded.

He entered the car and put on his seat belt. The other man closed the door and then walked to the driver side and entered. He started the car and drove away. Murray looked at the windows of the prison walls, hoping that he would spot his friends somehow. There was still no sign of Master Liu or Mouse. He couldn't understand why he didn't get to say goodbye to his two best friends. Disappointed, he turned to the road ahead.

"My name is Schroeder, Mr. Bench. It's a pleasure to meet you."

"Do parole officers usually pick up new releases from prison? I thought I was going to have to take a bus."

"I'm not a parole officer, Mr. Bench. I'm your liaison to the Department of Corrections. Were you not told I was coming?"

"I was told I was being picked up by my parole officer."

"Typical communication breakdown then. No, you don't have a parole officer, Mr. Bench. Since you are now employed by the State of California and agreed to join our SSC program there isn't any need for such commonality."

Murray was confused. "I'm sorry, agreed to join what? I've never spoken to anyone about such a thing."

Schroeder pulled the car off to the side of the road and looked over at Murray and asked "You are Murray Bench, correct?"

"Yes," Murray answered.

"And you don't remember signing a release form for your entrance into the State of California's Department of Corrections Skilled Special Cases program?"

"It's not that I don't remember; I never signed any paper."

Schroeder reached into his briefcase and pulled out a stack of papers. He flipped through to a certain page and showed it to Murray.

"So you're saying that this isn't your signature and that someone else signed it, thus making this an illegal document and negating your release from Santa Mira?"

Murray recognized the writing that made up the forgery of his signature. It was Mitchell's handwriting. He'd seen it in the warden's office. Corenswet had set him up. He'd never talked to the parole board and there never were any special strings that he'd pulled for Murray. The State of California had released Murray without his influence. The fight with Rains had been just one last charade of Corenswet's. However, Murray didn't see any point in revealing the truth to Schroeder. If Murray had seen this agreement he'd have signed it regardless.

"Oh that's my signature yes. Sorry. I must still be a little hazy from the riot. Of course, I remember it now."

"Okay. Phew, you had me worried that I was going to have to turn around and take you back. We've invested a lot in your future, Mr. Bench. We'd hate to have to lose that." Schroeder started the car and drove on. "I am to take you straight to your new job at Hearst Castle. The tapestry department is all too eager to meet their new chief. They've been so happy with all the work you've done over the years for them at Santa Mira and can't believe that they are going to have a student of Jan Liu's leading the department. We should reach the town of San Simeon in about four hours and then another twenty minutes up the mountain to the Castle. I hope you can wait on eating, as the staff is preparing a large dinner to welcome their newest member."

As Schroeder spoke, Murray couldn't believe what he was hearing. He hadn't known what to expect when he left today but it sure hadn't been this. He nodded with each new detail, just trying to hide his surprise. A job. His first job out.

No, that wasn't true. He had another job. He had to find Mitchell's sister. Now that Graves was dead, he had no idea where to start. Not to mention finding the identity of this mysterious figure that Graves said had taken a special interest in him. Someone from Murray's past, he said. Could it have something to do with his father's murder?

The car pulled through the prison gates and back onto the road that had led Murray through the town of Santa Mira four years ago. Murray was leaving behind the prison and a chapter of his life that would end up defining him as a person. He just didn't know it yet.

As the car rounded the corner and put the prison out of view, sirens rang out from the towers and walls. An alarm had been raised. Two prisoners were missing. A hole had been found in one of the sewer lines that led out to the ocean. Next to the hole, the guards had found a makeshift chisel and hammer that had once been a shuttle hook and tufting tool; the trademark tools of a rug maker.

ACKNOWLEDGMENTS

First and foremost, I want to thank every single person who believed that this journey would come to an end with publication. Your faith in me kept me going when I wanted to quit. Thank you to those that helped with ideas, fact-checking, credibility expertise and putting up with a seemingly endless stream of emails and text messages. Thank you Amy Knight and Jolene Taaffe, especially.

To Jenny Bent, who taught me the meaning of literary sensitivity and how to achieve it, thank you.

Thank you to those that read version after version after version along the way and for sharing your ideas for improvements and your inputs on what you liked and didn't. Thank you to Bruce Heflin and Jaime Mauchline who always helped when asked.

A big thank you to my sister, Casey O'Connell, who stepped up when I needed her help, all thirty-eight times. This book wouldn't have happened without her.

To my film friends who gave me a bevy of ideas and creative desires by sharing stories with me. Thank you for showing me the line between art and entertainment and when that line disappears.

Thank you to Sam Heflin. Without him, Murray Bench wouldn't exist.

Lastly, thank you, Jackie. Your patience, your willingness to do whatever you could, your belief in me, your belief in the characters and the story, your partnership and your love not only kept me working but keep me living for each new day.

www.ingramcontent.com/pod-product-compliance
Lightning Source LLC
Chambersburg PA
CBHW021133110726
47900CB00002B/334